A PICTURE OF GUILT

A PICTURE OF GUILT

James Brownley

This first world edition published in Great Britain 2007 by
SEVERN HOUSE PUBLISHERS LTD of
9–15 High Street, Sutton, Surrey SM1 1DF.
This first world edition published in the USA 2008 by
SEVERN HOUSE PUBLISHERS INC of
595 Madison Avenue, New York, N.Y. 10022.

British Library Cataloguing in Publication Data

Brownley,   James
  A picture of guilt
  1. Women journalists - Great Britain - Fiction 2. Serial
  murder investigation - Great Britain - Fiction 3. Women
  serial murderers - Great Britain - Fiction 4. Infanticide -
  Fiction 5. Detective and mystery stories
  I. Title
  823.9'2[F]

  ISBN-13: 978-0-7278-6562-5   (cased)
  ISBN-13: 978-1-84751-040-2   (trade paper)

All Severn House titles are printed on acid-free paper.

Typeset by Palimpsest Book Production Ltd.,
Grangemouth, Stirlingshire, Scotland.
Printed and bound in Great Britain by
MPG Books Ltd., Bodmin, Cornwall.

Acknowledgements

I know that novel-writing is supposed to be a solitary task but in this case it has been anything but. Quite simply, I wouldn't have got anywhere without the assistance and support of a large number of people. I am very happy to have the chance to acknowledge some of them by name here, and for anyone who I have omitted to mention, my profound apologies.

For all their kindness and inspiration I am truly grateful, and of course, any errors, factual or otherwise, are mine alone.

A long time ago I lived in north-east Norfolk where some of this book is set, but the Norfolk (and Norwich) which I have described is purely imaginary. None of the characters are based on or intended to resemble any real person, living or dead.

My thanks and appreciation first to Fay Calladine, who assisted in Alison Glasby's birth. And, in no order except alphabetical: James Attree; Michael Brodie; Susan Bunn; Isabel Calle; Jonathan Davies; Noelle Deschamps; Dimitrios; Deanne Edwards; Anette Funch; Paul Oneile; Juan Pita; Carol Price; Roger Rushton; Lucy Scher and Sian Smith.

I have been really lucky to work with Julian Friedmann, the most helpful, patient and nicest agent that any writer could wish for, and to have had the support, enthusiasm and confidence of Megan Roberts and Edwin Buckhalter at Severn House.

And finally, and most importantly, I owe everything to my parents, Gerald and Ruth Solomon, to whom this book is dedicated.

One

Very little work got done that day on features at the *Sunday Herald*. The building was alive with rumours of job cuts. Circulation was on the slide and an executive committee meeting had been going on since mid-morning, with editorial staff summoned in one by one to discuss the performance of their teams.

By five thirty when Tom Lear, who headed up features news, disappeared upstairs to the board room, only Alison Glasby was still trying, doing her best to concentrate on the usual dead-end stuff that Lear had given her. The new hospital league tables were due out soon, which was not exactly the story of the year. She'd spent the day looking at last year's tables to pick up possible points of interest, then phoning around the different health trust press people to see what had happened to them in the meantime. Big deal. But it was a job, at any rate, Glasby reminded herself, and if anyone was going to lose theirs, it better hadn't be her.

The noise levels around her were going up as the speculation got more fanciful. Glasby glanced up. Mike Marshall's sense of humour was intact as always – smart arse 'Jack' (real name Joe) Daniels was guffawing at something Marshall had just showed him.

'You don't think that Tommy might be on the chopping block, do you?' This from Serena Hamilton, the Sloane on Loan, whose daddy just happened to be an executive editor and who was given all the cushy jobs, going to gallery openings, junkets and new restaurants. When there was a space in her social calendar which allowed time for a little work, that was. She had a perfect tan, beautiful clothes and a great figure. And millions of friends, of course.

None of the others referred to their boss as 'Tommy'. Probably not even the long-suffering Mrs Lear did; he was

Tom to his face, the Leer behind his back (like Serena's nickname, this was a Mike Marshall invention).

'Don't be funny, Serena,' Marshall threw back at her. 'If
they got rid of the Leer, think of the all the extra that Ellington
would have to spend on toilet paper to wipe himself with. Our
Tom comes with built-in cost savings.'

Even Glasby had to smile at that. Politics were as rife at
the *Herald* as in any other office, and getting on well with
Mark Ellington, the editor, had certainly done Lear's career
no harm.

She made a last attempt to get back to work.

Alison Glasby was a tallish, slim woman of twenty-five,
with wavy brown hair, sharp cheekbones, watchful brown eyes
and a rather severe look. She didn't relax easily and until she
did her clipped manner could be off-putting. Another woman
might have described her as striking, or poised, but some men
found her difficult to respond to; she was a bit too serious,
too intense. She wasn't exactly disliked by her colleagues but
she was not exactly liked by most of them either.

A couple of minutes later she felt a hand on her shoulder.
Without even turning to see his face she knew that it was
Marshall; the freckles which it was covered in told her that.
Tall with blond hair and a cheerful disposition, Marshall was
– according to him – popular with girls. But even though he
didn't do much that way for Glasby, he was one of those
people who always seemed to find something amusing to say.
He was as close as she had to a friend in the office.

'Are you going to come with us, Ali?' he asked her.

'Come with? Where?'

'For God's sake, Ali, don't tell me that you've been doing
trivial things like work while we've been engaged in essential gossip?' Serena and Jack Daniels, standing together the
other side of the beige sound screen that marked out Glasby's
territory at the *Herald*, both laughed. 'We all decided five
minutes ago that we're downing tools and going to the pub.
And that goes for you too, Miss Perfect.'

Glasby wasn't sure whether this was meant as a compli-
ment or not. She looked at her watch. It was only six fifteen;
much earlier than she usually finished. The others were already
putting on their coats. There was still no sign of Tom Lear;
maybe he'd gone for the day.

Marshall looked over at her again. 'Come on, Ali, it won't be the same without you. We all owe the *Herald* a clear duty to go and get hammered, fast.'

Glasby wasn't much of a drinker – she'd hardly been inside a pub since she moved down to London – but she certainly didn't feel like working. She could have just gone back home, but other than the occasional pizza with Marshall when his wife took their boys back home to Brazil, she never went out after work with any of her colleagues. The rest of her social life wasn't overactive either. She got up to a round of applause from Serena and a sarcastic cheer from Daniels and Marshall.

Serena was drinking something pink which went with her nails, and the boys (as she called them) were on pints. Glasby, who couldn't manage more than one beer in an evening, opted for G&Ts. She'd had nothing more than a banana and a latte at lunch.

All the warning signs were there. After the third drink Serena's posh-girl drawl, which was normally so grating on Glasby, stopped being noticeable at all. Glasby found her foot tapping energetically to the output from the juke box across the bar. Daniels' leg brushed against hers, not for the first time. As before, he looked across to try to make eye contact; this time she spotted it and smiled back at him, not seeing the face that Mike Marshall pulled at Serena or the raised eyebrows that she gave him back. With a little effort, Glasby looked across to Marshall and tuned back into the conversation.

'Yes, you mean a tontine,' he was saying to Serena.

'What's a tontine?' Glasby interrupted.

'It's a sort of group thingy', Serena answered, 'where the last person to stay alive gets all the dosh. I was saying, that's what will probably happen to the four of us. The one left standing wins the goldfish, you know.'

Glasby had only the smallest idea of what she was on about but supposed that it must be something to do with them losing their jobs. Even this didn't seem quite as important as it should have done. She started to giggle, for no particular reason.

'Well, in case any of you lot is contemplating killing us all off, I'm going to love you and leave you,' Serena announced. And, ignoring Marshall's and Daniels' pleas and threats, she gathered up her Burberry mac and her black Prada bag and sashayed out into the rain to look for a taxi, followed by admiring glances from the table of bankers near the door.

It was Glasby's round. Daniels joined her as she headed slightly unsteadily to the bar. He was dressed in his usual Leer wannabe style: pinstripes, patterned shirt and loud tie. (Marshall, like most of the other men in the office below executive level, stuck to a uniform of chinos and an open-neck shirt.)

'You're not worried, are you?' Daniels asked her. 'About all this rubbish about job cuts? I mean, I think it's important that none of us let it affect personal relationships, don't you?'

Glasby wasn't sure what he meant, and said so. Even on a Monday evening the bar was pretty full by now with a press of people waiting to be served. She squeezed in front of a wooden pillar to a place in the barman's line of sight.

'What I meant is, Mike and Serena, and you especially, Ali. You know that we all really respect you. Your work, I mean, as a journalist. You're so good at doing the hard stuff that most of us don't have the nose for, the discipline to really get down to it. Mike, you know, he's a really good guy, but he's got his wife and his kids, that's where his heart really is. And Serena, well you know as well as I do that it's just a hobby for her. She doesn't even need the money like the rest of us. So there's only you and me, I care about the job the same way as you do.'

At some point in this speech Glasby noticed that his hand was on her arm, holding her just above her elbow. Strangely, it didn't feel that bad. She looked away from Daniels towards the shaven headed young man behind the bar, but didn't make any move away from him.

'And,' Daniels continued, 'I like you as well, a lot. As, as a woman, I mean.'

'Yes, love?' The barman, who like most barmen in London was an Aussie, had finally come her way. 'What'll it be?'

'Two pints of Special, please,' Glasby ordered. 'And a gin and tonic.' Daniels' hand was gone from her arm now as he moved in next to her at the bar.

'Better make that gin a large one,' Daniels said, 'if you're going to keep up with us, drinking pints.' And to her surprise he insisted on paying. Daniels had a reputation as being a bit careful with money, despite the flash clothes.

*   *   *

She'd lost count of how much she'd had to drink and certainly didn't care. Marshall announced that Fabiana would be expecting him and disappeared so quickly that Glasby found herself back at Daniels' Docklands apartment – conveniently just a few minutes' walk away down Westferry Road – without quite knowing how.

She badly needed to lie down and sleep but he had other ideas. It wasn't until the next morning that she noticed the Natalie Imbruglia poster on the wall and the remote control Ferrari on the floor next to the bed, her clothes scattered around it – most of them, anyway; her bra had somehow ended up twisted around her waist.

Looking up at Daniels' face she saw the same smile that she remembered from the night before, more triumphant than affectionate. And then she looked at her watch. Half past eight, when she would normally be arriving at the office! Throwing her clothes on, she fled, barely waiting to say goodbye, and got lucky outside with a taxi that she could hardly afford.

By the time she was back home in Stockwell, several miles away through the morning traffic, it was well gone nine. She bolted past the Indian shop and up the stairs to her rented flat, fumbling with the lock, feeling second-hand, cheap and thoroughly unprofessional.

After a lightning fast shower and an even quicker change of clothes she half ran to the Tube, her head pounding with every step, two thoughts in her mind. No one must notice that I'm late; and Daniels better hadn't say a word about it to anyone. Ever.

Two

'**Y**ou're late this morning, aren't you?' Glasby managed a watery smile in response to the security guard's cheerful greeting and stepped into an empty lift. Her stomach lurched unpleasantly as she began the ascent to the twenty-fifth floor.

Her little cubicle was just the other side of the glass doors from the hallway so she didn't have far to walk to see her colleagues snickering. None more so than Mr Cocksman Daniels himself, who had clearly told the others the score from his encounter with her last night. Humiliated didn't begin to describe the way that Glasby felt. She avoided everyone's gaze, most of all the now hateful Daniels', sat at her desk and switched on her computer for the day.

Mike Marshall came up and asked how she was. He got nothing more for an answer than a shrug of her shoulders.

'The Leer's been looking for you, Ali.'

'Why? What does he want?' was the ungracious reply.

'Don't ask me.' Marshall pulled a face and gave her what was supposed to be a seductive grin.

Ignoring this, Glasby headed for Tom Lear's corner office. Despite being twice her age, her boss often lived up to his nickname where Glasby was concerned, but today he was all business.

'Have you heard about Leonie Dellar?' he asked her.

'No, what about her?'

'She's not going to last out the day. They've moved her to the prison hospital. She's had a heart attack or something.'

After the postgrad journalism year at City University, Glasby had got in on the *South London Press*. Mostly she had covered nothing more exciting than local politics. But she did get to do the occasional hard news story – there was plenty of crime to go round. She had worked on a series on a local children's home scandal which, together with the strong personal recommendation of her tutor at City, had helped her on to the newsroom at the *Sunday Herald*. But since then all she had been given was the soft stuff that no one else wanted and she was starting to wonder whether she would have been better on some local rag after all.

Until today. 'You'll be working on the Dellar story, with Bill Davenport,' Lear told her.

Bill Davenport was a legend. Some people said he was past it, but the fact remained that he was still the best known name on the *Herald*. His book on the Dellar and Jarmy murders was a classic. It had even been a set text on Glasby's course. Rather than just cover the basic facts, Davenport had really got to know everyone. He had talked to the families, the police, and crucially he even got close to 'Mad Bitch' Dellar herself.

If Leonie Dellar was about to die now it would be a big story. And who better than Bill Davenport to work with on it? It was a chance for her at last and Glasby was going to grab it with both hands. If all the talk about job cuts proved true, it couldn't have come at a better time.

'Happy now?' the Leer asked her, trademark reptilian smile flashing across his face. And she was, for about five seconds. She actually believed that after eighteen months of waiting he'd kept his promise and put a decent job her way.

Glasby lowered her guard and he caught her with the sucker punch.

'Oh, and Jack will be covering it as well, of course. He's already got the ball rolling.'

Typical. Absolutely pigging typical. Daniels was not as experienced as her, not as bright and he didn't put in the hours like she did. So how come he did 'Footballer Tells of Son's Kidnap Horror' while she got 'Size *Does* Matter: The Men Who Admit They Prefer Size Zero'?

Daniels wasn't at his desk when Glasby got back. Marshall was sympathetic when Glasby told him what had happened. 'If Davenport, Jack Daniels and I are a team, it's pretty obvious who's going to be number three out of three, isn't it?'

'Oh come on, Alison. There's no way that Lear would have put you on to the job unless Ellington had approved it. And if the editor wants you on it, you must be doing something right.'

'Isn't Bill Davenport supposed to be retiring soon?' she

asked him. Unlike Glasby, Marshall was generally very well informed about what was going on at the paper.

'Yup,' he confirmed. 'There's some sort of do for him next week, I think. The story is he's not too happy about it. You know that when he took over Ellington booted Davenport up to crime editor. Some people said that it was a real non-job. But Ellington likes him, I think, and it was the best that he could do to save him. Anyway, what I've heard is that they're pushing him out altogether now. It's probably part of this cost saving stuff. So if the Dellar story runs for a while you could be on to a good thing.'

Glasby's mood was considerably improved. Until she bumped into Jack Daniels, even more full of himself than the night before and one step ahead of her as usual.

'Oh hi, Ali, it'll be great to have you on board,' he greeted her. 'Bill and I have had a quick chat and we've agreed the angles that I'll be doing. I'm going to be talking to the victims' families, the police, reactions to Dellar's death, that sort of thing. He needs me to freshen things up a bit, you know.'

'Right,' she replied, trying to sound more positive than she felt. 'I'd better find Bill as well.'

'You won't get him today. He told me that he's out until the morning now. But he wants you to go up to the prison once she finally pegs it. They'll hold a press conference up there after her death. I expect it'll be totally routine.' He paused, and went for the jugular. 'Oh, and by the way, thanks for last night. You're quite a girl, when you let yourself go.' And, unforgivably, he grinned.

Glasby bit her lip and walked away. Fast.

'Totally routine'. It summed up her life so well that you could have written it on a sign and hung it around her neck. Nonetheless, she got on with what she did best: getting down to it, working the cuttings, reading anything she could find on the Dellar and Jarmy murders, and any article on Dellar since then, most of them written by Bill Davenport.

It wasn't so much his trial coverage that was good. That was basically standard stuff, albeit nicely written – and anyway they didn't go in for much in the way of gory details those days. It was the way Davenport had stayed with the story over the years. He had got all the exclusives. Dellar's confession, even before the police had it. Jarmy in Broadmoor, glowering at the world and talking to no one but Davenport. And all the stuff from the victims' families, lots of it over the years. Some of it fillers: anniversaries, that sort of thing. And some anything but.

The case had made Davenport, although even at the time of the trial his byline was 'Crime Correspondent'. It had happened in 1969, so he must have been . . . Glasby hesitated, not sure how old he was now. At any rate, even if Mike Marshall was right and Davenport had been kicked upstairs since, it didn't look like a bad career from where she was sitting.

Why the hell they hadn't computerized all the old copy was beyond her. It took her hours going through piles of manual cuttings. But she knew that Daniels would never have the patience or the determination to do this sort of thing. Maybe it would give her the edge over him that she needed.

It was nearly nine by the time she got home. Glasby had been telling herself on the Tube that she must go out to the huge Sainsbury's up the road to get something decent for dinner. But when she got in, after glancing at the answer machine out of habit – it wasn't blinking, of course – the first thing she did was to find Davenport's book on the murders, *Children Carried Away*. Soon she was lost in it.

Just after midnight her mobile rang. It was the night news desk. 'Hello, Alison Glasby? This is Peter Buxton. Bill Davenport left me a note to call you when we got the news on the wire. Leonie Dellar died, a few minutes ago. The press conference is at eleven tomorrow.'

She realized that she was hungry but couldn't be bothered to go out to the supermarket. It stayed open twenty-four hours but that didn't make shopping there any more bearable. Dinner was some Swedish Krisprolls with peanut butter, propped up in bed while she read. They were a bit dry but the only butter she had was yellow and didn't smell good.

It was about two by the time she finished *Children Carried Away*. She knew that she had to sleep but her mind was racing. She *had* to do a good job. By about five she was finally tired enough to switch off.

The alarm went at seven fifteen. Twenty-five minutes later she was in the car. There was no time for breakfast, beyond half a cup of tea.

*   *   *

Marsham House wasn't equipped to deal with an influx of journalists on its premises. Security was stringent, as you would expect from a place that housed the most dangerous female prisoners in the UK. Glasby had imagined a Victorian building, dark-red brick and gothic towers. Her first sight of it was a bit disappointing. In the mid-distance, it looked more like an industrial estate: grey, featureless blocks and large expanses of concrete which could have been car parks. Closer by, she could see the huge banks of barbed wire and flood-light towers, the bars at every window. Set against the equally grey November skies and the bleak, empty landscape of the Fens, it was oppressive, ominous, almost overpowering.

Getting her ID validated, being searched for contraband and weapons, it had taken an age for her to be admitted on to HMP premises. Glasby shuddered at the thought of it: Dellar had been locked up there for years before she was even born.

The small room where the press conference was to be held was already quite full when she arrived. It was painted in institutional off-white, dingy even under the rows of strip lighting suspended on steel rods from the ceiling. About thirty wooden chairs had been squeezed in, with two chairs behind a Formica-topped table facing the others. It gave her the feeling for a moment of being back at school.

A few heads turned her way as she walked in but there was nobody she recognized. From the look of them they were much the same as her. Young hopefuls, sent to do the donkey work.

Glasby was normally to be found in trousers and trainers but today, conscious of the inquest to come, she had decided on a rather formal suit. Instead of giving her gravitas as she had intended, it seemed to emphasize a gawkiness in her build and her slightly long face, making her look like a girl in her first school uniform.

The press conference took a long time to get started, but Jack Daniels was right: it was pretty much for form's sake only. A Prisons Department press officer made a brief summary. Leonie Dellar had died in the prison hospital wing at 11.02 p.m. the night before, aged fifty-eight, having been found unconscious in her cell early that morning. She had been serving life, imposed in 1969, for abduction and murder. Cause of death was a coronary. This was subject to the findings of the coroner, who was required by law to investigate all deaths in custody. The spokesperson then introduced Senior Prison Officer Alan Dack to add some further details and answer any questions.

P.O. Dack was a large man in his mid-forties with a fleshy build, a red face and heavy eyebrows. His accent revealed that like both Glasby and Leonie Dellar herself, he came from Norfolk. He was obviously self-conscious about it, being very careful to lengthen the vowel in words like 'room' and 'news'.

In fact, he had very little to add. After repeating the bare facts, which had mostly been already covered by the press officer, he gave them a little background on the prison and then took questions. Most were routine, until two of the tabloids decided to outdo each other.

'Luxury cell?'

'Huge TV and DVD?'

'Internet access? Is it true that she could get into chat rooms and talk to young children?'

No, no and no. None of this was permitted. She was in a standard cell, ten feet by twelve, small television as with any long-term prisoner with full privileges. Nothing more luxurious than that – to the contrary, she'd had hardly any personal possessions: 'I've just supervised their removal, in fact. I would describe her conditions as humane –' *hew*mane – 'but austere. Nothing fancy at all.'

Questioning came to an end. The press officer confirmed the starting time and location for the inquest, and that was it. And even the inquest would be no more than a formality; it would be adjourned until the post-mortem results were available, more or less as soon as it began.

It seemed almost absurdly mundane. Leonie Dellar was a killer, and not just that: she was without doubt the most hated woman in the country. She and her boyfriend, Brian Jarmy, had abducted, tortured and killed four young children in the summer of 1969. Three had been local children from villages outside Norwich. One had been from the West Country, holidaying near the Broads in a caravan with his parents. All of them had been ordinary little kids, who lived in bungalows or on modern estates, children who rode bikes and played football or hopscotch.

Even in those more innocent times, the death of a child

at the hands of a stranger was not unheard of. But for a woman to be involved in such wicked perversions, no one had even thought of such a terrible thing.

Stories circulated during the trial. People said that some of the evidence had been suppressed as being too much of a danger to public order. Hanging hadn't long been abolished. People said they should bring it back, just for her. And if they didn't want to do it officially, why, we'll do it the old-fashioned way. He might be a nut job like they say, but she, she's plain evil, wants burning like they used to.

In his book Davenport stated definitively that there was no such secret evidence but the stories continued to be told.

Photographs of Dellar from the time have her wearing a longish bob. Years later when Glasby was at school they would still refer to a 'Leonie' cut with the contempt for bad fashion that only twelve-year-old girls can muster. In almost every photo Jarmy wore a dark suit and tie, his blond hair cut much too short for the fashions of the late Sixties. Dellar dressed as if to match, with knee-length skirts and twinsets. It looked almost as if she was impersonating another, much older woman.

Leonie Dellar was remarkable only in retrospect, for her complete normality. Perhaps this banal little gathering was a fitting ending for her after all.

As the room cleared, Glasby decided to take her chance. Going up to P.O. Dack, who was tidying his papers at the front of the room, she slipped into her best Norfolk accent. 'Nice to hear a voice from home for a change.'

He looked up, and grinned shyly at her. 'You aren't all from London then, you press boys? And girls, I mean.'

'No, they let a few of us bumpkins in every now and again. What a job you've had, looking after Black Shuck herself.'

He grinned again, this time more confidently.

'Well, she weren't no trouble really, you know. More like a school ma'am than Mad Bitch Dellar. Always beautiful and tidy with her things, everything had to be clean as a whistle. Not that she had much, as you heard.'

'She really didn't have a lot of possessions, then?'

'She didn't, no. She used to spend her time doing cross-words out of the newspaper, real ones I mean, like the *Telegraph* or *The Times*. Who are you with, by the way?'

'The *Herald*,' replied Glasby. 'Not a real newspaper like *The Times* or the *Telegraph*.'

'No offence, miss, I'm sorry. Anyway, I like the *Herald* myself. That's Bill Davenport, isn't it? I met him here more than once, a real gent.'

'That's right,' said Glasby, with a trace of self-importance. 'I'm working on this assignment with Bill.' Which was more or less true, although strictly speaking she hadn't actually heard a word about it from 'Bill' yet. 'What have you done with her possessions now that she's gone? There must be plenty of sickos out there that would pay good money for them, I bet.'

'We release them to the next of kin, or if they don't want them, we destroy them all. Shouldn't be surprised if that's what happens to these. After all, you'd hardly want family mementoes of Auntie Leonie, would you? We're waiting to hear at the moment, and they're all bagged up in the ops room.'

Glasby looked around ostentatiously to show that there was no one left to overhear them and leant in closer to the prison officer. He could smell her shampoo, see a mole on the side of her neck through the strands of hair. 'You mean the operations room, the one next door?'

'Yes, but there's no way—'

'It would be completely off the record. Bill, you see, he asked specially if it would be possible. Just for him to add, well, some atmosphere. You know his book, *Children Carried Away*?'

'Yeah, but—'

'This is for the final chapter. We'd be helping him with it. You know that he's someone you can trust, don't you? Even if you don't know me, you know him.'

'Miss, it ain't that I don't trust you. I didn't mean to say that. Well, that would be for two minutes only. And heaven help me if it got out, you know I'd get wrong.'

'It won't. I promise you that you won't get into any trouble. And two minutes would make all the difference. For Bill, I mean. Thanks!'

The prison officer unlocked the door and pulled a cover off a table, Formica topped like its fellow in the other room. And as luck would have it, at that moment his bleeper went off.

Glancing down, Dack said, 'I'm going to have to leave you.

I'll be five minutes max. I'll lock you in, OK?' And rushed off, turning the key in the door behind him.

Now she really could talk about working with Bill Davenport. He was a small man, shiny faced and a bit short of breath. Fair hair fading into a pale grey, thinning in places. Not ageing particularly well. Tatty tweed jacket with threads pulled on the shoulders and lapels and crumpled brown woollen trousers. But even if his eyes were a bit bloodshot they still looked the same as on the cover of his book, knowing and inquisitive, as if he had seen a lot but still had an appetite for more.

Davenport's office was piled high with cardboard boxes and large envelopes full of papers, ripped in places and threatening to spill over. Despite the clutter there was a lot more space than she was used to working in, but she felt overlarge and awkward as she sat down.

His first words to her couldn't have been any worse if he'd been trying: 'You're Daniels' friend, aren't you?' But as she told Davenport of her coup Glasby forgot her nerves.

'I had time to look at everything, and I've even got photos of most of it.'

'Photos?' he queried. 'I thought you said they searched everyone for cameras on the way in?'

'I used my phone. My mobile.'

'You took photos with your phone? Aren't they really bad quality? Anyway, what did you get?'

'I can show you them now. The camera on my phone is pretty good, actually. The only trouble is,' confessed Glasby, 'they're quite small. On the phone, I mean. You don't think that there's anyone who could help with them, do you?'

A couple of calls from Davenport and ten minutes later they were looking at the twelve shots she had taken on the screen of his PC. Quite a contrast to the last time Glasby needed technical support; it had taken her a full week to get her keyboard fixed after it broke.

'I remember that cushion, you know. "Forgive Them For They Know Not What They Do". Hmmm. Leonie told me that she'd embroidered it herself, donkey's years ago, it must have been. They've really torn it to bits, haven't they?'

They switched to the next image. Immediately Davenport was on his feet.

'What's that picture?'

'It's the third victim, isn't it, Donna Bacon? And I think that it's her older sister that she's with, Lynette. There's a photo of the two of them in your book, I recognized them from that. Although they're a bit younger in that one.'

Davenport said nothing, but just stood there with a strange look on his face.

'I asked the prison officer about it,' Glasby continued, 'because it was the only one. I mean there weren't any other photos. He told me that they didn't know what the photo was.' Davenport was staring at her intently. 'But they only saw it by chance. It was inside the cushion, must have been there for years they think. When they found Dellar in her cell she was already unconscious and she was clutching it – the cushion I mean – and she'd ripped it right open. And when they looked inside, the photo was there, she had her fingers round it. There wasn't anything else in the cushion. Was there a reason why you didn't use this photo for your book?'

He was standing over Glasby now, looking suddenly younger and taller.

'The thing is, Alison, I don't reckon I've ever seen that photo before. There were never that many pictures of Donna, you see. The family was dirt poor; I don't think they would have had a camera of their own. We used a few in the book, and of course in the paper at the time. I remember that Patricia, the mother, she had some she didn't want used, but they were baby photos, nothing with Donna older than that. I know I'm getting on a bit now, but even so . . .'

'Can't we look and see if we can find any trace of the photo, Bill? I mean, in your book, and the archives, and do you still have your old records? Maybe there's a reference to it somewhere. I think that I should look, don't you?'

Davenport looked thoughtful for a moment and then replied, 'Me? Still have old records? You obviously haven't been talking to the powers that be round here –' this with what might have been a slight edge in his voice. (Glasby, who had never even had a conversation with the *Herald*'s editor which went beyond 'Hello', tried to look as if she did.) 'Last time I threw a piece of paper out was about 1958. And you don't need to bother with their archives. If I had it, it's here. In this room.'

Glasby looked around her. Cardboard boxes, some bearing fading trade names of products she didn't recognize, were piled on top of each other and on every surface bar the small desk they were sitting at. Some reached as high as the ceiling. On one wall there were three large walk-in cupboards. Judging from the way that they bulged open, all were fully occupied.

'Don't you worry,' said Davenport, following her gaze. 'I know where everything is. When they transported us out to this godforsaken wasteland I had them move every box individually so they didn't mess up the system. Now, you're in luck, young lady. The boxes which you need, you'll find that they're in the left-hand cupboard, middle pile. Not the bottom one, but the next three up from that. You shouldn't have to move much.'

This turned out to be something of an exaggeration. Davenport departed to the pub for a meeting of his retirement party committee and she had the impression that he would not be back soon. Which was probably a good thing; there were several stacks of boxes between her and her quarry. As soon as she tried to move one, the whole pile threatened to topple over. By climbing on a chair she could move them one by one, but even then it would have been easy to set off an avalanche, and she was terrified of getting them out of order.

Some had clearly not been dusted for many years, and her suit would probably need dry-cleaning before she could use it again. But with persistence and at the cost of one bruised elbow when she grabbed an escapee from a particularly wobbly stack, she extracted the three as he had told her, and settled down with them.

The child was frightened, lying in the dark

Three

First there was a disappearance, then another. Two little boys, both lived in villages in north-east Norfolk, but they were twenty miles apart and there didn't seem to be any connection between them. The first, Kevin Yallop, was eight. He was out playing on his bike in a dusty lane behind the house. His mother had heard him, shouting and laughing with some other kids. And then, nothing. Just his bike, lying at the side of the lane in the sunshine of a late July evening.

Not much more than a week later the next boy went missing. His name was Matthew Starling, and he was ten. Just like the first, he had been out playing. What else would you expect children to be doing on a perfect day in the long school holidays?

This time there was a little more. Matthew shared a Jack Russell with his younger brother, Gary. She kept running off from the boys, excited by the scents and noises coming from the field of broad beans across from the bungalow where they lived, squashed together with two older sisters and their parents.

The dog had wandered, chased by Matthew the whole way across the field. Left behind, Gary saw what he later described as 'a lady, like Mum only a bit taller' talking to Matthew. But there were a thousand things more interesting than adults to occupy their thoughts and when boy and dog returned, neither brother mentioned the woman to the other. An hour or two later, after Matthew and the terrier had disappeared yet again, Gary grew bored with waiting. Dragging his heels through the dust of the field, he trudged home.

It wasn't until after teatime that anyone really worried about the boy. By the time the police were called it was already nearly dark so there wasn't much they could do until the morning. Well into the next afternoon, the Jack Russell was found, cowering in a dense thicket. But Matthew Starling had gone, as if the dark-brown, fertile earth had simply closed in on him.

The press immediately linked the two cases and so, apparently, did the police. Hundreds of volunteers scoured ever larger areas but there was no sign to give anyone hope, nothing. In the parched summer of 1969, the hardened ground couldn't even offer a single suspicious footprint or tyre track.

Parents throughout the county were tense. For a few days after Matthew's disappearance, so were their children. Frightened to go out alone, frightened to go to sleep. But children are children, and in a little while, even for those who were quite close to either of the two boys, the fear started to fade and the summer went on like a lunchtime drinker, drowsy in the sun.

Then it struck, like a four o'clock hangover. This time it was a little girl, Donna Bacon, only seven years old. The same story: she was there, and then she wasn't. It was nine o'clock at night and Donna was playing outside. Her older sister Lynette shouted for her to come in. Somehow there was a mix up between Lynette and her parents. All three of them thought that one of the others had seen Donna to bed. By eight the next morning they realized she was missing. Donna's parents were incoherent with grief, so it was mostly left to the teenaged Lynette to talk to the police. Not that there was much to say.

The television news was ready this time. The latest disappearance was the main story on *Look East* that night, and it even made the national news as well. It was the third in a series, the police were baffled and the family was in shock. Sir Stephen Blofeld, the Conservative MP for Norfolk North-East, called for the death penalty to be reinstated, immediately. Mr Stuart James, Labour representative for one of the Norwich constituencies, regretted the depletion in police numbers caused by the irresponsible policies of the (Conservative) county council.

The policeman in charge of the investigations was comfortable with television and the press, unusually so for the time. A local man, slow spoken and steady but thoughtful and incisive with it, Chief Superintendent Mullins tried to reassure people: 'There is evil afoot in our county. It is our job to track it down and catch it, and we will. We will.'

Parents were advised to exercise the greatest of care; Mullins had to admit that the police were no closer to catching the killer, or killers.

And then, the very next day, they did. The road from Norwich up to Yarmouth is long, straight and the scene of many bad accidents. So when two policemen from Acle passed a Morris Minor van broken down at the side of the road, they went to help. In the front, waiting for the engine to cool again, they found Brian Jarmy and Leonie Dellar. In the back was Michael Summer, with a piece of old carpet thrown over him. He was a day short of his twelfth birthday. No fewer than seventeen stab wounds were later found, but it was the belt around his neck that had caused his death.

Michael hadn't even been reported missing. It had all happened so suddenly. Two families were on holiday together. They had hired a cruiser on the Broads. The two boys were on bikes, going to meet up with the others at a pub along the river. The older boy went on ahead but Michael never turned up. By the time the police got the call, they already knew what had happened to him.

Neither of the murderers said a word when they were arrested. According to Constable Robert Jones, a married man with twenty-two years' service, they were 'like bloody aliens, or on drugs or something. All they did was just look straight ahead of them, like they were the only two people in the world'.

Chief Superintendent Mullins was lying down trying to catch an hour's sleep after spending all but two of the last thirty hours on duty. He heard his wife shouting up the stairs: 'Adam, quick, quick, they've got them!' Three minutes later he was in his car and he reached Acle police station only moments after Jarmy and Dellar were brought in.

It didn't take long for some more news to come through. A search of the terraced house shared by Jarmy and Dellar in Norwich revealed nothing much. But in the lock-up garage at the end of the street there was a pile of old carpet. Later the police would establish that it came from the same roll as the piece found in Jarmy's car. Underneath the pile was a boy's body: Matthew Starling. And with it, a fresh horror. What sort of person could have burnt a swastika on to a little boy's leg? With a cigarette, twenty-six separate times?

Both Dellar and Jarmy remained silent, in Jarmy's case,

almost literally. He refused to speak to anyone, about anything, for the whole of his first week in captivity. It was only after they brought in a psychiatrist and transferred him on remand to Broadmoor that he agreed to talk. And then, on the express condition that nothing would be said, or even asked, about the killings themselves.

Dellar was less confrontational but the effect was the same. She was polite and cooperative about the routine business of arrest and detention. But neither of them would shed any light on why they had done such things. Not when they were questioned, not when they were charged, not when they were on trial and convicted.

It didn't make much difference really. The police had their killers. Norfolk was a safe place again.

In the first box Glasby found two blue box files marked 'Interview Notes'. Despite the appearance of chaos in his office, Davenport was obviously very organized. There was an index at the front listing each interview, by person and date. First of all the police: Mullins; PC Jones and his partner PC Parker who had arrested them; the sergeant at Acle. The victims' families: Kevin Yallop's mother; Matthew Starling's mother and father and his older sister Alison; Patricia Bacon and her daughter Lynette. Michael Summer's father, followed by a note: 'Summer family – no interviews and requested none from relatives etc.'. Friends of the children; neighbours; teachers. There were separate files with 'Leonie Dellar' and 'Jarmy Transcript' written in ink on the front, which Glasby put to one side for later.

Davenport's interview notes seemed mostly to have been transcribed from tape recordings. (Glasby wondered what they used to record on in those days – did they even have cassettes?) In amongst the typed pages, which looked as if they'd been done on an old manual typewriter, were occasional handwritten notes. Some less formal occasions when the tape recorder would have got in the way, she assumed.

The obvious place to start was with the Bacon family. There were two transcripts of interviews with Mrs Bacon, one much longer than the other. Lynette had been present at both of them. There were also records of conversations with Lynette, a thick pile of them, some typed, some handwritten.

It seemed strange to Glasby that there was nothing with the father. Then she realized why. None of the Bacon notes were dated until after the trial, which finished on 20th November 1969. On the 19th, John Bacon had dropped dead on his way home from the village pub, having suffered a massive heart attack.

The first interview of Mrs Bacon and Lynette had taken place on the 26th. Davenport had begun by offering his condolences for Mr Bacon. 'It's a terrible blow for you both, so soon after the tragedy of poor Donna, and I'm very grateful to you for seeing me now.'

'That weren't no tragedy!' Patricia Bacon threw back at him. 'That were the devil that did it. That poor little angel . . . How could I have let it happen . . .'

'Now Mother,' said Lynette. 'You know there was nothing any of us could have done. They told you not to blame yourself, didn't they? Those evil murdering bastards – they're fiends, no better than fiends, aren't they, Mother?'

'You're right, dear. She's such a good girl, Mr Davenport, so strong – and now she's all I've got!'

Glasby skimmed the rest of the interview. There wasn't much more. The mother was close to hysterics from the look of it – the only wonder was that she had agreed to see Davenport at all. Especially at that time, so soon after the husband's death.

'Funny thing, grief,' she said to herself.

'What's funny about it?' asked Mike Marshall, making her jump.

'Oh my God, Mike! You shouldn't creep up behind people like that!'

'You shouldn't sit with your back to the door, talking to yourself, should you? I'm off now, and I thought I'd see how you were doing. Are you OK?'

It was nice of him to ask, but Glasby had more important things to do. 'Thanks, Mike, but I can't really stop to talk. Bill's asked me to go back through some of his notes, and there's a hell of a lot of them. Thanks anyway, though.'

'Please yourself. I wouldn't want to get in the way of your work with *Bill*.'

Ignoring the sarcasm, Glasby turned back to the next package of interview notes, and Marshall wandered off, whistling out of tune.

The next interview with the Bacons was dated 2nd December. It was much longer, and Mrs Bacon had been a lot calmer. After asking a lot of questions about Donna, her hobbies, what subjects she liked at school – settling them down, thought Glasby approvingly – Davenport had turned to the events of the terrible day when the little girl disappeared.

From the sound of it Donna had been a rather solitary little girl. Lynette, who had gradually taken over the conversation from her mother, said that she had been playing outside on her own for most of the day.

'She had her Sindy doll, with all the different dresses. Dad used to get them for her. She loved it, you know, and she liked to take it outside and play down by the stream with it. It's next to the rec. We didn't hardly see her often, she'd be out there for hours by herself. She come in for tea, and we all watched telly. Then Dad went out about some job – he was always after what work he could get, weren't he Mum? – and Donna must have gone back outside. They found her Sindy down at the stream, you know.'

Glasby read through the rest, but there wasn't much in it that she didn't know already from the cuttings or the book. Towards the end, Mrs Bacon had described family life: 'We never had much. John, he always worked when he could get it. That was only bits of work on the farms or fruit picking, or driving if he was lucky. He always done everything he could, you know, ices, fish – that didn't half pong, d'you remember, Lyn? He loved us, we loved each other, we did, we did. And now there's only us two . . .' Even Glasby was moved by that.

It wasn't until the very end that Glasby found what she was looking for. Davenport had asked the Bacons if there were any family photographs he could look at.

'Go fetch us the picture album, Lyn,' said Mrs Bacon. There's a few in there of Donna, such a pretty little girl she was.'

'OK, Mum, but don't you go getting upset again, will you?'

Davenport had admired them all – 'such a sweet baby' – and broached the subject of borrowing them and having them copied for the paper. It was before the days of chequebook journalism, obviously; there was no mention of money, which would be unthinkable nowadays.

'I don't want you printing them three, not when she was only a baby, that don't seem right. But you can take the others if you like, but be sure to take good care of them, won't you?'

Davenport had promised that they would be returned in good condition, and offered to have a spare copy made for the Bacons. Meticulous as ever, there was a note in his handwriting on the transcripts: 'Photo file 7'. Glasby scribbled it down, hoping that Davenport's cross-referencing would prove to be as efficient as it seemed.

Before she started the search for the photos, Glasby leafed through the 'Lynette Bacon' notes. There really were a lot. In the first, dated 6th January 1970, Lynette had begun by explaining to Davenport that her mother did not want to be interviewed again.

'She said to say sorry to you, Bill. She thinks that you're a real gentleman – not all of them have been like that, you know, really rude some of them, no manners at all. Mum said that you're welcome to come round any time, but please no more tape recorders or making notes, nothing like that. I do hope you understand; she don't mean to be rude or nothing, it's just she's so upset. The doctor came round and he give her some pills, to calm her down, and he told me she mustn't let herself get stressed. You do understand, don't you?'

Davenport had said that he did, of course – not that he had much choice, thought Glasby, cynically.

'Anyway, I suppose,' Lynette had continued, 'now that it's all over, you'll not be round here again, will you? You're the only one left, you know. All the others, they got their stories in the newspapers and they was off. What, 'ave you taken a fancy to our beautiful landscape?'

Glasby thought of the flat, windswept fields of north Norfolk, bare of crops and desolate in the arctic east-coast winter, and smiled. Norwich had been all right to grow up in when she was a kid, but it was miles from anywhere, and the countryside! Some people said they liked it, but she couldn't wait to get out.

'No, Lynette. Do you remember, I told you that I'd like to write a book about it all?' Davenport had replied. 'Well, now I've been given the go-ahead. The publisher has told me to start now.'

'A book? I didn't think you meant it, when you said that. You aren't putting any of us in it, are you?'

Davenport explained: it would be a book on the case. Not just on the trial, but on everyone whose lives had been touched by Jarmy and Dellar, including herself and her own family. Lynette had reacted badly.

'Bill, no offence, but we don't want that! That's the last thing what we need, Mum and me. I know you're not like some of them others – that Tony Scace off the telly was the worst, always trying to stick a microphone up your nose: "How do you feel?" You know better than anyone how we feel, Bill, we just need some peace now. I worry about Mum, I really do. We don't want no book. I'm sorry, but you can't put us in it.'

Davenport had reassured her, promised her that he would never use any material that she had told him in private, would tell her who he was talking to, and keep her informed of what he was doing.

'Lynette, I have never betrayed a trust in me, and I never, ever will.' Glasby could imagine him saying it, with his long vowels and his 'man of the people' estuary twang. You had to admire the way he had brought her round.

He seemed to develop quite a relationship with the family. There were notes from more than twenty different conversations with Lynette, some dated well after Davenport had finished writing *Children Carried Away*. Occasional references in them showed that Davenport had taken up Mrs Bacon's invitation to visit. But beyond a bit more background to family life, there wasn't much in them.

The Bacon sisters had clearly been close, considering the gap in their ages. There had been precious little money to go round, with John Bacon often out of work. Maybe because they didn't have much else to divert them, Lynette and Donna seemed to spend a lot of their time together, Lynette reading to Donna or them both playing with her dolls. But she seemed to have nothing of any consequence to tell Davenport, and Glasby found herself getting bored, wondering where Davenport had found the patience to take all this time with her.

Maybe he fancied her? To Glasby's mind, there wasn't much in the photo she had seen to bear this out. It must have been taken not long before Donna's death, by the seaside in the summer sun. Donna was a pretty, slender little girl with delicate features, her hair blonde in the strong sunlight. Lynette was darker, squarer faced, and from what Glasby could see, her figure was shapely but a bit on the solid side.

Anyway, it was hard to see Davenport as much of a Lothario, and there was certainly nothing in any of the notes to indicate any flirting. Although he might have been quite good-looking when he was younger – you could imagine that Lynette might have had a crush on him.

Working back from a conversation about birthdays, Glasby calculated that Lynette would have been eighteen when her sister died. A very mature girl, obviously.

Glasby decided to look for the photographs, but as she got out of Davenport's chair its normal occupant returned, looking surprised to see her.

'Ah, you're still here,' he said, carrying beer and cigarette fumes in with him. 'You're a glutton for punishment. Did you manage to find anything interesting? Or is it just a load of boring old twaddle?'

'Of course not,' said Glasby, blushing slightly – could he have read her mind? 'I've located the Bacon notes, and been through all of them. Here's where you cross-referenced the photos. I was just about to start looking for them.'

'Well, that shouldn't take you too long. But it's quarter to nine, and if you've been here the whole time you must be starving. Wherever it is that Leonie is now, she'll still be there in the morning, won't she? You can look for the photos then. Don't worry, you can leave everything out. The cleaners know better than to touch anything in here until I tell them to.

'You did say that no one else but you found out about it – the photograph, I mean?' he added, after a pause.

'Yes, that's right.'

'That's first-class work, it really is! Let's keep it that way, then. If there is a story in it, we don't want somebody else pinching it, do we? Just you and me, OK?'

'You mean, not even Jack Daniels, or Tom Lear?'

'No need at this stage. Not that I can see.' Glasby was more than happy to agree.

'Now, it's time you were getting home, Alison, and me too. Where d'you live, anyway?'

'Stockwell.'

'Oh, I'll drop you off then, if you like. I'm in Kennington, just up the road.'

They went down in the lift together, and through a door at the side of the foyer. Glasby hadn't even known that there were parking spaces under the building.

Davenport's car was a bit like him: small and not very tidy. As they crawled along the Embankment, clogged with traffic even at that time of the evening, Davenport asked Glasby about herself, how she had come to journalism, why she had chosen the *Herald.*

'Mind you, when I started, I was desperate. I didn't know anyone; I couldn't even get anyone to talk to me about a job on Fleet Street. I gave the bloke on the reception desk half a crown to point out the editor to me when he walked past. It was Hillier in those days. Then I followed him into the lift and carried on talking right the way to his office. I think he gave me a job just to get rid of me.'

Disarmed, Glasby told him more than she had meant to. About her father, who had told her it was a waste of time her going to university, and who refused point blank to support her then or during her postgraduate year in London. How she'd worked in a McDonald's, practically seven days a week for the whole time. About the job she had found herself on the *South London Press* but how she always wanted to be on a national. Working with Tom Lear, of course, was *great* – Davenport gave her a quizzical look at that point – but she'd always hoped to do investigative reporting, crime and so on. And somehow those stories never came her way.

Then, feeling self-conscious, she asked him instead about the Dellar and Jarmy story: what had it felt like, working on it?

Davenport just gave a little half laugh. 'We'll have plenty of time to talk about all that tomorrow,' and instead started telling her at length about his retirement party, planned for the end of the next week. 'I asked them not to bother with anything,' he said, unconvincingly, 'but you know how they are.'

He dropped her off at home on the Wandsworth Road, insisting on taking her to the door, even though it was a mile or more out of his way. Where she was renting was nothing special, right on a busy main road heading into South London, but it was nothing to be ashamed of either. Or so she told herself. Davenport didn't seem like a snob.

It would have been nice to have someone around to share the day with. There were times when she carried a radio around the flat with her, just so as not to hear the silence. It had been her choice to live on her own, which was not the easiest of things to do, for a young woman without many friends in a city as big – and as expensive – as London.

Meanwhile, Davenport finished his journey home, wondering who it was that the young woman reminded him of. There was something in her manner, but he just couldn't place it.

The child was frightened, lying in the dark, listening –
but what was it?

Four

At work earlier than usual the next day, Glasby forced herself to wait until a decent time before phoning Davenport. She sat with her elbows on her desk, bare of veneer where someone had pulled strips of it off, chipboard showing through underneath. The sound screens which surrounded her little cubicle were dotted with holes from drawing pins and small rectangular patches less faded than the rest, left behind from old postcards or perhaps family photographs put up by her predecessors. Nothing was there now, except for a list of phone numbers.

'What time did you get off last night, then?' asked Marshall, who always arrived just before nine thirty.

'Oh, poor Alison, have you been working awfully hard again?' asked Serena. She probably didn't mean any harm but as usual Glasby did her best to ignore her.

'About half nine. Though Bill and I carried on discussing things in the car. He dropped me home.'

'Bill Davenport drove you home? Maybe the Leer's got some competition!' Marshall liked teasing Glasby; she was thin-skinned at the best of times and could usually be relied upon to rise to it. She gave him a dirty look but could feel herself going a bit pink.

Jack Daniels looked up from his desk at Marshall.

'Careful, Jack, you'll all be fighting over Ali soon,' Marshall threw his way.

'Who's fighting who?' asked Davenport, who had walked in unnoticed. Glasby had the exquisite pleasure of seeing Marshall and Daniels turn bright red, both at the same time, like a pair of traffic lights.

'Come along, young people, we'd better get you started.' Glasby leapt to her feet, grabbing her notes from the night before, and followed Davenport down the corridor without a backward glance at her colleagues. Daniels was right behind her, of course, but for once it didn't bother her. This time she was one up on him with a story, and he didn't even know it.

Davenport's office looked a bit more grimy in daylight than she'd remembered from the evening before. There were notes everywhere, some typed but most in his now familiar, rounded handwriting. Thankfully he had been right about the cleaners; everything was exactly where she had left it.

He talked to them as he filled the coffee machine. 'OK, Jack. You've spoken to all the families now?'

'Yes, Bill. As far as I can get, anyway. Mrs Summer still won't talk. And I phoned the Bacon sister, but she won't say anything either. Mrs Yallop is fine, but she's basically rent a quote, you know – everyone'll have her if they haven't already. But I've got something really good from the Starling brother and sister. Gary and Alison. They both say that the police told their parents that it was Dellar that did Matthew Starling and Donna Bacon – not Jarmy, I mean, just Dellar alone. They never talked before while Dellar was alive, and I've told them not to say a word to anyone else. So I'm going to have to make them an offer for an exclusive, and I think we should do it today.'

'But there's nothing in *Children Carried Away* about that being a police theory!' Glasby protested.

Daniels glowered at her and addressed himself pointedly to Davenport alone. 'The Starlings are very convincing, Bill. They won't change their story, and if we don't get them, the *Chronicle* will.'

Davenport thought for a while. He had a strange look on his face which Glasby couldn't read. Then he smiled broadly. 'You're right, Jack. It sounds like a great angle and we should definitely nail it down. Let's hope they're not going to get too greedy. So, call them right now and tell them you'll be ready to talk business with them later today. And get a meeting with Ellington fixed up. You, me and him. We'll get him to OK making them an offer and you can go from there.'

Daniels looked even smugger than usual as Davenport turned to Glasby.

'Alison, let's see. I assume that the inquest was routine? Just a formal opening and then postponed until the post-mortem stuff's done?' Glasby nodded. 'OK, so nothing there.

And the press conference was a formality as well. So you can carry on going through the background papers. Jack, we'll catch up with you later.'

Throwing a broad smirk in Glasby's direction, Daniels was off down the corridor towards the editor's office, striding jauntily like a man should who had just landed an exclusive that would go straight into the paper, leaving Glasby with . . . more research.

Davenport looked at her and held her gaze for a moment. But there was nothing in his face that she could read.

'What do I need to cover, Bill? Which files, do you think?'

'Hmmm. Well, you're going to need the photo files – the second from top box there, orange cardboard wallet. They should be sorted by subject, and they'll all be referenced on the back. Date acquired, subject, age, source. Photographer, date taken and any other details if known. It shouldn't take you too long, I wouldn't think. I won't be long either. Help yourself to coffee.'

'Oh –' an afterthought on his way out of the room – 'if I'm not back by then, you can make a start on the Dellar and Jarmy interviews. That's the only other place to look.'

'OK,' she replied, trying not to sound surly. Glasby had expected to be working with him, not another solo stint. However it was that he spent his time, it didn't seem to involve much in the way of work. Daniels would be strutting his stuff for Ellington, while she was stuck in an office on her own, with a load of papers that were older than she was.

Luckily the files she needed weren't too bad to get to, and Bill Davenport's knowledge of his personal archives was, as usual, immaculate. There were precisely six photographs of Donna Bacon. A couple were of her as a baby, marked 'Donna Bacon, photographer unknown, taken c. June '62. Age, c. 3 months. Source, Patricia Bacon (mother), 2nd December 1969'. These must be the two Davenport had agreed not to use. Glasby checked her copy of *Children Carried Away*. The other four were all featured in the book.

Only one had Lynette in as well. Like the one Glasby had found among Leonie Dellar's possessions, it had been taken at the seaside. But the girls were clearly younger in it, and it was marked as taken c. August 1967. Donna's wispy blonde hair was blowing across her face, an almost knowing look in her eyes, incongruous in such a young child. Lynette's face had a bit more life in it than in the later picture.

Glasby allowed herself a thrill of excitement. Bill was right; she really had found something new!

She poured herself a cup of coffee from his machine and took a sip. It was bitter, much stronger than she was used to. She winced and tensed her stomach but eventually the warmth of the liquid soothed her and she relaxed again.

There was no sign of Davenport, so she got back down to work. It was time for the Mad Bitch herself.

The Leonie Dellar interview file was thicker than any of the others. Before the first transcript was a handwritten note of Davenport's: 'Interview requests refused by LD' and a list of dates, covering the periods before and immediately after the trial. Then, 'Interview requested by LD, Jan. 70'. The first interview was dated 22nd January 1970. It wasn't by any means long, but it had made Davenport's career.

Davenport had begun, courteously as usual. 'Thank you for seeing me, Leonie. Do you mind me calling you Leonie?'

'People call me a lot worse than that, Mr Davenport. And I think you're the first person to say "thank you" to me for quite some time.'

'Are they treating you badly in here? I mean, have you had any problems?'

'You mean, has anyone tried to stick a knife into me? Or are they spitting in my food? No, not that I've noticed anyway. Nothing like that, thank you. The warders are OK, they'll give you a quiet life unless you're looking for some trouble. Broadlands was pretty bad, they've got some right mental cases in there. Mind you, that's what half of them think I am. Is that what you think I am, Mr Davenport?'

'I'm here to find out what I think, and to listen to you. I'm not a psychiatrist, and I'm not here to judge you either. Just to ask questions, listen to the answers, and try to understand a little bit more than I do at the moment.'

'Yes, I'd heard that you were pretty fair. Not like some of them: "The *Mail* says, string her up. Let the Mad Bitch die". All that sort of stuff. You're not going to write that sort of rubbish, are you?'

'No. I'm going to write about seeing you, about everything we talk about. It will be in the *Herald* this Sunday. Being as

it's you, and you haven't talked to anyone before now, they'll
probably put it on the front page. But the *Herald* doesn't
favour capital punishment, and whatever they call you it won't
be "Mad Bitch", I can promise you that.

'Of course,' Davenport added, shrewdly, 'if you want people
to give you a fair hearing, you've got to do some talking first,
haven't you? Maybe that's why you decided to see me now?'

'Well, I'm sorry for the short notice. But I heard how you
wanted to know about everything, so I thought that I ought
to see you. I hope you'll think your journey here is worth it.'

Without waiting for an answer, she continued. 'You're right,
Mr Davenport. If I want people to listen to me, I have to talk.
So now I'm going to say what everyone keeps on asking me.
Are you sure that tape recorder is working?'

'Quite sure, yes.'

'All right then.' She spoke without any emotion. 'This is
my confession. We did it. We killed them. Brian and me. All
four. Kevin Yallop, Matthew Starling, Donna Bacon and
Michael Summer. Brian did most of it, but I helped. I'm guilty
too. I helped him catch them. I suppose I told myself that he
wasn't going to kill them.'

'Even after the first one?'

'Yes. Yes, even then. I knew it, but I didn't know it, if you
understand. I loved him, you know. He's the only man I've
ever loved.'

'Why didn't you tell the truth before?'

'I wasn't ready to. That's all. I wasn't ready before, but I
am now.'

'Kevin and Donna. Are you going to say where the bodies
are?'

'Mr Davenport, I hope you feel you've got what you came
here for. I'm really tired now. And I'd like to stop. Perhaps
we'll talk again another time.'

That week's *Herald* was triumphant. 'Leonie: The Truth at
Last' screamed the front page. 'By Bill Davenport, the Man
Who Knows.'

But although this may have been the truth, it certainly wasn't
the whole truth. Dellar had given nothing away about their
motives, their methods or, most crucially, where the remaining
two bodies had been hidden. Bill Davenport, never one to give
up easily, continued to request interviews, and periodically

Leonie agreed to talk to him. Indeed, sometimes she seemed to have asked to see him.

A lot of this material was familiar to Glasby from the book so it made quick reading for her. To be honest, in between the two big revelations, there wasn't a lot there. Even after hours of meetings, spaced over many years, Leonie hadn't ever said why she had committed such terrible crimes, or how.

Occasionally she would let slip – if that's what it was – the odd piece of information about the killings themselves. For example, in 1978: 'The knife Brian used on Michael Summer, it was an old kitchen knife of my aunt's. We'd chucked it in the ditch, a while before they stopped us. It's probably all rusted away by now.' (There was a note of Davenport's next to this: 'Informed Dep. Ch. Con. Mullins – nothing found'.)

It wasn't until 1982 that Leonie had given Davenport his second real breakthrough. The transcript was marked '27th August 82 – Interview at LD request'. Knowing what she would see in it, Glasby read it from the start.

'Thank you for coming to see me, Mr Davenport. I was sorry to hear about your mother.'

'Thank you, Leonie. How are you? How's the angina?'

'Much better, thank you. They've finally got a permanent doctor in here again. Much better than the last few months, they've had all these kids, looking at me like I was in a freak show.'

Then she got to the point. 'Mr Davenport, there's something I want to tell you. The bodies. You know when you've asked me before, I couldn't remember where they were?'

'Hmmm.'

'Well, I've been thinking a lot lately. About Brian, mostly. Him and, well, no, that's nothing. You see, I know I'm responsible for, well, you know, the things I did. But I was always trying to do what he wanted me to. And I've been thinking, I can't do anything about it now. But there was something.'

Glasby could picture Davenport waiting, patient as ever.

'Mr Davenport, I remembered something. About that little boy, Kevin Yallop. It was on Mousehold Heath – do you know it, in Norwich? Underneath where the prison is. Brian drove up there once, with me, I mean, and there was this big patch of rocks, sticking out quite near the prison. The left side, if you were looking at the entrance way. And there was a bog, in between the rocks, and Brian kept saying what a good place it was. And when I was thinking the other day, it came to me. I think that might be where Kevin Yallop is.'

There was another of Davenport's notes: 'Informed Ch. Supt. Anderson. Body found, 2nd September '82'. Once again, the front page boasted: 'World Exclusive: Leonie Gives Up Her Secrets to The *Herald*'.

All very convenient for Dellar, Glasby thought. She remembered things when she felt like it, and not when she didn't. Obviously she was trying to manoeuvre her way to parole, or privileges inside prison or something.

There were still some more Dellar interviews, all of which she dutifully flicked through without needing to concentrate on every word. There was nothing in any of them; not a clue as to how the photograph of Lynette and Donna came to be in the possession of Donna's murderer.

It was quarter past twelve, Bill Davenport still hadn't reappeared, and Glasby was starting to worry that he'd forgotten about her. He was quite nice, but all he'd really done was listen to her for a while, waffle on about his retirement do, and leave her to do all the work.

Still, he'd told her to read Dellar and Jarmy, so that's what she'd better do. Maybe she'd find something he hadn't – she already had, after all – and then Daniels could smirk all he wanted. Rather wearily, she turned back to the files, and found the one marked 'Jarmy – Transcript, 15th Apr '70'. As she opened the cover, she forgot her indignation. This was the record of the one and only interview Brian Jarmy had ever given, in more than thirty-seven years of imprisonment.

The interview ran to only four pages, even in the double spacing favoured by the Broadmoor stenographer. Each one was stamped in red: 'Approved: Broadmoor Special Hospital'. The interview was printed verbatim in *Children Carried Away*. But seeing the original, holding it, was a completely different experience for Glasby. One of the old *Herald* articles had called Jarmy 'the enigma of evil', and although the phrase was over-coloured to Glasby's taste, it wasn't a bad description. Barring an occasional diary of – in the words used by Davenport in his book – 'almost calculated banality', and the odd 'wholly unrevealing' letter to a relative, these four pages

represented almost the entire recorded words of one of the
most notorious criminals alive.

Broadmoor Patient Relations
Patient Access Visit
Official Transcript
Patient: Brian Jarmy
Visitor: William Davenport
**   (*journalist* – Daily Herald, *London*)**
15.04.1970

'Good morning, Mr Jarmy. Thank you for agreeing to
see me.'

Silence – by the stenographer. [*I wonder how long a
pause before they type 'silence' in?*]

'Mr Jarmy, might I start [*A bit pompous. Not like his
normal style at all. Maybe he was intimidated by Jarmy?*]
by asking why I'm here? I mean, why me, and why now?
I first requested an interview months ago, and I've done
it many times since. You must have had half of Fleet
Street knocking on your door.'

'Why don't you tell me? You're supposed to be the
smart one, aren't you?'

'Mr Jarmy, I think that you are an intelligent man.
You know as well as I do why I'm here. They tell me
that you get the newspapers in here, or most of them,
anyway. So you've seen some of my stuff on the case,
and on Leonie. She trusts me a little, you know. Maybe
you might decide to do the same.'

Silence.

'Whatever you tell me, it'll get fair treatment in my
newspaper. I can guarantee you that. If you want to talk,
that is.'

'Aren't you supposed to get me off my guard first?
Ask me about life in here, and stuff like that?'

'If you like. Tell me about the hospital, please.'

'The *hospital*, as you so politely call it, is a shit hole.
Run by morons, who think that they're going to make me
better. There's hundreds of them, everywhere you look.
Funny really. No one gives a monkey's until you do something *evil*, and then they want to make you *good* again.'

'And how about the other patients?'

'"Patient" is right. Patient as in "don't be impatient". We all spend every day hanging around, waiting for the geniuses who run the place to think of something to do with us. You know they say that if you come in here completely sane, nothing wrong with you, and everyone agrees that you're fine, it would still take about two years for them to let you out again? Pedestrians, that's what they are. Plodders. Did you have anything planned for the next two years, Mr Davenport?'

'Do you have many visitors?'

'Tut tut, Mr Davenport. You took the trouble to ask around enough to know they don't always give us the newspapers in here, but you haven't got round to asking anyone about my visitors? Let's not try to play games. My mother and I, as you undoubtedly know, have decided to maintain our relationship at a slight distance. One hundred and fifty miles, to be precise, and a few brick walls in between us, like that rather large one you can see out of the window there. And since I haven't felt like talking to any of your colleagues, or all those lovely people who want to save me, or marry me, or burn me at the stake, then no, visiting time has been a little quiet.'

'And how about the other patients? There must be a fair cross section in here, aren't there?'

'That's funny, I thought we'd already done that one. The other patients – well, there are some right nutters in here. Not a very superior type of person, on the whole. There's one or two who you can have an intelligent conversation with, but nothing special, nothing at all. Why, are you hoping to find an informant? Someone to fill in all those evilly enigmatic gaps?'

'And Leonie, Mr Jarmy?'

'Leonie. Well, we haven't had much contact lately, have we? In fact, I hear that you've seen a good deal more of her than I have. Do you get on well with her?'

'I told you before. I said to her that whatever she told me, it would be written up fairly, and I don't think she's had any reason to think differently.'

'So it's true then, is it? That she's told you that we did them?'

'What I wrote is what she told me. You must have seen it, haven't you?'

'Well, no, I haven't, actually. The morons seem to have decided it might upset me. And believe me, in this place, if they don't want you to see something, you don't see it. But they can't stop people talking. One of my fellow *patients* may have mentioned something about it to me. Why don't you tell me? What exactly did she say? Word for word I mean – or are you going to tell me that you can't remember?'

'I can remember exactly what she said. Word for word – that I promise you. She said, "This is my confession. We did it. We killed them. Brian and me. All four. Kevin Yallop, Matthew Starling, Donna Bacon and Michael Summer. Brian did most of it. But I helped. I'm guilty too. I helped him catch them. I suppose I told myself that he wasn't going to kill them."'

'So it's true then. It's true. "I helped him catch them" – that's a laugh. Always liked a joke, little Leonie did. You're sure, absolutely sure, those were her exact words? "We did it. Brian and me. All four?" And all the rest?'

'Mr Jarmy, I have it on tape, the same as we are now. It was exactly as you said it: "We did it. We killed them. Brian and me". She told me that it was time, that she was ready to talk. And how about you? Are you ready?'

'Ready? What I'm ready for, Mr Davenport the journalist, is a little quiet reflection. But if I want to talk some more, you can be sure that I'll be in touch. No need to ring me, you know.'

Reading the transcript out of the context of Davenport's book for the first time, Glasby was struck by a sudden revelation. Jarmy had agreed to the interview just so he could find out what he wanted to know, which was whether Leonie really had confessed.

Just then Davenport finally reappeared. 'Ah, Alison. How are you enjoying all my old boxes for company? Have you found anything new?'

'Not on the photos, no. It's just as you said: all the ones that you ever had from Patricia Bacon are there, only six of Donna, and none of them are the one that I found. It really

is one that you haven't seen before.' He looked at her thoughtfully, but didn't speak, so she continued. 'I've read through
all your interviews with her, and the one with Jarmy. I finished
Jarmy just a moment ago.'

'Hmmm, Jarmy. Not a pleasant character, Alison, not by a
long chalk. Leonie, I wouldn't ever pretend that I understood
her. I mean, after all the years of talking to her, I still have
no idea of how she could have done it. She was a close one,
very close, but you did feel that there was some point of
contact with her, some sort of humanity. But him, he was
cold. Through and through.'

'Bill, don't you think he was using you? When you saw
him, I mean. All he wanted was to hear about what she'd said
to you, and once he'd got that, he lost interest. Like, maybe
he was hoping to appeal, and her confessing spoilt his plans.'

Davenport looked distinctly put out and Glasby flushed.

'Appeal? He'd have a job to do that, with one body in his
car and another in his garage, wouldn't he? Why do you think
anyone talks to a journalist? Don't you think that they're all
using us? Everyone's got their own axe to grind, you know.
And let's be fair; we're using them too. Don't you think?'

'Yes, of course, you're right, Bill. I'm sorry, I didn't mean—'

Davenport rescued her. 'You're right, though, Alison. He's
a manipulative little creep, without a doubt, a real little know-
all. He thinks he's part of a master race, some sort of superman.
You know about all that Nazi crap he had, don't you? The
National Front backed away from him fast, but he'd been a
member at one time. I don't know how political he really was
but he had all the SS gear. You know, the Aryan superman
look: long leather coat, boots, the lot. Oh, and the swastikas
of course. Have you seen the post-mortems yet?'

'No. Should I look at them?'

'It's up to you. I wouldn't unless you have to. Some of the
worst stuff I couldn't use in the book. Times have changed,
I know, and the publishers talked to me about adding some
of it in for a new edition. But I haven't got the stomach for
it, really.'

'Anyway', he continued, 'where were we? Your photo. Well,
we're no closer on it, really. It looks like it might be another
mystery that Leonie's kept to herself, doesn't it?

'I've got a lunch now, I'm afraid, all part of the long

goodbye, you know. Why don't you give me till, let's say three thirty. We'll meet here, and wrap things up then. All right?'

'OK,' said Glasby, sounding anything but. What did he mean, 'wrap things up'? What about the photo? Feeling miserable, she left the papers as they were in Davenport's office (if he wanted to forget all about it, she wasn't going to make it easy for him) and trudged back to her own desk, hemmed in by the pockmarked screens on the other side of which Mike was working and Serena wasn't.

Surely Bill bloody Davenport didn't give up on a story just like that? She might just be on to something, something that would blow Daniels and his stupid 'angle' to bits, so why the hell wasn't Davenport being more helpful? No wonder they were pensioning him off.

The child was frightened, lying in the dark, listening –
but what was it? Quick, let's get under the sheet.

Five

S erena was having one of her rare breaks from chatting on the phone. 'Alison! Hi! Are you excited, working with Bill? He's such a sweetie, isn't he? It must be so thrilling for you!'

'Yes, it's great, thank you. I'm very excited,' Glasby replied, trying not to sound sullen.

Marshall looked up from his terminal. 'What's the matter? Are you bored with life on the executive floor already?'

'Give it a break, Mike, please. I'm not in the mood,' she snapped.

Daniels cut in. 'You haven't hit the wall already, have you, Ali?' He added, without waiting for an answer, 'Things are going very well on my story. Mark Ellington lapped it up, he didn't have a problem at all with the payment. "Cheap at the price," he said, actually.'

Getting no reply, Daniels asked, 'And how's your archaeology project going? Are you enjoying the excavations? More fun being a historian than boring old newspaper work?'

'It's not history!' she snapped back at him. 'Maybe if you put a bit more work into researching your stories, you'd get them right more often.'

Daniels walked over to her, looking angry now. 'What's that supposed to mean, Alison?'

'It *means*, that if you're ever going to learn to be a proper journalist, you'll have to learn how to check your source's credibility. That's all. It's obvious that the Starlings are making all that up so that they can cash in.'

'Oh, I'm sorry. Maybe you'd better let the editor know that the story he wants in as an exclusive doesn't live up to your high standards. And Davenport too – have you taught him how to be a proper journalist yet?'

'Oh for God's sake grow up!' Glasby shouted, and Serena hastily intervened.

'You poor thing! Is Bill being a demon? Daddy says he works like a . . . like a dog.'

Serena probably meant well but it was all too much to bear. Glasby felt like exploding.

'Mike, have you got time to go and get a pizza? Now, I mean. I'll buy, if I can pick your brains a bit.'

'For the price of a pizza you can have all the brains I've got. In fact, you can have my body as well if you want it.' He grinned at Glasby and Serena, whose mobile was just starting to ring. 'Justin, hi! How *are* you? No! In *Tatler*! You bad boy!'

'Let's go *now*, Mike. Please.'

The Portuguese girl who showed them to the table can't have thought much of their potential as tippers. The Isle of Dogs branch of Pizza Express was reasonably full – to be fair, there wasn't much in the way of competition within easy reach – but there were plenty of tables free, and she had no real need to seat them next to the entrance to the kitchen. Glasby tried hard not to let her irritation show. At least it meant they would be served quickly.

And they were, by a charming boy with an Eastern European accent who was so friendly and efficient that not even she could find fault. Marshall ordered an American Hot and a beer. Faced with the smell of food, Glasby remembered the nagging ache in her gut which had been there all morning. She didn't have much of an appetite at all. Probably she should eat if she wanted to have the energy to keep on working. But what was the point if Davenport cared more about his lunch than her story?

'So what's the problem, Ali?' asked Mike, cheerfully. 'You're not very communicative. Let me guess: Davenport's asked you out on a date, and you don't know what to wear. I'd recommend the "nice girl but still up for it" look.'

Glasby gave him the thinnest of smiles. 'You are so not funny, Mike. Ha ha.'

'OK, hold on, let me try again. You've impressed him so much, he wants you to do his next book with him.'

'Yeah, right!' she replied, with far more emphasis than she had intended. 'His bloody party is all Bill's interested in!'

'Yes, Jan mentioned there's some big do they're putting on for him – not that we'll get invited, of course.'

'Jan' was Mark Ellington's PA, who Marshall was pally with. A real Essex girl, so far as Glasby could see. High heels and a big chest.

'Well, it's really frustrating – he's hardly got his mind on the story at all.'

'Really?' Marshall replied, surprised. 'You know that everyone says that he was a real terrier. Never married, worked all hours . . .'

'"Was" is right,' she interrupted. 'He certainly isn't working all the hours this week, that's for sure.'

'Oh, come on, Ali. I mean, it's great that Ellington chose you to work with him, it's a really good step for you. But Davenport must know this story back to front. I mean, he *wrote* it. Aren't you just helping him tie up the loose ends so he can knock out his retrospective piece?'

Glasby didn't want to admit it, but Mike had a point. Luckily the pizzas arrived just then so she was spared a reply. Mike had his smothered in black pepper, the thought of which made Glasby's stomach even worse. She made herself take a mouthful anyway.

'What's he like? As a person, I mean?' asked Marshall, wolfing his food down as he talked.

'Oh, he's been all right. I think he likes me. He's down to earth, very polite. You know that I was reading some of the old interview transcripts?'

'Mmmm.'

'Well, he spent ages talking to people. Time and time again, I mean. Even after he'd finished the book he went back to see, like, the families and everyone. And he has been nice to me as well,' she conceded.

'So what's the problem, then?'

'Mike, if I tell you something, it's just between us, OK? Off the record, I mean, completely. OK?'

'OK, Miss Mysterious. Trust me, I'm a journalist. Off the record. What is it?'

'You know I went to the prison? For the press conference? Well, while I was there, I found . . .' She hesitated. Only Bill and she were supposed to know about the photo. 'I found something, something that Leonie Dellar had, which seemed a bit strange. Something connected to one of the victims. I talked to the prison officer, and he showed me some of her things. In confidence, of course, because they weren't supposed to do it.'

'Clever you! What did you do – use your feminine charms on him?' He wiggled his chest, pouting at her.

'No!' Glasby was indignant. 'I just chatted to him, that's all. And he showed me some things that were found when she died.'

Marshall raised his eyebrows. 'Some things?'

'Yes. Anyway, what I was saying is, when I talked to Bill about it afterwards, he couldn't work out how Dellar had this thing. He was, like, she just shouldn't have it. It didn't make sense. So he and I were going to investigate it. But now he seems to have lost interest. I don't think he can be bothered to take it any further. He's gone off for a boozy lunch, and he's talking about getting the story wrapped up for today. And I really feel like we're on to something.'

'Well, since you obviously don't want to tell me what this *thing* is, I can't really comment, can I? If you think you've got a story, I suppose it's up to you to convince him. If he doesn't want to do the work on it, the least he could do is let you do it for him. Why don't you tell him that?'

'Yeah, maybe you're right! Thanks Mike. I'll try, anyway, when he's back from his lunch. You won't say anything to anyone, will you?'

Marshall started on about his latest domestic problems while he finished his pizza. He was only a year older than Glasby but he had two baby sons. He'd got married to Fabiana very shortly after he met her in Brazil. His wife didn't like London and couldn't understand why they only had a cleaner once a week, no one to cook for them or look after the boys. Glasby had heard most of it before. 'Marry in haste, repent in leisure' could have been written for him, except that he didn't seem to get much leisure.

Rather shamefully she thought about her own problems while pretending to listen to his, chewing slowly on small pieces of dough. She gave up eating when she had got about a third of the way through. They ordered some coffee, which arrived almost instantaneously. The smell of it reminded her of the cup she had had earlier in Davenport's office, and her stomach growled loudly enough for her to hear it above the clatter of cutlery and conversation in the restaurant. Leaving

Mike to practise his Portuguese on the girl who had given them their table, she sought relief, and a bit of thinking time, in the Ladies.

Walking back to the office, she told Marshall about how she had read the Brian Jarmy transcript and her impression that Jarmy had wrapped Davenport around his finger.

'Who got the most out of it, Ali? Think! Davenport wrote a best-seller, and Jarmy's still in Broadmoor!'

Mike had a point, she thought, once again. He really was a decent guy, as well. He never seemed to get wound up like she did. Probably because he had a real life outside work. For the first time, Glasby felt just a touch jealous of Fabiana and her two baby sons.

Glasby walked up to Bill Davenport's office at three thirty on the dot. She could see him framed by the doorway, hunched up over his desk, deep in thought.

'Did you have a good lunch, Bill?' she began, having resolved to be diplomatic with him.

'What? Oh, lunch. Yes, it was very nice, thank you. Another of those "They don't make 'em like old Bill" speeches.'

'Listen, Alison.' He was out of his chair now, pacing around the cramped office, avoiding boxes and piles of papers as he did so. 'The thing is, you've found us a puzzle, and we don't know how to fit the pieces together, do we? And we can't even use it as it is, can we? I mean, some people would write it up just as we have it: "Dellar's final secret – mystery of the hidden photo". But you can't do that, because you told Dack you wouldn't. And anyway, it's a cheap story – no answers, just a picture that might be something or nothing. All we'd be doing is to set the hounds on Lynette and Patricia Bacon for no reason. So . . .'

He hesitated for a moment and Glasby seized her chance. 'Bill, I was thinking. There isn't one puzzle; there're two. First, what is the photo? What I mean is, when you talked to Patricia Bacon, she showed you all the pictures she had of Donna. And there were only six. She even let you see some she didn't want published – the photographs of Donna as a baby, I mean. So if there's another one, why didn't she tell you about it? Why did she keep it secret? Or even if she didn't know about it somehow, Lynette must have done. She's in it,

48 *James Brownley*

after all, and it's not like there were lots of photos of her and Donna so that she could have just forgotten about it.

'Then we've got the second question, which is how did Leonie get it?'

She hurried on, feeling slightly breathless from letting all this burst out.

'They must know something about it, Bill. Or Lynette does, even if her mother doesn't. Don't you think that we have to talk to them? Couldn't we go up to interview them? We've still got a clear day to work in – if they'll see us, we could go up first thing tomorrow.'

'Tomorrow? No, I couldn't do that. Even if I wanted to, I couldn't possibly get away.'

'Well couldn't I go in your place? I mean, I know that they wouldn't talk to Jack when he tried phoning them. But if you called them and told them it was something important, maybe they'd see me then.'

'You *have* been thinking this through, haven't you? Well, we're still on good terms,' Davenport conceded. 'We keep in touch, you see. We exchange Christmas cards, Lynette's birthday and such like. In fact, I got this in the mail from them today.'

He picked up off his desk a rather garish card with a large shiny gold clock on the front. Inside was printed 'Best Wishes on Your Retirement'. It was signed in a scratchy hand: 'Lynette and Patricia'.

'And you're right,' he continued. 'If I ask them to do it, they'll probably see you. Let me think.'

Glasby, bursting with impatience, forced herself to be quiet while Davenport slumped into his chair, gazing for a full minute at a spot on the wall just above the coffee maker. Could he trust her if he let her go? On the other hand, could he trust her if he didn't? Eventually, he turned to her.

'Alison, when you were a kid and you thought you wanted to do this job, did you imagine yourself having to deal with things like this? Talking to the families, the neighbours? When you get close to evil, not just some lowlife, but evil, real evil, it doesn't easily leave you alone, you know. When you rub up against it, it's dirty, filthy, and it sticks.'

His voice was quiet, with nothing of his usual lightness of tone.

'I got to know a lot of people in Norfolk when I was working on the book. Adam Mullins – Chief Superintendent Mullins he was then – in charge of the investigation and bringing the case to court. He became Chief Constable of Norfolk, until he retired a few years back. A very decent man, you know. A lot of people, when Jarmy and Dellar wouldn't talk, they wanted to beat the truth out of them, and he wouldn't have anything to do with it. He said it would bring all of us down to their level and he wouldn't let anyone touch them. It can't have been easy to do that, with all the pressure he had on him.

'Adam Mullins said to me once, "People like us, we always have to remember, we made a choice. We went looking for evil, for all the right reasons, don't get me wrong, but all the same, we went after it. The victims, their families, they didn't do anything. Evil came hunting them, when they'd done nothing to invite it in, and now it will never leave them alone, not until their dying days."'

'He was right, of course. I got to know Lynette Bacon . . . I knew her quite well, you could say. There was only her and her mother, you see, and her mother, well, I don't think she's even half got over what happened to her family. First her little girl, then her husband. How could anyone manage with the shock of that? Lynette still lives with her, she always has done, and they're as close as could be. But from time to time, especially in the early years, Lynette needed another pair of ears to listen to her and sometimes that's what I was.

'I'll ask her to talk to you. And I'm sure she'll see you, and Patricia too if she's up to it, but if you go to see her from me, you'll go as a human being first, and a journalist second. There's plenty of people around here will tell you differently, and some of them have had very good careers from it. But if you have to do something dishonourable, something you wouldn't like being done to your own family, just to get a story in a newspaper, it's not worth it. Never.

'Now, if you're happy with that, I'll call Lynette.'

The child was frightened, lying in the dark, listening –
but what was it? Quick, let's get under the sheet.
Trembling, but it was a hot summer night, so sweating
as well.

Six

Glasby was in her car and heading east for the first time in several years. In fact, she had never driven herself up to Norfolk before; she hadn't had a car of her own, the last time she had been back home. Her father, who was quite a few years older than her mother, had taken early retirement from the accounts department of the Norwich Union insurance company in her final year at university. They moved house to a small town in Hertfordshire, barely mentioning it to her before they did it. When she went to see them that summer, she found that her mother had cleared out most of the things she had left at home. ('We didn't think you'd want all that old clutter, dear'.)

So now she was struggling to find the way on to the A11 and out of London. She had checked her *A–Z* carefully before leaving Stockwell, but the route she'd chosen along the river turned out to be a mistake. 'Damned traffic,' she said to herself, looking anxiously at her watch and then, for the twentieth time that morning, at her handbag, next to her on the front passenger seat. Inside it was a copy of the photograph of Donna and Lynette that she had printed off, with Davenport's agreement, to give to the Bacons.

She had struck lucky yesterday. Patricia's health was very variable, so Davenport said. Kidney problems. She spent a lot of time in bed or at the hospital. But when Davenport spoke to Lynette she told him that her mother was doing fairly well, and yes, they would both be willing to see Miss Glasby on his behalf.

Mrs Bacon was addicted to a soap opera that came on after lunch so it had been arranged for her to see them at eleven o'clock, in their home in the north Norfolk village of Coltishall. Glasby had allowed four hours for the drive, setting off while the sky was changing from black to grey and the streetlights were still on. But she was starting to worry that she would be seriously late.

To her relief, as she turned into Tower Bridge Road the traffic eased. Before too long she was through Aldgate and on to the start of the dual carriageway. Steering her Punto (she hated the adverts, but it had a very good write-up in the car magazine) through the East End, she found the left turn at the Bow roundabout and settled herself for the journey up the M11.

Predictably enough it was raining hard as she followed the motorway through the green Essex countryside. Glasby, who wasn't a particularly experienced or confident driver, had to concentrate hard to keep a reasonable distance between her and the large commercial vehicles in the middle and slow lanes. She didn't like the fast lane, using it only if it was absolutely necessary to keep up a decent speed.

By the time she passed the M25 junction she could relax a little. It had been almost overwhelming, the way the week had gone. She'd started it worrying about whether she would be made redundant (that all seemed to have gone quiet, anyway), getting drunk and making an idiot of herself with Jack bloody Daniels. Well, Daniels or no Daniels, she was finishing it by working her own lead on the Dellar story, which was awesome. It would be great to have someone to talk it through with. But there wasn't anyone that she could think of, no one who would understand what it all meant.

A huge royal blue HGV appeared out of the spray to her left, and she realized that she had let her speed drop to less than 50 mph. 'Get a grip,' she told herself sharply.

Just then her phone rang. She hadn't got round to fitting the hands-free kit that you were supposed to have but she had an ear plug connected to the phone on a length of wire, which was almost as good. Glasby had placed it within easy reach before she set off, thinking that Bill might need her, perhaps want to discuss the article.

'Hi, Ali. I'm not calling you too early, am I?' It was Kate Hall.

'No, of course not. I've been up for ages.'

They had met on the first day at Leicester, enrolling for English, and became friends – best friends according to Kate in a drunken moment, the first and only time anyone had ever said that to Glasby – but that was a few years ago now. While Glasby had gone off to City University in Islington for the journalism course, Kate was at Roehampton training to become a teacher. When she was there she met and eventually moved in with Simon Sheppard, a self-satisfied sort of bloke with a beard and a way of talking that Glasby often found patronizing.

Somehow, little by little, Simon's presence had changed everything. He didn't stop Kate from doing anything, of course; except that somehow, he did. Going to see a film, for example – unless it was French, or Iranian or something, which was definitely OK. To start off with, Kate would laugh about it: 'Simon would have *hated* that!' These days, everything was 'we'. As in, 'We don't like Hollywood much. It's all tosh, when you think about it, isn't it?' Glasby still got on with Kate, but it was very clear that everything had to be fitted around him. 'Simon says' used to be a joke between them, but it just wasn't funny any more.

Kate was calling to invite her to dinner, no doubt to introduce her to another of Simon's colleagues or friends, but social engagements were about the last thing on Glasby's mind. 'Kate, I'm driving, on the motorway. I'm having to go somewhere on a story. Can I call you back?' And she immediately forgot all about it.

After dithering uncharacteristically the night before about what to wear to see the Bacons, she had decided on the same grey suit that she had worn on Wednesday. She thought that Bill would approve; it would show respect for his sources. She had succeeded in removing the dust from Bill's office by giving it a thorough going over with Sellotape.

The important thing was to get their trust, right from the beginning. That's how he would do it. Manners. Thank them for seeing her, especially at such short notice. What should she say to them about Dellar's death? Remember to call her 'Dellar', not 'Leonie'. If they call her 'Mad Bitch', maybe even do that. 'You must have been pleased' – no. 'It must be a relief to you to know that she's gone now, where she can't hurt anyone else.' When we talk about the photo, 'such lovely girls'. Bill would do all that so naturally; you wouldn't ever think it was just part of the job.

Davenport had offered Glasby one piece of advice which she had clung on to hopefully, expecting some sort of insight into how a legend like him worked his sources. But she had been disappointed. 'Whenever you go out on a story always take an overnight bag. I always have one ready. You just never know.' She had dutifully packed a bag and put it in the boot of the Punto. It didn't seem particularly likely that she'd need it. But, as Davenport said, you just never knew.

The plan was, she'd get there at eleven, be finished before lunch and call Davenport immediately. If there was anything that could be included, he would write it into his Dellar article. Not for the first time, she wondered what sort of a byline he would give her. She had tried to convince herself to ask him yesterday after the interview with the Bacons was arranged. But it would have been too cheeky.

She was making good time now. She decided she could indulge in a favourite of her childhood; a stop at the Red Lodge transport cafe at Freckenham and a fried egg sandwich for breakfast. She deserved it!

The ring road around Norwich is well signposted from the A11, and Glasby quickly found herself on a B road heading north out of the city to Coltishall. She had dim memories of going there as a child. Her father, resentful as ever that she was not a boy and probably acting under the instructions of her mother, had taken her to an open day on the RAF base nearby. She had soon got bored with looking at banks of dials and knobs in the cockpit, and the noise from the planes was ear-splitting. Eventually even her father had noticed this and they had gone back home, earlier than planned.

Coltishall was larger than she'd expected; maybe people commuted the nine miles into Norwich for work. She stopped to ask the way of a very jolly and helpful traffic warden (why would they need a traffic warden out here, for God's sake?). The rain was so hard it was pouring in a little stream off the peak of his cap, but it didn't seem to have affected his spirits at all.

'Recreation Road? Keep going, past the old school on your left, and it's the next left after that. I suppose that you're going to see Mrs Bacon, are you? Yes, I thought you weren't from round our way.'

'I grew up in Norwich, actually,' Glasby replied, a bit miffed to be so easily identified. Then, remembering her vow to be well-mannered and friendly, 'Thank you so much for your help. I do hope you can get in out of the wet soon.'

It looked like a prosperous village, not really what Glasby had in mind from Davenport's description of the Bacons. Recreation Road was easy to find from the traffic warden's directions. She slowed down, looking for number 53, the rain making it hard to see any of the house numbers. They were semis, ex-council maybe, but they looked pretty decent. Crawling along the street in second gear, she reached 39. There was a gap after that, given over to allotments. Then the houses started again, just three of them. They were single storey, detached, strange square-shaped constructions. Glasby had never seen anything quite like them before.

Thankfully, they had the numbers on the front gate posts: 51, 53 and 55. Number 51 was a mess. One of the front windows was boarded up with plywood. A caravan with the wheels off, and seemingly a piece of one side missing, had been dumped in the front yard. Next to it was a rusting old Ford Capri. She parked her car outside the Bacons' and made sure to lock it. As she walked up the pathway – there was no gate, just the posts – she could see a child with its face pressed up against the glass next door, staring out at her.

She hadn't thought to bring an umbrella. Shoulders hunched against the rain, she knocked on the door of number 53. She checked her watch for the umpteenth time: 10.59. 'Get a move on,' she implored silently, worried about her suit. Footsteps, and the door opened.

'You're Miss Glasby, are you? Come on in out of the rain. I'm Lynette, Lynette Bacon. Come in.'

The first thing that Glasby noticed was the smell, a mixture of boiled cabbage and old washing. Mindful of Davenport's strictures she put aside the thought that the house might not be very hygienic. Lynette led her down a dark hallway and pushed open a flimsy door which had been patched up clumsily with unpainted hardboard. 'Come into the lounge, Mum's in here.'

It was stiflingly hot inside, so hot that Glasby felt momentarily dizzy. Opposite the door was a fireplace surround decorated in a bad imitation of wood, with two large electric fires balanced on the hearth, both full on.

'I hope it's not too warm for you in here. Mum likes it this

way, she finds it comforting. Mum, this is Miss Glasby, who
Bill phoned us about yesterday.'

'I won't get up, Miss. It's my kidneys you see, they make
my legs go all swollen. They give me terrible aches, especially in this weather.' Through the haze across the room Glasby
made out a small, elderly woman. Her face was half-hidden
behind large round glasses. She was wrapped in a pink blanket,
a pair of tartan slippers poking out underneath it.

'Have you come up all the way from London this morning?
You'd like a cup of tea then.'

It was a statement rather than a question, but Glasby stuck
to her script: 'Thank you. It's very nice to meet you and Mrs
Bacon. Thank you very much for seeing me, especially at
such short notice. Bill Davenport said to say thank you, and
to send his best wishes to you both.'

'Sit down, won't you. I'll put the kettle on. Do you want
a cup, Mum?'

Lynette didn't seem to expect an answer and Mrs Bacon
gave none. Her breathing was loud enough to be heard from
across the room.

Glasby sat down on an old pvc-covered sofa, choosing a
corner as far away as possible from the two fires. Just above
her head she could hear the rain beating against the window.
The sofa creaked and subsided alarmingly and she shifted
uncomfortably, eventually perching on the edge with as much
of her weight as possible on her elbow, resting on the wooden-
faced arm.

Her senses having at last adjusted to the heat, she looked
around her. The room she was in was about three metres wide
and five or so long. The walls were covered with some sort
of textured paper which had been painted in a gloss finish, a
rich chocolate brown, which was peeling in places. There was
water trickling down inside the window to her left; the metal
frames were spotted with rust. The floor was carpeted in a
rough cord, a similar colour to the walls. There was one other
chair in the room, across the fireplace from where Mrs Bacon
sat, a wooden standard lamp with a pink floral shade behind
it. To her right was a large television. The aerial lead trailed
along and up the wall.

'It's a prefab,' said Mrs Bacon, startling Glasby out of her
inspection of the room. 'Built them after the war, they did.

You wouldn't remember them. The council, they've knocked most of them down now. But they kept ours, us and Mrs Willis. Number 55, at the end. And them next door.' She jerked her hand dismissively in the direction of number 51. 'No good, they ain't, no better than Dids.'

From the little Glasby could see of her, Mrs Bacon didn't look at all healthy. Even in the orange glow of the fires her skin looked pasty, like old dough. Magnified by her spectacle lenses, her eyes were milky and clouded over. Possibly she was a little cross-eyed. Donna didn't get her looks from her mother, that was for sure.

The kettle must have been ready for her arrival, because before Glasby could say anything to Mrs Bacon, Lynette had returned carrying a large wooden tray. On it was a brown teapot and three cups and saucers and a plate with some sugared biscuits. Having put the tray down, Lynette sat herself on the sofa next to Glasby. There was a brief silence while everyone sipped at their tea, which tasted like half a bag of sugar had already been added. It was also horribly strong. Glasby had neglected to pack any Imodium in her overnight bag.

Lynette was obviously determined to take control of the situation. 'Now, Miss Glasby,' she said, 'if Bill Davenport wants Mum and me to talk to you, then of course we're glad to. He told me that it would be "off the record" – that's what you call it, isn't it? So you won't be putting nothing in the *Herald* what we say, will you?' Glasby, taken by surprise, just nodded. Davenport hadn't said anything to her about that.

'We don't want no notes, or quotes in the newspapers. Since, well, since the other day, you can imagine, we've had a lot of newspaper people calling, and television n' all. We don't want no one upsetting you, Mum, do we?'

While Lynette was talking Glasby took the chance to have a look at her. She was still recognizable from the old photos, but only just. If her charms as a youngster had depended on her shapeliness, the years had not been kind to her. She must have been about 5'3", bordering on dumpy, with the same frizzy hair as her mother. Her eyes were brown and shrewd, her jaw square. She looked liked she knew what she was about.

Sensing that she should try to take the initiative, Glasby jumped in hastily. 'It must be a comfort to you, Mrs Bacon.

To both of you, I mean. Knowing that Dellar is, er, gone. So that she can't do anything wicked to anyone else again.' Why did it sound so lame? She cursed herself. If Davenport had done it, it would have sounded so much more genuine.

Mrs Bacon stirred at this, leaning forward in her chair, half making as if to get up. 'Her? Gone? She'll never be gone. She's evil, she is, nothing but evil. Evil doesn't go. Once it's in this world, it never goes, it lives on. You don't understand nothing. Tell her, Lynette.'

'Now, Mum,' cautioned Lynette. She turned to Glasby, her jaw set. 'Like I said, we're only talking to you because Bill asked us to. We don't see people like you, we don't like it. They're always coming here, asking the same questions, stirring it all up again. No offence to you, but we don't like it at all.'

'I'm sorry,' Glasby stammered, taken aback. 'I didn't mean—'

'Don't you mind,' Mrs Bacon interrupted. 'How is Mr Davenport? We haven't seen him for quite a while, have we Lynette? Such a nice man, really kind. Him so important, down in London on the newspaper, and he always remembers us, don't he? Always a card, Christmastime. Is he all right?'

'He's very well, thank you.' Glasby, recovering her poise, was grateful for the change of subject. Her Norwich accent coming back to her, she continued: 'You know he's retiring from the *Herald*, don't you? We're holding a big party for him next week, in his honour. Everyone thinks the world of him. But that's why he couldn't come up to see you himself, so he asked me to come instead.'

While she was saying this a picture on the wall caught her eye. It was Prince Charles and Princess Diana on their wedding day. Idiotically, she had to fight the impulse to smirk; this must be the only household in the country still to believe in the fairy tale royal marriage. Next to it was a colour photo of Mrs Bacon and Lynette, taken fairly recently from the look of it. They were sitting at the end of a large table in a pub or restaurant with the remains of a meal and drinks in front of them. Both were smiling broadly; a birthday party, Glasby guessed, maybe Mrs Bacon's seventieth.

Above the fire was a picture of Lynette and Donna, taken at the seaside, the one from 1967. Glasby was struck again by how pretty the little girl was; hair sparkling in the sunlight, the sea breeze blowing wisps across her face and tugging at the hems of the girls' summer dresses. It was hard to imagine this delicate little pixie in the stale stew of the living room, let alone being the fruit of Mrs Bacon and her presumably equally unappealing husband.

'What exactly did you want to ask us about then?' Lynette had relaxed a little, but her eyes had lost none of their shrewdness. How many smart-suited, well-spoken so-and-sos had she seen in the last thirty-eight years? Each one of them looking for a quick human interest quote to justify an update on the murders, and then on to the next story. Some of them, like this one, even had the nerve to pretend that they *cared*. If she'd learnt one thing it was this: it never bloody ends. Answer one question, you get another. Finish with one of them and the next one's knocking at your door – if they even bothered to do that before they barged in on you.

Glasby drank some more of the disgusting tea. The cloying sweetness and the closeness of the room were beginning to make her feel sick.

Before she could reply, Mrs Bacon started again. 'That woman. They said on the news that she was dead. She ain't dead. She weren't never alive. She's the devil, that's what she is. She came round here, with that nutter, and she took our little angel. Our little darling, she was, our Donna. Prettiest little thing alive she was. When she smiled, she sent the sun down from the sky to us. And that bitch, she took it all away. We were such a happy family, we were so happy . . .' To Glasby's horror, she began to sob, and then gasp for breath.

'Mum,' said Lynette sharply. 'Mum!'

The old lady stopped crying as quickly as she had started.

Glasby didn't see how she could produce the photo just like that but to her relief a telephone rang, an old-fashioned one with a bell, and Lynette went to answer it. From the other room, she called out, 'It's just Mrs Willis. Shan't be a moment.' Glasby seized her chance.

'Mrs Bacon, when Leonie died – I mean Dellar – when she died they found a photograph she had. This is a copy of it. You see, it's a picture of Donna and Lynette.' Slipping the photo from her bag, leaning out of the sofa and handing it to Mrs Bacon, she continued, 'I wasn't sure, that is, Bill wasn't sure, we didn't know how Dellar could have got it, and we were wondering . . .'

'What! You what? What's this photo? What are you doing with a picture of my Donna? I ain't never seen this before! What d'you mean, that bitch had a photo of my Donna? What sort of squit is that? Who are you, anyway?'

The old woman was shrieking, on her feet, her eyes wild, face almost purple, her whole body shaking. She was panting for breath, chest heaving. There was a crash from the other room as Lynette dropped the receiver and ran back in to the lounge.

'What the hell are you doing? What is that? Give it to me!' Lynette grabbed the photo from her mother then dropped it on the floor as if it had burned her. She grabbed Glasby with both hands and physically lifted her from the sofa by her shoulders, fingers digging into her flesh.

'You, you'd better go. Now!' – as Glasby tried to speak. 'Haven't you done enough? Upsetting her like that, you should be ashamed of yourself, you should! Who d'you think you are anyway? Get out! Get right out!'

Lynette shoved Glasby down the hall, more or less throwing her handbag at her. She turned and ran, slamming the front door behind her. Trembling, fighting back tears, she fumbled in her bag for her car keys, dropped them in a large puddle, and finally got herself into her car.

'Shit!' She banged both hands on the steering wheel, hard enough to hurt. 'Shit, shit, shit!'

With an effort she controlled her breathing and forced herself to calm down. It wasn't her fault. Davenport couldn't blame her, she'd only done what they had both agreed. But he would, anyway. Lynette would probably be on the phone to him now. She'd be lucky if she still had a job by the time she got back to London. Daniels would be laughing out loud when he heard the news; first she'd let him have her, then he'd got her story and now he was going to get her job.

'Calm down,' she said viciously to herself. 'Think!' The first thing was to get out of here, before they set a lynch mob on her. The next was to call Davenport. He would know what to do. Wouldn't he?

The child was frightened, lying in the dark, listening –
but what was it? Quick, let's get under the sheet.
Trembling, but it was a hot summer night, so sweating
as well. What was that noise?

Seven

Wouldn't it just be her luck to bump into the jolly neighbourhood traffic warden? Partly to avoid him and partly to make sure she wasn't spotted by any vengeful friends of the Bacons, Glasby found a close to turn into across the main road. It was lined on one side with 1960s bungalows and houses. At the other side, where she was parked, was a small stretch of woodland. She checked the reception on her phone and switched off her engine.

She tried Davenport's mobile. It went straight to voicemail. He must have switched it off. What was the use of having the wretched thing if you didn't keep it on? She called the *Herald*.

'Be in your office, please be there,' she whispered. 'Herald Newspapers, may I help you?' came the voice at the other end of the line. It occurred to her that she hadn't phoned the office from outside since the day that Tom Lear had interviewed her for her job. Well, she'd better get into practise now – if this went badly, she was going to need some more job interviews, soon.

Davenport answered on the first ring. 'Oh, hello Alison. Have you finished with Lynette and Patricia already? Or have you had a problem finding the house?'

'No. Well, yes. There was a problem. I went to the house, and I saw them, but . . . It was really bad, Bill. I'm really sorry. Maybe I did something wrong, I don't know, but they were really angry with me. I don't think there was anything I could have done. Actually, I thought that you might have already heard about it.'

'Heard? Why would I have heard anything? You didn't take the News at Ten team in with you, did you?'

'No, but I thought maybe Lynette might have called you or something, to complain.'

'The Bacons aren't much for telephoning, I don't think.

Listen, why don't you begin at the beginning and tell me what's happened. I'm sure you haven't done anything you shouldn't have, so just start at the beginning, please.'

Somewhat comforted, Glasby told him. How she had got there on time, passed on his regards, and received their best wishes for him, drunk the awful tea, the heat in the room, Mrs Bacon's state of health, the telephone ringing – 'The next door neighbour? I remember her, nosy old bird. I bet she was just trying to find out who you were' – then the photo, Mrs Bacon on her feet, Lynette dragging her off the sofa – 'I thought she was going to hit me, Bill' – and throwing her out.

'Alison, I'm sorry. You've had a bad experience, but these things happen to everyone. It won't be the last time, and I'm sure it wasn't your fault.

'Now listen,' he continued. 'I'm writing up the Leonie piece now. Whatever happened today, we can't use anything to do with the photograph, can we? So get back to London, and drive carefully. Don't worry about coming in today, just go home and have a rest and a good weekend. We'll talk on Monday.'

'Don't come in? Why? There isn't . . . there isn't a problem, is there?'

'No! Alison, I told you, stop worrying! Actually, I was going to talk to Lear, to tell him that you've done a damned good job this week.'

'Oh. Thank you.' She still felt deflated, though.

'Look,' he added, 'there's a lot of things happened with the Bacons, with Lynette actually.' A pause. What did he mean? 'We'll talk on Monday. I'll tell you what, are you doing anything for lunch then?'

'No, I'm not.' Of course she wasn't.

'Right then. We'll have a bite, and talk it over after the weekend. Come to my office at twelve forty-five, OK? But you've reached the end of the road on the photograph.' The line went dead as he hung up.

Glasby sighed, the sigh of someone who still had a job, hadn't screwed up after all, and was going to be taken out to talk things over by her boss. She sat for a few moments, listening to the rain on the Punto's windscreen and watching the bough of a tree swaying as it was hit by gusts of wind.

Then she started to think. It was still not midday. She needed a drink, anything to get the taste of Lynette's tea out of her mouth. Maybe she could find a café or something. Having manoeuvred her car around the turning space at the end of the close, she headed back into the village.

Sitting over a cup of milky coffee in the Broadland Tea Rooms, she tried to picture the scene at number 53 Recreation Road. A medical emergency, the ambulance arriving, Mrs Bacon fighting for breath, Lynette telling the grim-faced neighbours: 'It was that cow from London. She did it.'

She told herself not to be silly. More likely, they were both glued to some drivel on daytime telly, knocking back some more delicious tea.

Having got over her relief at how decent Davenport had been, it suddenly hit her what he had said. 'End of the road on the photograph.' So that was it. The end of her amazing week, and nothing much to show for it after all. To be fair, she couldn't really argue with him. They had tried, gone back to the source as it were, and there was nothing doing. No answers.

'Just more questions.'

'Sorry, dear, what?' asked the old lady behind the counter.

Glasby hadn't realized that she had spoken aloud. 'I'm sorry, I was talking to myself.' Noticing that she was the only customer in the place she looked down quickly, not wanting to be drawn into conversation. But she was right. There were more questions now than when she'd started. Reaching into her bag for pen and paper, she wrote them down:

1. Where and when was the photo taken?
2. Who took it?
3. Why did Patricia Bacon say she'd never seen it before? Was she lying? Surely she couldn't have forgotten it – there were only six other photos of Donna, after all?
4. What, if anything, does Lynette know about the photo?
5. The one they'd started with: how did Leonie Dellar get it? Why had she kept it hidden for so long? Why was it so important to her that she had ripped open the cushion to get to it as she was dying? Was there some connection between her and Donna – or Lynette – as well as the obvious one?

On reflection, she added another:

    6. What does Bill know about the Bacons that he hasn't told me?

She was no closer on 1 and 2 than when she'd started. And she wasn't exactly likely to get any answers on 3 or 4 from the Bacons. Or 5. On 6, hopefully Davenport was going to tell her something on Monday. She would just have to wait until then.

Then she had one further thought. If there was some connection with Leonie, some reason why she should have had the photo, maybe people in the village would know. Villages were small places after all, even smaller years ago. Everyone knew what was going on in everyone else's lives. Presumably the police must have asked around at the time, but who knows how thorough they were? Anyway, there was no harm in trying. Come to think of it, she might as well start here.

'Thank you,' she said, getting up to pay. 'That was very nice, especially on such a dismal day.'

'You're welcome, dear. Just passing through, are you?'

'More or less', said Glasby, vaguely. 'I don't suppose you're from Coltishall, are you? I mean, have you lived here a long time?'

'Not really, dear. I'm from Norwich originally, it was my husband who was from the village, we moved here when he was made redundant, Doston and Poole, they closed down the whole yard, 1983, we moved here, he's passed away now, Mr Whiting, emphysema, I always told him, no cigarettes, but you know what men are like . . .'

Glasby waited impatiently for Mrs Whiting to pause for breath, eventually eliciting the information she was looking for: 'You want to try Mrs Brighty, down at the post office, she's Coltishall born and bred, ever such a nice lady, very helpful you'll find her I'm sure, she knows everyone from round here . . .'

Glasby thanked her politely and fled.

The post office was only fifty metres down the street, so she braved the rain on her good suit and made a run for it. She arrived at the doorway just before a rather plump old lady who was protecting a hairdo that looked like it had been welded on to her head, under a large, incongruous blue and white striped golfing umbrella. Leaving her struggling with her umbrella, Glasby pushed open the door and stumbled into the shop.

It was dimly lit and smelled a little musty. The floor was bare concrete. Ahead of her was a rack of shelves which contained a rather odd conjunction of greeting cards, wrapping paper and tins of cat food. It was where Bill Davenport's retirement card had come from, almost certainly.

At the rear of the room was a metal counter. Behind it, protected by a thick glass panel which ran up to the ceiling, was a tall, thin-faced woman who looked to be in her sixties, wearing a blue nylon overall and a pink polonecked sweater. (There didn't seem to be anyone young in the whole village.)

'Hello, are you Mrs Brighty?' she asked, walking up to the counter. A drop of rain found its way along the parting in her hair and down under her collar.

'Yes, dear, that's me. What can I do for you?'

'My name is Alison Glasby. I'm from a newspaper, in London. I work with Bill Davenport, on the *Herald*, perhaps you remember him?'

'Yes, I knew Mr Davenport, that was an awful long time ago. What was it you were wanting?'

'Well, I know that you come from Coltishall. So I suppose you must know the Bacons, Mrs Bacon and Lynette, very well. Bill Davenport is a very good friend of theirs, I expect you know that. But unfortunately he's indisposed at the moment, and he asked me to talk to you, because he said that you were someone who everyone in the village respects. Just to get some background.'

'Background, dear? On Pat and Lynette? Whatever for?' Mrs Brighty sounded surprised and a touch suspicious.

'From what I heard, you've asked quite enough questions about Pat and Lynette, without going snooping around behind their backs.' This was from the golf umbrella lady, who must have followed Glasby into the shop without her noticing. 'It was you who was there earlier, wasn't it? I saw you from my window as you ran out. Don't you think those two have suffered enough already, without you poking about? We look after people round here, you know. Do you want me to shout for my nephews, so we can see what they thin'< about your sort?'

'Mrs Willis, you're quite right,' said Mrs Brighty from behind her counter. 'Now young lady, were you wanting to buy anything, or . . .'

Glasby muttered an apology and left, her face bright red. She didn't even notice the rain as she walked back to her car. Without remembering to switch on the lights, she swung it round in a sharp U-turn and headed back home.

At least she hadn't got a parking ticket.

Her reward after a miserable – and wretchedly slow – journey was a cold flat. It looked like the boiler had gone again. So much for Robin Hutley and his 'utmost good faith'. Having a landlord who ripped you off with cheapjack repairs was bad enough, but why did the man have to be so unctuous while he was doing it? He didn't answer his mobile number when she tried it, needless to say, and although she left a message there was no chance whatsoever that he would call her back before Monday. Her father said that she was an idiot not to be started on the property ladder. Probably he was right. But Glasby had no idea how you found places – agents, mortgages, solicitors and everything. It all took so long. Who had the time?

Ironically, time was the one thing Glasby did have that weekend, when she least wanted it. She chucked off her shoes and threw her jacket over an upright chair whose fellows were arranged around three sides of the small table in the kitchen. The idea was, if she had a dinner party for four, she would move the table into the sitting room and squeeze the fourth chair in. It hadn't been a problem so far; Kate was the only person other than her who'd eaten here.

Without bothering to take off the rest of her clothes she climbed into the only warm place available, which was the bed. And lay there for a long time, brooding.

It had been a real stretch, moving in here on her own. What with the rent and the repayments on the Punto, there wasn't much left over for the basics, let alone buying clothes or going out. So it was a good job that she didn't do much of either. The landlord had put a few bits of furniture into the flat after he'd finished the conversion; show-homing he called it. Nearly all of it was bottom of the range Ikea (surely no one could have *chosen* a purple sofa?), but she had persuaded him to leave it there without putting the rent up, which was a godsend really.

Alison Glasby was certainly no socialite. Her parents made lots of time for their interests, especially her father's golf obsession, and she had grown up knowing that she wasn't one of them. With no brothers or sisters, she had learned to depend on no one but herself. But even for her, London could be a lonely place. When she had moved down after Leicester she only really knew Kate and Helen, and Kate was miles out, almost in the suburbs.

Helen lived in a big house in Camden, sharing with a bunch of medical students. There had been a room available for Glasby, just when she needed it; small, dark and right over the sitting room, so that she had to wear earplugs every night, but it had been home for nearly four years. Helen had stayed, happy with her job in a big bookshop on Piccadilly. The medics came and went, to be replaced by others who were just as noisy. The lack of privacy grated on Glasby, though; that and the way that you never knew who was going to be there, or who would have helped themselves to your food.

The burglary was the last straw. Someone (no one owned up) hadn't locked the front door properly, so the insurance company wouldn't pay out, and Glasby had lost a television and her camera.

A place on her own was the obvious answer, even if Helen had been pretty uptight when she told her about it. It would be nice if the phone rang a bit more often, though. Sometimes she had morbid thoughts of herself lying dead: 'Single girl Alison's tragic end: only the smell alerted neighbours'. Still, even with the traffic noise outside she could hear herself think these days. And boy, did she have plenty to mull over.

Looking back, her encounter with the Bacons was like a nightmare. Her being as polite as she could be, handing over the photo; the old woman, rising from her deathbed (more or less) to curse her; Lynette manhandling her (she prodded at her shoulders. They still ached from Lynette's fingers; surely there would be bruises in the morning); the smell; the heat; the disgusting tea which had left her stomach in knots.

Davenport had held back on something; he'd as good as said so himself. Something between him and Lynette, maybe?

She wasn't exactly an oil painting, but she was a tough woman, and probably when she was young she would have had some sort of appeal for him. Or maybe he'd done something out of line, something she was now being set up for?

'Stop it!' she told herself sharply. 'You're tired and cold and getting hysterical. Get some food and some rest.'

She obeyed the first instruction. The remains of yesterday's Chinese, heated in the microwave, made a passable meal. She sat on the hard wooden chair, looking at the white wall above the table. The floor was tiled with padded lino, white with small black diamonds, and she noticed that it looked grubby. She even considered getting the mop out from the cupboard behind her, but only for a moment. Instead, she dumped the dirty dishes and cutlery in the sink and headed for the bedroom.

Her first waking thought was that it was cold. Absolutely freezing. Luckily the shower was heated electrically, so she was able to get up, wash and breakfast without too much discomfort. But a weekend hanging around the flat seemed out of the question.

Over some mouthfuls of toast from a sliced loaf at the bottom of the freezer, it occurred to her that her parents might like to hear from her.

The mobile had been a birthday present from them a couple of months ago. It was an expensive phone and the video-messaging facility made it a great present for someone with a lot of friends and a frivolous frame of mind. Neither of which, unfortunately, described Glasby, and she hadn't been very diplomatic when they gave it to her. But the superior camera quality which it had boasted had now turned out to be incredibly useful after all, and it would be nice to tell them about it. In fact, it would be a good weekend to go and visit them, something she hadn't done since Christmas.

'Oh, hello dear,' her mother answered, sounding a little surprised. 'How are you?'

Glasby told her about working on the Dellar story and how she had hopes of finding a new angle on it. 'And it wouldn't have happened without the phone you got me.'

'Oh good, we were afraid you didn't like it very much. I'm glad that you've been using it. What did you say you were writing about again? That terrible Dellar woman?'

'That's right, Mum. I told you already. She died, and I had to go and . . . Well, anyway, I was thinking I might come up and see you today, if you're not busy. I could stay over, if you like.'

'Well, we'd love to have you, Ali, but your dad's in a competition this weekend. Fourballs. You know, at the club. We were just about to leave, actually. And there's a dinner tonight. I'm sure he'd like it if you came to watch, of course.'

Spending a weekend watching her father play golf was not what she had in mind. Instead, she switched on her mobile, and found a voice message from Kate Hall. She sounded annoyed.

'Ali, this is Kate. It's Saturday, just after nine. I won't call your home number in case you're asleep, since you're having such a busy time.' (Sarcasm wasn't like Kate – she was obviously angry with her.) 'Remember you were going to call me back, when I phoned you? We're having an old friend of Simon's to dinner this evening. Simon says that he's terribly serious, always working, so we thought you'd get on and it would do you both good to relax for a change. We're hoping that you can come for dinner tonight, about seven thirty, give me a call back as soon as you get this, won't you?'

Damn! She had completely forgotten Kate's call. But a dinner party, making conversation with some friend of Simon's, feeling like a wrung-out sponge . . . Mentally preparing an excuse to go with the apology which Kate deserved, she pressed the call return button and heard the number start to ring.

On the other hand, she had no other plans whatsoever for the weekend beyond catching up on the washing and ironing and getting some decent food in the house. So when Kate answered, she apologized handsomely and thanked her for the invitation.

Kate was pleased. 'Oh, great! It'll be nice to see you. And it will be good for you to relax a bit.'

Glasby started telling her about the Dellar story and her work with Bill Davenport but it was obvious that Kate was more worried about what to cook than what Glasby was saying. The conversation petered out rather soon, Glasby already starting to regret her decision to accept the invitation.

*   *   *

She tried to put work out of her mind and concentrated instead on domestic chores. Sainsbury's would be a nightmare, but it had to be done; with the stupid Sunday opening hours, it would be even worse tomorrow. She hoped to have another very busy week next week, so it made good sense to get the shopping done now. Not to mention washing some clothes, cleaning the flat, getting some petrol and taking her suit to the dry-cleaners. Thank God it had stopped raining.

The flat hadn't got any warmer while she was out. Kate and Simon had moved six months ago to a two-bedroom conversion in a Victorian house in Crouch End, presumably a prelude to marriage, babies and Glasby having to be a godmother. It was the other side of London but even so it shouldn't take more than forty-five minutes on a Saturday evening. So Glasby had time to spare.

She turned on all four gas rings on the stove for some warmth, and made herself a cup of camomile tea to help her relax. It had no effect whatsoever. All she could think about was Leonie Dellar, Donna Bacon, the photograph and what it all meant.

If Davenport wouldn't put her in the picture, she would just have to work things out for herself. And he thought that she'd reached the end of the road! Fishing in her bag, she found her copy of the photo, and the list of questions from the day before:

Where and when was the photo taken?

Where? At the seaside, somewhere on the Norfolk coast almost certainly – given that the Bacons weren't likely to have been holidaying in the Seychelles at the time. When? That was relatively easy. Donna was seven when she was murdered and Glasby had worked out the other day that Lynette was about eighteen, and that was pretty much how they looked in the photo. She died in August. Glasby knew from *Children Carried Away* that it had been a hot summer in 1969, which also tied in with the photo; the girls' shadows were black on the pavement behind them. They were both wearing summer dresses, and Lynette was holding a rather ugly handbag. So, they'd had a family outing to the seaside, sometime between about June and late August, 1969.

Who took it?

That was tricky. But she almost definitely knew who *didn't* take it. Mr and Mrs Bacon didn't own a camera so it wasn't likely to have been them. Other than that, she had no idea. Whoever had taken it knew what they were doing, though. It was nicely framed, with no missing feet or tops of heads, and the girls were in focus, both smiling at the camera. There was good depth of field as well; the buildings behind them were sharply defined. The original print was on decent quality paper, so far as she could remember, albeit crumpled from its time in the stuffing of the cushion, but it had no studio name or anything like that on the back. Probably someone in the *Herald*'s picture room could get more out of it than she could, but the chances of getting her hands on the original were remote. Presumably either it was still in P.O. Dack's custody or it had already been destroyed. At a guess, therefore, it was taken by an amateur who was an experienced photographer, or a professional, but not one who had a studio of their own.

Why did Patricia Bacon say she'd never seen it before? Was she lying? Could she have forgotten it?

The most obvious answer to this was that Mrs Bacon was telling the truth. She surely couldn't have forgotten the photo. And she would have to be a very good liar and a quick thinker, because she had been taken by surprise big time when Glasby had produced it. Remembering the old woman's puce face, almost fighting for breath as she staggered to her feet, Glasby was certain that it wasn't a put on.

What, if anything, does Lynette know about the photo?

Lynette had her wits about her. No doubt about that. Obviously she knew the photo was being taken. No telephoto lenses had been used, or anything like that. And if she knew about it, she wouldn't have forgotten it, for the same reason as her mother: there just weren't enough photos of Donna (or, presumably, Lynette), let alone of the two girls together. So she knew about it at the time, and when she had seen it again she would have remembered it, even if she didn't know what had happened to it since.

Which left the last questions: *How did Leonie Dellar get it? Why had she hidden it, and why did she try to get to it as she died?*

A thought struck her. The picture had been sewn up in the cushion. Davenport said that Leonie had made the cover herself, a long time ago. Surely the photo had been hidden there at the time and had stayed there ever since? So if Davenport knew when the cushion had been embroidered, that would definitely narrow down when she had been given the photo. She couldn't possibly have been able to hide it during the arrest, and trial, and transfer to Marsham House, all under maximum security. So almost certainly she would have sewn the photo into the cushion very soon after receiving it.

As to how she got it, everyone knows that it is possible to have things smuggled into prison. But that would mean third parties involved, not very honest ones presumably, and given the sum any number of newspapers would have paid for the story, surely they would have cashed in and spilled the beans by now? It was inconceivable that the prison authorities would have given any sort of official permission for Dellar to have it – and if they had, she wouldn't have needed to hide it so carefully.

So however she got it, it was illicit, but involved as few people as possible. And the smallest number of people who might know, other than Leonie herself, was one. The same person who had the photo on the outside would have brought it into the prison and secretly given it to her. Which meant a visitor, almost certainly.

Why anyone would want to do it, and why it had meant so much to Leonie that her last act had been to try to reach it, Glasby had no idea.

She realized suddenly that she was cold and it had got dark outside. She glanced at the clock on the cooker: seven o'clock. Kate's dinner party! If she changed quickly, with any luck she wouldn't be too late. At least she had bought some wine earlier, so there was no need to stop on the way. She had forgotten to ask whether to bring red or white.

*The child was frightened, lying in the dark, listening –
but what was it? Quick, let's get under the sheet.
Trembling, but it was a hot summer night, so sweating
as well. What was that noise? Please God, take me in
your care, keep me safe and hear my prayer.*

Eight

The traffic was a complete nightmare. Glasby got lost twice en route and arrived at quarter past eight.

Kate's welcome was on the frosty side, although Simon was OK about it, which meant that Kate had to pooh-pooh any suggestion that her beef Wellington had been spoiled by the delay.

The evening turned out rather differently from what she had been expecting. The friend wasn't how she had imagined him at all. Simon and he had been mates at Reading University, but they had lost touch until they'd bumped into each other by chance at a football match a couple of weeks before. Her first impression had been that he was, like Simon, tall, with slightly wavy dark-brown hair; but unlike Simon, was slight rather than weedy. He looked probably to be in his late twenties, the same as Simon. A rather beaky nose and piercing eyes gave his face character; deep lines in his forehead suggested to Glasby that he was a man of intellect.

'Let me introduce John, John Redgrave – no relation to the actors, or the Olympics man,' Simon made a point of telling her. From the look on Redgrave's face it wasn't the first time that he had heard it. 'This is Alison Glasby. We'll have to be careful what we say tonight. John's a copper, and Ali's a tabloid hack. Between the two of you, you could get us all into trouble!'

Simon was the last person she would have expected to have a policeman for a friend. Redgrave was a detective sergeant in the murder squad, which sounded interesting. But before she'd had a chance to ask him anything about it Simon started a long discussion about football, which was as boring as it was incomprehensible. Then he turned the conversation to old university chums which was no more exciting and took even longer. Kate disappeared into the kitchen, rebuffing any offer of help.

By this time Glasby was having to remind herself that with a policeman at the table, she probably shouldn't be drink driving. She got through two large glasses of Chianti more quickly than she intended and wandered into the kitchen to ask Kate if she could have some mineral water instead.

'Of course, you're driving, aren't you? Actually, Simon said to John that you would probably drop him home afterwards. If you don't mind, that is. John left his car so that he could have a drink.' It felt suspiciously to Glasby as if she was being set up, something she resented intensely.

Things improved a bit when dinner was finally ready. Everyone assured Kate that her pastry, which was a bit leaden, was perfect, and she cheered up for the first time since Glasby had arrived.

'So you said that you're working on something to do with Leonie Dellar?' she asked Glasby. 'Isn't Bill Davenport very well known?'

'Bill Davenport?' Redgrave interrupted. 'You work with him, do you? On the Dellar story? That must be interesting, I imagine.'

'That's right,' said Glasby. 'Why, do you know him?'

'No, but I've read his book. *Children Carried Away*. It's superb, don't you think? The way he got into people's lives, he really made you feel like you were in their shoes. How it touched all of the people involved, I mean. The families, neighbours and the police, of course. He must be a fascinating bloke.'

'He is,' Glasby agreed, before realizing that she actually knew very little about Davenport.

'What have you been covering on it?' Redgrave asked her. 'Dellar's death, or something more specific?'

'Her death, of course, but there is something specific as well. I'm sorry, but I can't really talk about it at the moment.'

'See? I told you,' Simon put in, to no one in particular. 'I said we'd all have to mind what we talked about, didn't I? The fourth estate likes to expose any sordid little secret that the rest of us may be hiding, but when the boot's on the other foot . . . Well, since Ali's so hush-hush, why don't you tell us what sort of things you're working on at the moment, John.'

'It's exactly like they show on the TV. We spend all of our time bonking each other, and in between we solve the odd murder.' Kate and Simon laughed. To be polite, Glasby joined in. Redgrave glanced at her and continued.

'I'm joking of course. It's very pressurized when a case comes in. All murders are bad, but sometimes, when it's a child, you wonder what human beings are made of. And you can't stop, not until you've caught the bastard who did it. A lot of the time we work with other areas, uniformed, or one of the regional squads, forensics, ballistics, you know. So you have to be able to motivate your team to get the best out of them. But often it's down to you, just sitting and thinking things through. We've got one like that at the moment, an eight-year-old boy, taken off the street, stabbed, dead. No witnesses, nothing. And that's when it really gets to you. You know there's an answer – you just *have* to find it.'

'When you hit a logjam like that, what's the most important factor in breaking through it?' asked Glasby, leaning forward.

'Hard work really, and sometimes intuition. You just run with it. Of course you need guts because sometime or other you're going to make a prat of yourself. But if you're not prepared to take a risk you might last out as a cop, but you'll never make a decent detective.'

Then, as politeness dictated, Redgrave asked Kate and Simon about their work. Simon's usual anecdotes of classroom life followed, expanding as always to fill the remaining available conversational space of the evening.

Glasby tuned out and pursued her own thoughts.

'Is there ever a situation when the police can get permission to use a truth drug on someone?' she asked. 'Say, if someone knows something really important about a murder but they won't tell anyone.' Without realizing it, she had cut into the middle of a long explanation by Simon as to the merits of something called SAT tests for seven year olds. All three of them stared at her.

'No, I don't think we'd ever be allowed to do anything like that,' replied Redgrave. 'You're not thinking of the Dellar case, are you?'

'It's a bit late now!' said Simon. 'She's pegged it! Or does your Mr Davenport have connections on "the other side" as

well?' He and Kate laughed uproariously, and eventually
Redgrave too. Glasby did her best to join in the joke but gave
up rather soon. Looking back, she was embarrassed to
remember that she had basically sulked for what was left of
the evening.

Not long afterwards she announced that she had better be
getting going. There didn't seem to be any way of avoiding
it so she offered Redgrave a lift back to Kentish Town.

As soon as they were in the car he apologized.

'What you said about someone knowing something about
a murder, from the look on your face you're serious about it,
aren't you? I didn't mean to make fun of it at all. I was
surprised when you said it, that's all.'

Glasby was considerably mollified but couldn't think of
any way of confiding in him that wouldn't have broken her
agreement with Davenport.

'It can be aggravating for us, though,' he continued. 'Don't
take it wrong, but there's nothing more tempting for the press
than to drive an investigation. They whip something up and
then demand that we look into it. Then they get an extra story
– "Police follow up on *News of the World* lead", that sort of
thing – and if we can't do anything with it they can always
slaughter us for lack of effort. But there's only one rule for
any good detective: always follow the evidence.'

The conversation stayed on safe ground until the Punto
drew up outside his flat, yet another nineteenth-century conversion just off Tufnell Park Road.

Before Redgrave got out of the car he added, 'Let me give
you my number, Alison. If there's anything that you'd ever
like to discuss, as a friend I mean, I'd be happy to hear from
you. And if you'd like to give me your number, maybe we
could meet up again sometime?'

She drove off feeling rather satisfied with the evening.
No doubt Davenport, who had been pals with a chief
constable and probably knew lots more, moved in rather
more exalted circles. But having Redgrave as a friend felt
rather good.

'Lady Penelope, please!' Davenport had indeed spent the
earlier part of the day in circles, circles around his sitting
room, to be precise. Lady Penelope, known as Penny except

when he was annoyed with her, had somehow found a sparrow arthritic or brain-damaged enough to allow itself to be carried in through the cat flap and up the stairs. Now the bird was flying around desperately looking for a way out, pursued energetically by cat and man. A book went skidding off the coffee table, taking his tumbler of scotch and ginger with it.

Eventually he managed to grab Penny and hustle her out of the room. At the same time her brother, Lord Jim, woke from his slumbers upstairs and poked his head in to see what the fuss was. 'Jimbo, out!' he shouted, waving a foot in the direction of the indignant black and white cat, and closed the sitting-room door. He opened the sash window as wide as it would go, having fumbled with the security grill which the insurance company had insisted he had fitted after a burglary, and finally coaxed the terrified bird outside.

Then all he had to do was close the window, reinstate the grill (whose existence he resented) and start the delightful job of cleaning up bird mess. It was halfway up the stairs and in six or eight large splodges all round his sitting room, one of them surrounded by a little puddle of whisky. When he had done that, ruing the waste of a good Glenmorangie, it occurred to him that Penny might very well go back for seconds of sparrow. He looked out into his garden and there she was, half-hidden under a large potted hydrangea and looking very predatory indeed.

He bribed her inside with some tinned tuna and hoped that the sparrow would go and die somewhere else.

Davenport had lived in the Victorian terraced house in Kennington for almost thirty-five years. It was part of the Merceaux Estate, around one hundred houses which had been funded by an ancient bequest to the Church and managed by a board of trustees. The houses had been rented out and although the trustees' high ideals were not always matched by their willingness to spend any money on upkeep or new-fangled improvements such as central heating, the rents were low. As a result, people tended to stay, and there was, unusually for London, a real community on the estate.

More recently, and in keeping with the politics of the day, the trustees had begun to sell the houses. Sitting tenants had first choice. Davenport didn't really approve, but there wasn't anything he could do to stop it, so he bought his in the early nineties, and a few of his neighbours did the same. Following the lead of the government they were even offered a discount as an incentive to buy. But most of the tenants didn't want to, or couldn't afford the asking price. As anyone moved away or died in situ their house would be put up for sale on the open market.

The inevitable result was a gradual change in the character of the estate, as the usual young professional types moved in, stayed for two or three years and sold on to others, more or less identical to themselves. A few years ago, Davenport had renamed the area as the 'Mercedes Estate' in honour of the vehicle of choice of his new neighbours.

He settled back in the leather chair which he had leapt from when the feline excitement had started. The room was not so much book lined as book infested. Shelves had gradually encroached on every wall, but all were overflowing, and piles of books and other papers were all over the floor and most of the other available surfaces.

In one corner was an old dark oak desk which was particularly swamped. On top, as if it was floating on a sea of papers, was a framed photograph of a racehorse with a beaming and much younger Davenport standing next to it. The walls were painted in a smoky yellow but most of the available spaces between bookshelves were hung with black and white photographs of jazz musicians, a large study of Ella Fitzgerald taking pride of place. A saxophone stood in one corner. It was covered in dust.

Davenport had been deep in contemplation before Penny and her unwilling little playmate had disturbed him. He'd been able to reach one conclusion. There was something about the young woman he had been working with, something about her attitude, which had reminded him of someone from a long time ago. Now he had worked out who it was.

At Glasby's age he had been as thin as a greyhound and had the energy to match. Having caught the editor's eye in more or less the way he had described to Glasby, he progressed rapidly and became the *Herald*'s crime correspondent while still in his late twenties. His colleagues, admiringly or otherwise, nicknamed him Billy the Kid. He wasn't necessarily the most popular man in the office but the hours he put in and his determination in pursuit of a story were unrivalled.

Maybe Glasby had something of the same single-mindedness? If so it was about the last thing he needed now. But if it was going to turn into a battle of age against beauty, he'd back himself. Every time.

Penny, now full of tuna and tired from her acrobatic display, was preparing to settle herself on his lap. 'If you can just wait for another week or two, you can do some proper hunting. Let's see how you get on with seagulls, shall we?'

The house was long since paid for. Davenport had never worried about money when he didn't have any, and he felt much the same now that he had plenty. But even so, he needed some security for his retirement. Knowing nothing and caring less about the stock market, the obvious choice was property. A keen walker, he had spotted a cottage for sale a couple of miles outside Ditchling in Sussex. It had spectacular views over the South Downs, rambling roses around the front door, and was otherwise a complete dump.

A year or so later it was his, and almost completely renovated. Or, as his builder regularly told him, rebuilt. The plan was to rent it out, but having got this far, he didn't want to part with it at all.

Also, if he really was going to retire, people kept telling him, he would need a complete change of scene and some hobbies. Walking would certainly keep him busy – and in better shape than he was now – and a house on the South Downs Way could hardly be better. And it would be handy for the occasional trip to Goodwood.

He also fancied the idea of writing a novel. It had always struck him as a lot easier than being a journalist. Let's face it, he shouldn't be short of material, after forty-odd years of writing about criminals. There would be no deadlines, no sub-editors counting every word and hacking your piece around without bothering to tell you about it. But it would require a certain peace of mind, time for contemplation.

So the plan had changed. He would move to the cottage, taking Penny and Jimbo with him. They would grow sleek on country living, he would write or ramble as the mood took him. The house in Kennington would be tenanted, although he was tempted to leave it empty instead. After all, if there *was* something that needed him to be in London, some crisis on the paper, for example . . .

Five pinpricks in his right knee brought him rudely back to the present. Penny was in her getting comfortable phase, which generally involved some padding around or worse. Unfortunately, she had huge feet for a cat of her relatively modest size and claws like multiple hypodermics. 'The sooner you get some proper outdoor life, the better,' he told her, as she looked up adoringly at him.

Meanwhile, he had a more pressing problem. Glasby finding the photo really was a sensational development, and that rare thing: a genuine exclusive. It had taken him completely by surprise – why did Dellar have a picture of Lynette and Donna, for Christ's sake? And he couldn't just pooh-pooh it; if he'd have pretended that he knew about it, she would have started asking why it wasn't mentioned anywhere in his book. He'd had no option but to let her get started. Still, at least it was someone working for him that had discovered the bloody photo. And no one else knew – at the moment, anyway. Any number of people at the prison might get to know about it. All it took was for someone to recognize who was in it, realize its news value, and the Fleet Street chequebooks would open very wide indeed.

He wasn't happy with the situation at all but there wasn't anything that he could do about it now. He'd let Glasby go this far because he had to and that was that. The best thing was to give her a good lunch, a sympathetic ear, and persuade her to forget all about it. She really was a very promising girl and he could put in a good word for her with that berk Tom Lear and maybe even Ellington. She would be disappointed, but after all, there were more important things at stake than the ambitions of a young journalist.

The doorbell rang. It was Lisbeth Hunt, a retired district nurse from two doors away. She had been widowed in her fifties and had become very active in the Church of England. Something or other on the synod, in fact. But she never evangelized, had a warm wit, and most importantly, was an excellent cook. 'Pheasant? I'd love to, thank you. I'll be along at eight, shall I?'

After she dropped John Redgrave off, Glasby drove back towards the south at her normal cautious pace. Then she changed her mind, pulled into the side and when the road was clear behind her turned the car around and headed back to north London again.

A few years ago someone had asked her to go with him for moral support while he looked for his exam results in *The Times*. He was the son of friends of her parents, hoping to become a solicitor. She didn't know him well. Presumably he didn't have many friends in London either. They had driven up to King's Cross about this time of night because you could buy the next morning's newspapers from the stall outside the station. He had passed all his exams and swept away with enthusiasm had grabbed her and kissed her, embarrassing them both.

King's Cross at night was darker than Glasby remembered it. She had to park around the corner from the railway station and there were bodies lying in several of the doorways that she walked by, huddled up in blankets against the cold. Nothing to be nervous about, though. They weren't going to bother her. All the same, she put her hands in her pockets and walked quickly towards the lights at the front of the station.

Glasby stepped up the pace again on the walk back. A hundred metres before she reached her car, a man appeared, with dark greasy hair and long black coat, lurching towards her with both arms outstretched. 'It's cold,' he roared. 'Gimme something, gimme something.' She pulled back, frightened, and made to walk round him, but he followed her to the edge of the pavement and caught hold of her arm. He smelled stale and unwashed, of alcohol and something like engine oil.

'Get off!' she cried. 'Get off me.' She was angry, as much with herself as him. Why did she sound so feeble? He muttered something which she couldn't catch, his hand still tight around her arm, leaning right in to her face. Close up he was filthy, stinking and repellent.

'Get off me, you bastard! Bastard! Let me go!' This time she screamed at him, her body tensed up, breathing like a bull ready to charge. She kicked him hard somewhere on his leg, pulled away from him and rushed to her car as he fell on to the cold pavement.

Less than an hour later she was in her bed, the *Herald* in front of her. On the front cover was one of the usual pictures of Leonie from the late sixties, complete with bob and frumpish middle-aged clothes. The caption with it read 'Leonie – by The Man Who Knew Her'.

And there, starting on page four, was Davenport's article. At the top was his byline. Underneath, in smaller type but still quite prominent: 'Additional reporting by Alison Glasby'.

There were photos across the top of each page: Davenport (not looking too bad – quite dapper, actually); Leonie as a young child with her mother, and as a teenager; Leonie with Jarmy; the Morris Minor van in which they'd been caught; the victims: Kevin Yallop in black NHS glasses; Matthew Starling, minus a front tooth; the same grainy headshot of Michael Summer that Davenport had used in the book (the family mustn't have released any others; this one looked like a blow-up from a school class photo); Donna Bacon. And in the last photo Glasby recognized the main entrance to Marsham House prison, where Dellar had spent so many years, and where she had died that week.

She settled back to read it.

LEONIE DELLAR – A LIFE LIVED
IN THE SHADOWS

I knew Leonie Dellar for a long time. I first saw her on the last day of August, 1969. Only days before she had been responsible for the inexplicably cruel deaths of two children, and two others in the weeks before that. She was well dressed, outwardly respectable. And she said not one word.

Three months later she was on trial, accused with her lover, Brian Jarmy, of kidnap and murder. The trial lasted for five unforgettable days. They were convicted, of course. The jury was unanimous, the verdict never in doubt. The sentence, life, and only now has she finished that sentence.

But what we really wanted, all of us in that court-room, the judge, the police, the jury, the journalists, most of all the families of her poor little victims, what we wanted we did not get. We wanted answers, we wanted to know the truth, we wanted to know why, how. How could they do it? Most of all, how could she?

They didn't just kill (and it is a measure of their

depravity that we are forced to talk of 'just killing' four children). They used knives, ropes and even their bare hands, took them and tortured them and butchered them in ways that no one who sat through the evidence of their evil will ever forget.

And Leonie Dellar said nothing, for the whole week of the trial. She didn't say 'Guilty', or 'Not Guilty'; she didn't argue; she certainly didn't apologize or ask for forgiveness. Not one word passed her lips.

So although I first saw her in August 1969, it wasn't until five months later that I heard her speak. She wouldn't talk to the police. She ignored what must have been hundreds of requests, from me and other journalists like me. Then one day, out of the blue, she asked to see me. And she said (these are her exact words – I will never forget them): 'This is my confession. We did it. We killed them. Brian and me. All four. Kevin Yallop, Matthew Starling, Donna Bacon and Michael Summer.'

Why did she confess? I don't know. Why did she choose me, at that time? I have no idea. I saw her often in the long years she spent in prison. Sometimes it was at her own request. Neither I nor the *Herald* has ever given any money to her or anyone who knew her. Other newspapers have. But for all it got them, they might just as well not have bothered.

Many years later, in 1982, she chose me again. I was able to pass information to the police which led to the body of Kevin Yallop being recovered. Why did she reveal its whereabouts then, after so many years of silence? I can't tell you and neither can anyone else.

And now that she has gone, she has left behind her perhaps the greatest cruelty of all. Three of her and Jarmy's victims now lie in decent graves, where their families can care for them and remember them in their own ways. There is no such comfort for the family of little Donna Bacon, only seven years old when they took her. Jarmy could tell them where their loved one is – but he won't. Dellar could have said but now she never will.

'A Well-Mannered Girl'

Leonie Dellar was born in 1949, in the Norfolk town of North Walsham. Her father, a railwayman, died in an accident on the line when she was still a baby. Her mother Ida brought her up, an only child, on a widow's pension and a little extra that she could earn as a cleaner. It was a decent household.

They lived in the terraced cottage in which Leonie was born, number 11, Station Road. It was an un-remarkable life in a typically English small town. Rural Norfolk is a peaceful place even today but in the 1950s it was largely isolated, from some of the excitement but also from the wickedness of the rest of the world. There was no Internet, not much foreign travel or even television.

She went to school in the town, neither excelling nor giving any cause for concern. If you were to look at one of her school photos you would see a rather tall girl, serious looking but not unattractive, surrounded by other boys and girls who looked much like her.

Like her, and like the other children who only a few years later would become her victims. They too came from villages and small towns, all but one of them within a few miles of North Walsham. When Leonie Dellar looked for victims, the people she picked on were her own.

When she was eleven she joined the youth group of the Salvation Army. Every Sunday there were bible classes. She was given music tuition, learning the trumpet. 'A pleasant girl' was how she was remembered, 'shy, but always nicely spoken'.

She gave up the Salvation Army at fourteen. Nothing unusual there, either. It was (and is) an age when many girls start to think about more worldly things: clothes, make-up and boys. 'She was always very neatly turned out,' a classmate told me once. 'Some of the boys were quite interested in her. But I never remember her with a boyfriend. She wasn't unpopular, but she kept herself apart a bit.'

Her teachers agreed with this assessment. 'Not a

natural "joiner"', ran one school report, 'but not lacking in ability. Perhaps a little under-confident for her age. Would benefit from "pushing" herself rather more. A well presented, well-mannered girl.'

Mother's Death

She left North Walsham Secondary Modern School at fifteen, as was normal in those days, and went to the local technical college to study secretarial skills and bookkeeping. Her attendance records at the college were immaculate and she passed all of the normal proficiency certificates.

'She was a good student, quiet and hard-working,' was how the college principal described her to me. 'A lot of the students are easily distracted at that age. But never Leonie. She was always very serious about her work.'

If you had known her then, you would probably have predicted her future with some confidence. A first job in an office, or perhaps the accounts department of a factory or warehouse. Beginning to contribute to the household income, their standard of living rising a little. Pop records (it was the heyday of the Beatles, the time when the word 'teenager' was first to enter all of our vocabularies); new clothes; the cinema. Boyfriends, then a husband, a family.

And perhaps you would have been right, but for one sad event. In 1966, when Leonie Dellar was seventeen, her mother died, aged only forty-six. 'It was very sudden,' remembered a neighbour. 'We saw the ambulance, and then the very next day Leonie put a sign up in the window. I remember it well, it said: "Ida Dellar has passed away – thank you for your good wishes". It seemed so sad, a young girl all alone in the house, with just that notice.'

Moved to the City

Dellar had an uncle who lived in Norwich. Fred Dellar had been a footballer before the War, appearing on the wing for Norwich City. But by the 1960s he worked in a sportswear shop in the city. 'He was a smashing fellow with a really big heart.' according to a colleague of the time. 'He felt so sorry for Leonie, he couldn't do enough for her. It nearly killed him, what happened afterwards.'

Leonie moved to Norwich towards the end of 1966, lodging with her uncle and aunt. They were a popular couple, keen tennis players and active members of their local church. But there is no record of Leonie ever having joined them in either.

She found a job in the city as an accounts clerk at Caley's, the chocolate factory whose sweet smell used to dominate Norwich when the wind was right; it still does, although the name has changed many times since. She joined the Social Club and attended some of the events: outings to the Broads on a pleasure cruiser; to Yarmouth for the amusements; once, a trip to the Theatre Royal to see a musical.

'She was nice enough,' one of her colleagues told me later. 'She didn't go out of her way to be friendly, she kept herself to herself really. But no "side" to her – not like him at all.'

'He' was Brian Jarmy, soon to be her boyfriend, later her partner in infamy.

Nazis Were Their Hobby

'Jarmy was a nasty piece of work' – the verdict of one of his team in the finance department. 'If he could find a way to be snide, he would. He always had to show he knew more than you, smiling at his own private little jokes. None of us could stick him.'

Brian Jarmy was twenty-seven when he met Leonie Dellar, nine years older than her. He was born forty miles away in Ipswich and grew up there. He was excused from National Service on medical grounds, though colleagues told me that he always used to boast that he'd got one over the authorities.

After leaving grammar school at sixteen he studied finance and gained some qualifications. He began work locally but in 1966 took a job with Coleman's, the famous mustard producer in Norwich. The following year he moved job again, this time to become a supervisor in the financial department of Caley's.

He was thin faced, with hair which was unfashionably short for the time, and favoured dark suits and a dark tie, whether in or out of the office. When he was younger Jarmy had been an enthusiastic member of the National Front. He got tired of that, but there was no doubt where his sympathies lay.

'He was always talking about the Nazis. It was more than a hobby for him; he was completely obsessed. And when she was with him, she took it up too' – this from one of his neighbours in Norwich. The house was decorated with fascist regalia, swastika banners and iron crosses. There were photographs of Jarmy dressed in the uniform of one of Hitler's SS killers, holding a dagger or doing the Nazi salute.

It is not clear exactly when the couple first met. Although they weren't close colleagues, their paths would have crossed in the office and presumably on one of these occasions they must have recognized something in each other, something that brought them together.

As Leonie's colleague told me at the time: 'We had no idea about them. She didn't say anything. And then one day, she turned up at a Social Club trip, with him driving that van of his. They walked round with their noses in the air. And after a while, she was like that the whole time. She didn't want to know us any more.'

A Catalogue of Brutality

Leonie Dellar continued to live with her uncle and aunt, working at Caley's and making no close friends. But gradually she began to see more and more of Jarmy. 'He was so different,' she told me once. 'Not like anyone I'd ever met before. He had ideas.' But unsurprisingly, she didn't want to talk about what those ideas were.

Jarmy liked to read, but his choice of reading material was grotesque. Books on the Nazis were his favourite; histories of the period, Hitler's *Mein Kampf*, of course. Books on anatomy, with colour illustrations for preference. And books on murder, real and fictional. He started to believe that he was above the law; not just the criminal law, but the laws of morality, of religion.

Dellar began to dress more like him. She cut and dyed

her hair in the now infamous 'Leonie' black bob. After he took to visiting, relations quickly grew strained in her uncle's home. In February 1969 she went to live with Jarmy in a terraced house which he had rented, at an address which has become notorious: number 19, St Anne's Road, Norwich.

I don't doubt that she loved him as she told me she did. I am not convinced that he is capable of any normal emotion, for her or anyone else.

The couple became more and more isolated, interested only in themselves and their increasingly wicked notions. They set themselves on the path to what the trial judge called 'some of the most depraved brutality ever brought before any court in this land'.

A Life in the Shadows

A few months later they kidnapped, tortured and murdered four little children. Before they killed them, they stabbed them, burnt them, and broke their limbs. Jarmy remains alive, certified insane in Broadmoor, where he will undoubtedly end his days. He has never talked about their terrible crimes and I suppose that he never will.

Dellar spent the rest of her life in prison. She was a model inmate, giving no trouble of any kind. She was courteous, pleasant and always well turned out. In all the many times I met her, she never uttered a single word of remorse, self-pity or regret. She never asked for forgiveness, never asked to be set free.

Now Leonie Dellar is dead. She was touched by evil. Perhaps she *was* evil, in human form, as many people say. Probably no one will mourn her or miss her. Certainly she would have wanted it that way. Once she told me that when she died she would like to be forgotten, by everyone, as soon as possible. She lived her life, as she chose to, in the shadows.

It was OK, but no better than that in Glasby's view. It was basically a rehash of Davenport's book. None of her stuff was included, not even a hint about the photograph.

But if only that was the worst of it. Next to Davenport's final column was a box headed in bold type 'Exclusive'. Underneath was the headline 'May She Rot in Hell: Dellar Killed our Brother', the byline, Bill Davenport and Joe Daniels, a photograph of a middle-aged man and woman, and underneath that:

Yesterday the brother and sister of one of Leonie Dellar's victims revealed exclusively to the *Herald* a secret which they had kept for the last thirty-seven years. Matthew Starling was only ten when he was kidnapped and tortured with cigarette burns, a swastika branded on to his leg before he was butchered to death and his body dumped in a lock-up garage.

Leonie Dellar confessed to Matthew's murder (see main story above). But she always claimed that her psychopath boyfriend Brian Jarmy was the main culprit. Now after years of silent suffering, Matthew's sister Alison and brother Gary have spoken out.

'After the trial the police told Mum and Dad that they knew it was Dellar all along,' said Gary Starling, forty-four. 'They said that Jarmy had an alibi, but Dellar was there. It was her that killed our brother. And the little girl, Donna Bacon, too.'

Alison Starling, forty-nine, said that the family will never get over the pain of Matthew's loss. 'It drove our mum and dad into early graves. Dellar should rot in hell for what she did to us.'

Her brother agreed. 'We were sick when we heard that she'd died, all comfortable in a hospital. Matthew never had a hospital bed. Dellar should have suffered worse than he did. Why couldn't they just hang her?'

The other families shared their grief and anger. Doreen Yallop, mother of Kevin Yallop, who was the killers' first victim, slammed the treatment Dellar had received in gaol. 'She had an easy life and an easy death. Nothing was too good for her. They gave her anything she wanted. They should have hanged her years ago. And I'd have been there, to watch her die.'

There is speculation that Dellar and Jarmy might have made some sort of sickening pact to kill two children each. Police sources refused to comment but it is understood that they have not ruled it out.

With Dellar dead and Jarmy caged and insane in
Broadmoor, we may well never know. What is certain is
that the anguish of families like the Starlings and the
Yallops will go on.

An image of Daniels' smug face came to Glasby's mind. If
she had been kicked in the stomach with a hob-nailed boot
she could hardly have felt more sick.

*The child was frightened, lying in the dark, listening –
but what was it? Quick, let's get under the sheet.
Trembling, but it was a hot summer night, so sweating
as well. What was that noise? Please God, take me in
your care, keep me safe and hear my prayer. Not again
not again not again not again.*

Nine

Monday morning did not start the way Glasby had planned it. 'Unanticipated staff illness levels' (or skiving after the weekend in her view) meant that she had to wait forty minutes for a train at Stockwell Tube station. She had spent most of Sunday lying around the flat, wrapped in her duvet, feeling listless.

She tried sitting at the kitchen table with the cooker going full blast and the radio on but couldn't concentrate on anything. The chair started to dig into her back so she shifted to the sofa. The sitting room was freezing, but it was easier to keep the duvet wrapped around her. She switched on the TV.

Like her office, Glasby's sitting room was devoid of personal photographs with only minimal gestures to homeliness. There were framed posters from an exhibition at the Tate Modern and the Edinburgh Book Fair, and even ornaments: a pair of antique wooden ducks her parents had given her when she finished at Leicester (she hadn't gone to the graduation ceremony and they hadn't seemed to mind much).

But any intruder looking for a clue as to her character would have been stuck, at least until they examined the books stacked double high on the twin Habitat bookcases. In amongst the customary Austens and Brontës there was crime of every description, from Christie and Conan Doyle to Ellroy, Reichs and Paretsky.

Glasby found herself dropping off. She abandoned the old musical which she had found on BBC Two and crawled, duvet wrapped around her, into the ice-cold bedroom. She drew the curtains to shut out the view of other people's backyards and drainpipes and drifted into an uncomfortable sleep. When she woke in the late afternoon she felt lonely and tried to call an old friend in Norwich for a chat. All she got was an answer machine. She didn't feel like leaving a message. Basically, Sunday had been a wasted day.

Now, packed into an Underground train and on the way to the office at last, she was rapidly getting a headache. And the week hadn't even properly started yet.

She got to work after ten, meaning that for the second time in a week she was in later than Serena.

'Bloody Tube,' she said, to no one in particular. Mike was glued to his terminal, but Serena looked up.

'I think you're frightfully brave, living south of the river. All those awful people, I just don't know how you bear it. Oh, and I nearly forgot: Tommy was looking for you.'

'Tommy!' If the Leer was looking for her, maybe Davenport *had* said something about her disaster with the Bacons. Glasby steeled herself to go and find him but before she had left her desk, Daniels swung by.

'Ali, good morning,' he said, ostentatiously looking at his watch. She ignored him, so he addressed himself to Serena (making sure that he talked loudly enough for Glasby to over-hear).

'Mark's a good man, isn't he? You know, he praises where it's due. He couldn't have been nicer. Of course, Bill and I work to our own standards not for pats on the back, but it doesn't hurt to know that you've been noticed, does it?'

Serena's phone started to ring. Glasby marched off in the direction of the corner office before she was physically sick.

Lear was wearing a particularly nasty pink shirt, even by his own low standards. 'Come in, Ali, sit down,' he began. 'Bill's taken quite a fancy to you. Which of course we can't blame him for, can we?' He gave her his usual oleaginous smile. 'He left me a note on Friday absolutely singing your praises. So, well done! You and Jack have really upheld the reputation of the department.'

As if she gave a monkey's for the reputation of the depart-ment, aka the promotion chances of T. Lear Esq. At any rate Davenport had been good for his word, and she wasn't going to get a bollocking after all.

Then came the bad news. 'Now that the Dellar piece is done I've got something else for you. That piece you did before on computer dating, Ellington liked it, you know. He's looking for a younger female demographic and it fits right in. So I want you to map out a framework for a series, let's say five articles. You know, different aspects, from the lady's perspective of course. "Log on and flirt, ten top lies told by girls who date online", that sort of thing. See what you can come up with, and we'll take it from there.'

'Isn't it the sort of thing that would suit Serena better? She doesn't seem too busy.'

Lear looked at her with distaste. There really was no pleasing some people. 'Serena has some important projects. Some of them come directly from Mark, you know. We can't afford to take her off them now.'

Can't afford to upset Serena's daddy, you mean. Bloody typical!

'Oh, and one other thing, Ali. I gather that there's a lot of talk around, people worrying about their jobs. You know how that sort of thing gets out of proportion. As far as this department's concerned, so long as we keep our work to the highest standards, there shouldn't be any problems. So you will do a good job on the dating series, won't you?'

Glasby went back to her desk in a foul temper.

Her phone rang. It was Jan, Ellington's PA. Apparently she also did diary duty for Davenport. 'He says for you to meet him at one. The table's in his name, at the Oxo Tower. The restaurant, not the brasserie (she pronounced the first syllable to rhyme with farce). It's ever so nice, you know. Mark took me there for my birthday.'

Glasby had heard of the restaurant but she'd never been there. She looked at her watch. Twenty past ten. She booked a taxi on the newspaper account. They told her to allow the best part of an hour to get to the restaurant, so she had less than two hours to get herself ready to convince Davenport to let her run with the story. Otherwise it was bloody online dating agencies and if she messed that up she'd be out on the street, presumably.

First things first. She called Directory Enquiries. 'Marsham House prison, please.'

'P.O. Dack?' the prison switchboard operator said. 'Is it an inmate enquiry? Are you a relative or friend?'

'No, it's, um, a personal call. My name's Alison Glasby. I'm a friend of Mr Dack's.'

'I don't know if he's on duty at the moment. Let me see . . . Yes, but I don't know if he's available. I'll see if I can put you through. Hold on.'

A few moments later, P.O. Dack came on the line, friendly as before, Norfolk accent sounding even stronger over the telephone: 'Miss Glasby. From the other day, wasn't it? Are you all right?'

'Yes, I'm all right, thank you,' she said. 'I just had a question about those things that you showed me. You know, from Leonie.'

His tone changed abruptly. 'You know I said I couldn't talk about that no more. If you want another look, you're too late. We sent the whole lot off to incineration, Saturday.'

Glasby found a mirror in her bag and checked her appearance. She had on a decent jacket and a top her mother had bought her several years ago, with trousers not jeans, and luckily not trainers either. She had been expecting lunch to be at the pub or Pizza Express.

Going up in the lift, she felt a bit nervous. The couple who got in just after her looked as if they went to expensive restaurants all the time. The woman had a bag with a Gucci logo and an absolutely huge diamond ring, and they probably bought all their clothes from Armani or somewhere like that.

The girl who took her to the table was friendly enough, even if she had stepped straight out of *Vogue*. Thankfully Bill was already there. He was wearing his usual tatty tweed jacket and brown cords, looking completely at ease.

'Nice view, isn't it?' he greeted her. It was. Even on a dreary November day, London looked exciting from up here: the river; the Savoy hotel and the Law Courts opposite; and St Paul's, majestic if a bit grimy, scaffolding halfway up the dome.

'I'm glad you could make it today,' Davenport said, courteous as ever, his usual prelude before getting to the tough part. Except that this time, the trick was to avoid any sticky issues and ease her off the story gently. It would be best to give her the chance to get it all off her chest first, though.

'Would you mind telling me again what happened in Coltishall?'

This fitted Glasby's game plan perfectly, so she gave him full details of the drama in the Bacons' lounge, strategically edited as far as her role was concerned. It was more or less the same as he had heard on Friday, but he listened sympathetically, without interruption.

'So,' she finished, 'I had no option but to leave. I just thanked them for seeing me, and went.'

Then, before he could react, she went on: 'Where that takes us to, Bill, is as follows. The photo –' she fumbled for it in her bag and plonked it in front of him on the table – 'the photo was taken not long before Donna died, while she and Lynette were at the seaside in Norfolk, on an outing of some sort. It was probably taken by a professional, but not printed in a studio as such. Maybe it was a jobbing photographer, taking snaps of holidaymakers and printing them up quickly to sell to them later in the day. Like in *Brighton Rock*.

'Mrs Bacon never knew about it. But Lynette did. And either Lynette gave it to Leonie, which I know sounds weird but we can't rule it out yet; or if it wasn't her, it could have been whoever paid for the photo when it was taken. Whoever it was, they were one of Leonie's visitors in Marsham House, some time between December '69 and whenever it was that she told you that she'd made the cushion.

'Now, there are a few things we can check to take some of this forward, and I wanted to ask you how you thought I should get started. But I have confirmed the most important thing; no one else has got hold of the photo and the prison have incinerated all Leonie's things. You and I are the only ones who know anything, other than the Bacons, of course,' she concluded.

Davenport was taken aback, to put it mildly.

'Hold your horses, Alison! Do you want to take me through all that again, one step at a time?'

Just then, their starters arrived. Probably they were delicious, but neither paid them any attention, Davenport now as focussed as Glasby on what she had to say.

'You can see in the picture that Donna looks seven, which was how old she was when she died. And Lynette would have been eighteen, wouldn't she? Compare it to the picture from 1967 which you used in your book. Donna looks much younger in that one. And it's obviously taken in the summer, look at the sun. And the dresses the girls are wearing. And you see the curve on the terrace of houses behind them. Doesn't it look like a sea front? Seeing as how poor the family was, they wouldn't have gone far. It must be somewhere near Coltishall, on the Norfolk coast. I bet it would be easy to identify even now.'

'Hmmm. You're right. It would be. And I agree, summer 1969 sounds right. Keep going.'

'Like I say, there used to be seaside photographers.'

'I remember them, yes. I know you wouldn't think it, looking at me, but I am a bit older than you.'

She didn't know what to say to this so she ignored it and carried on instead: 'It's a good quality photo and a professional print. That's what John Lucas thought, too.'

'Lucas? When did you show it to him?' This wasn't remotely what Davenport wanted to hear.

'This morning. I didn't tell him what it was about, of course. But I thought that a picture editor should know a professional photograph when he sees one, and he did.'

'There's no way that Mrs Bacon was putting on an act for me. But Lynette couldn't possibly have forgotten the photo. Or even if she had, she'd have recognized it as soon as she saw it. So she definitely knows more than she's said so far. Do you think that she'd be capable of holding back, in the situation she was in with me?'

'Lynette is a very self-possessed woman, Alison, very strong. I always had the impression that she was as much like a mother to Donna as a sister. Some of that must have been because of the difference in ages, of course, but there was more to it than that. She's a very strong character, much more so than her mother.'

Davenport made as if to say something else but stopped and started again. 'I can't fault anything you've said. It's, well, admirable, really impressive.'

'Thanks, Bill.' But Glasby was in no mood to be soft-soaped. 'Now, you told me on Friday, when I called you, that there were some other things to do with Lynette, that you were going to tell me something more about. What were they?'

Davenport avoided her eye for a moment, then frowned and looked straight at her. 'Lynette? I'm not sure what that could have been, Alison. Nothing relevant now, at any rate.'

Glasby was unconvinced, but short of calling him a liar she didn't see what more she could say. She tried again, from a different angle. 'What I don't understand is how your piece with Jack Daniels fits into the middle of all this. What evidence have we really got?'

'Evidence? Oh, exactly what was reported, I'd say,' was

Davenport's response. This time he had the same strange expression on his face that Glasby had noticed before, when he had agreed to let Daniels run his story. Was this how he looked when he was trying to hide something? She pressed on again.

'Speculation about a pact between Jarmy and Dellar to kill two children each? The police not ruling it out? I mean, what does it add up to? Really?'

'What I told you, Alison. Exactly what we printed, a good angle on a major story. Now let me think for a moment, please. I need to take all this in.'

And in truth, he did. He had intended to tell her how well she'd done, make her feel that she'd got some brownie points and then put a lid on it: no more digging. But now she had got this far, there was not a cat in hell's chance that she was going to let it drop, not if she was worth her salt. If he told her to stop, she'd simply carry on behind his back.

Or even worse, she'd go to someone else, the *Chronicle* or one of the red tops. Someone might give her a job on the strength of this and then they'd really set the hounds running. No, he was going to have to work with her. But how?

Glasby interrupted his thoughts. 'Tom Lear and Mark Ellington have put me on to a series for features. So I can carry on for today, but we may have a problem with the rest of the week.'

So if he kept her busy now she'd be out of harm's way for a while after that. It would buy him some thinking time, if nothing more. After all these years, for this to come up now, just as he was retiring. For crying out loud!

The thing to do was to give her something to work on, something where she couldn't do any damage. 'There's one person that we haven't considered so far,' he said. 'And that's Brian Jarmy.'

'Jarmy?' Glasby was surprised and a bit wary. 'But all this happened after Dellar was jailed.'

'Yes. But you haven't mentioned where we started from on this. The fact that Leonie had the picture must mean something. And the one person who would know about that is Jarmy. The horse's mouth, so to speak.'

And so a couple of hours later Glasby found herself making a call to Broadmoor Special Hospital. 'I'd like to request a visit, please. On behalf of Bill Davenport and Alison Glasby. To see Brian Jarmy.'

Whatever else might be unusual about Britain's most infamous hospital for the criminally insane, as Broadmoor is usually (albeit wrongly) known, their on-hold music was boringly conventional. After the third repetition of whichever bit of the *Four Seasons* it is that phone manufacturers have bought up wholesale, Glasby was starting to wonder if the hospital had closed for the day and gone home early.

At last a male voice came on to the line. 'Ms Glasby? This is Roy Allen here. I am the officer responsible for patient/public liaison. I understand that you and Mr Davenport are making a public access request relating to Brian Jarmy?' He had the slow, careful voice of the career bureaucrat. Although he also sounded rather pleased to have someone to talk to.

'Yes, that's right. I work with Bill Davenport at the *Herald* newspaper. Bill once visited Mr Jarmy. Quite a few years ago. Would it be possible to ask Mr Jarmy if he would be prepared to see us?'

'Oh! So it is the same Bill Davenport, then. While they were putting you through, you see, I was just looking up Mr Jarmy's records, on our system – we're fully computerized now.' He sounded very proud of this fact. 'I don't know how much you know about Mr Jarmy, but you see he hasn't actually received a visit for rather a long time. In fact, Mr Davenport *was* his last visitor. 15th April 1970. Not that our current database was in place then, of course,' he added. 'But when we set it up, we transferred all of the old card-index system on to the computer. It took a great deal of time, even though we only transferred active entries. They call it migration, you see.'

'It must have been quite a job,' said Glasby, not wanting to spend the rest of the afternoon discussing his filing system. 'So you will put the request to Mr Jarmy, then?'

'Certainly. It's the policy of the hospital management to encourage patient/public interactions. Unless there are reasons for any restrictions of course.' (A vision of a mad axe man, foaming and ranting, came to Glasby's mind. There would need to be some restrictions, wouldn't there?) 'And no restriction has been entered on to Mr Jarmy's records. In fact, according to his assessment, the lack of any public interaction may be having the effect of holding back his treatment. So,' he continued, completing the bureaucratic equation, presumably in case she hadn't fully followed the logic of his response, 'there is no reason for the visit not to be approved, and I am able to process the request.'

'When do you think we will know? Could I call you later this afternoon?'

'Oh! Normal procedure is for the public access request to be put to the patient at their next supervisor's meeting, you see. Then the patient supervisor passes the information to me. And I write to the member of the public who made the request, actioning it. Or otherwise, of course. But procedures require that my response is put in writing.'

'When is Mr Jarmy's next meeting with the patient supervisor?'

'Patients meet with their supervisors a minimum of twice daily.'

'So it should be possible for the request to be made to Mr Jarmy later on today then?'

'Yes, I expect so. I imagine that that would be possible, yes.'

'Oh, I see. Well . . . maybe if you're not supposed to phone me with your response, you could email or fax it to me instead? It would be enormously helpful, if you wouldn't mind.'

'Oh! Well, we certainly don't have external email facilities in the patient/public liaison office. But I suppose that there's no reason why I couldn't use the general office fax machine. Although I would still have to send the response by post as well. Just to comply with procedures, of course.'

'Of course,' Glasby agreed, trying to match the seriousness of Mr Allen's tone. 'Thank you very much for your help. If I haven't heard from you by then, I'll call you again, just before five,' she said, guessing correctly that this would mark closing time for patient/public liaison.

'Please don't trouble yourself, there's no need for you to do that. I'm sure that I can respond to you by then. Of course, there are extensive guidelines – requirements I should say – relating to access visits. But unless you would like me to, I don't think we need to go through them now, do you? After all, Mr Jarmy hasn't agreed to a public visit for more than thirty-five years. So he's not very likely to start now, is he?'

Glasby's pleasure at working the Broadmoor bureaucracy was almost completely deflated by this last comment. She had to admit that it seemed fully justified.

Still, she thought that she might as well get some background information on the hospital so she dialled the switchboard number again. This time she asked for their press office. 'Press?' The voice sounded perplexed.

'Yes, please. Or PR, maybe?' suggested Glasby.

'Putting you through. Hold please.'

The phone rang for a very long time and she was about to give up when a man with a thick Scottish accent came on the line. 'Hello?'

'Hello. Is this the PR department, please?'

'PR, did you say? I don't think we have one of those. This is C and R – control and restraints. I don't think that was what you were after now, was it? Shall I put you back to the switchboard?'

She shivered: manhandled into a straitjacket, surrounded by lunatics, screaming . . . Without even answering the man's question she slammed the phone down, hard enough to hurt her hand.

The child was frightened, lying in the dark, listening – but what was it? Trembling, but it was a hot summer night, so sweating as well. Quick, let's get under the sheet. What was that noise? Please God, take me in your care, keep me safe and hear my prayer. Not again not again not again not again. If I close my eyes it will go away.

Ten

While she waited impatiently for the fax from Mr Allen, Glasby was able to move forward on one question. She found the file where she had stored the picture of the two girls, emailed it to her parents, and called them.

'Hello, Dad. How was the golf?' she asked, not listening to a word of the answer. 'That sounds great! I'm sorry to bother you, Dad, but I just sent you an email. It's a thing from the newspaper, a sort of competition, and I wondered if you might be able to help. It's a photo, a copy of an old photo, and I'm trying to work out where it was taken.'

'A competition, you said? It can't be too hard, if it's in the *Herald*. Is there a prize?'

Glasby did her best to ignore the inevitable put down. 'I'm not sure, actually.' She thought that appealing to her father's sporting instincts would be the quickest way to get him interested, and she was right. A damned sight easier than having him show any respect for her or her work, that was for certain. 'But the thing is, I'm almost sure it was taken in Norfolk, on the coast. It was somewhere small from the look of it one of those seaside places like Sheringham or Cromer. And quite a while ago, the late sixties, probably.'

'All right, Ali. I'll have a look and call you back. I don't know if I'll recognize it, but I'll try. And Mum might be able to help as well, I suppose.'

When she got off the phone, Tom Lear was standing over her, looking down the front of her shirt. He was wearing a Prince of Wales check suit and a lime-green striped tie.

'Well, Ali, I've some fantastic news for you. I had another chat to Mark about this dating series, and the more we talked, the more it sounded like the business. We need you to put your research together this week. When you're scoping it out, why don't you cover the traditional ways as well? You know, agencies, Miss

Lonely Hearts, that sort of thing. Mark was thinking that it might work well if you enrolled in something different for each piece, like a sort of road test. You'll keep it light, of course. You never know, you might even meet someone you like the look of.'

He treated her to his smile again. Glasby made no effort to return it. 'OK, Tom. I'll move on to it first thing tomorrow and start putting some ideas together. I've mentioned it to Bill Davenport, and he's all right with it. Although,' she improvised, 'he might need me back again on Friday.'

Lear looked irritated with her. 'Friday? Isn't that when his party is? What are you doing, practising? Are you going to be jumping naked out of the cake?'

'You patronizing bastard,' she managed not to say. But he was right. Friday was when the party was; it must be Davenport's last day. How were they going to get to the bottom of everything by then? It hadn't even occurred to her.

Before she had time to think the phone rang. It was her father.

'It was easy,' he told her. 'I'm surprised you needed any help with that one.'

There was nothing he loved more than a competition. Unless it was being able to put her down at the same time.

'I checked in my slide library. You know that I've uploaded them on to my PC and indexed them all? It was quite a job.' He was starting to sound like Mr Bureaucrat of Broadmoor. 'It's Helmswick. Your mother and I used to drive up there regularly at the weekend. Before you were born, of course.' Of course. After she was born, it had been completely impossible for him to do anything nice at all. Until she had the decency to turn eighteen and move out. 'But if you look carefully at the background, just about in the middle, above the end of the terraced houses, you can see the top of the clock tower. You didn't say what the prize was, by the way.'

'I don't know if there will be one. It's something they were thinking of trying out, just an idea. But thanks anyway, Dad. Say hello to Mum.'

Glasby's landlord, Robin Hutley, had still not returned her call from Friday evening. She tried him on her mobile but it just rang until it went through to his voicemail. She was about to leave a message but had a second thought. She called his number again using the office phone. This time he wouldn't recognize who was calling him.

It worked. 'Alison! I got your message this morning. I've been trying all day to get hold of my heating man. I'm not a builder, you know. Boilers are a bit too technical for you and me to get our hands dirty with, aren't they?' Glasby said nothing to this. 'But I've got some good news. He's just coming off a job and I should be able to talk to him in a few minutes. Give me your number, dear, and I'll call you in five or ten.'

It was obvious that he had intended to avoid her for as long as possible. The chances were that he wouldn't ring her back, either. However, she wasn't in any position to argue the toss with him, so wisely she did as he said and thanked him instead.

She found a roadmap of Norfolk on the Web and looked at how you would get from Coltishall to Helmswick. The B1150 which she had taken from Norwich simply continued through Coltishall to North Walsham. Then it went almost straight on to Helmswick.

'North Walsham!' she exclaimed, out loud. That was where Leonie came from. For the first time, she realized how close Leonie Dellar's childhood home had been to the Bacons' – no more than seven miles or so. And Leonie was only a few years older than Lynette. There *had* to be some connection, something to explain why Dellar had the girls' photograph. But wrack her brain as she might, she was no closer to knowing what it was.

From the map, it looked as though there would be an easy bus route between Coltishall and Helmswick. In other words, her theory of a seaside outing by Lynette and Donna was completely plausible. They might not even have been with their parents. Could it have been Lynette, being a good older sister, keeping Donna amused during the school summer holidays?

In fact, they would have passed through the town where Donna's murderer grew up. Glasby had a sudden thought, grabbing *Children Carried Away*. The other photo of the two sisters was also taken by the seaside. In 1967. But unlike her photo, there was nothing on this one to identify the location; just beach and sea behind the girls. And then it came back to her; Leonie Dellar had moved to Norwich by the end of 1966, several months before the photo had been taken. Glasby had just found herself another blind alley.

It was no good. She needed more information. That reminded

her: Brian Jarmy. Four fifteen, and no news from Mr Allen
on her request for an interview. Maybe she should call
him?

But instead her phone rang. To her surprise it was Hutley
with news of a repair for her boiler. 'I've managed to get things
straight with Wayne now. Don't worry, we'll have you snug
as a bug in no time. Wayne will be round first thing tomorrow
and he'll have you right as rain. Half seven all right for you?'

Glasby thanked him with a little more feeling than before.
Apparently she was only going to have one more night of
arctic conditions to endure.

The fax machine near her desk started to chirrup its greeting.
Roy Allen! She leapt up, and stood over it anxiously while it
finished communicating and started to print.

The letterhead came through first: 'Broadmoor Special
Hospital, Patient/Public Liaison Office'. It was addressed to
William Davenport Esq. and Ms Alison Glasby, and headed
'Re: Your Public Access Request: Patient Brian Jarmy'.

In the time it took her to read the letter Glasby's good mood
evaporated.

> We refer to your request made earlier today by telephone
> to the undersigned, for fully supervised restricted public
> access to Patient Mr Brian Jarmy. Your request has been
> approved by Mr Jarmy's Patient Supervisor. However,
> we regret that Mr Jarmy does not wish your request to
> be granted. Accordingly, your request has been rejected.
> Yours sincerely
> Roy Allen
> Public/Patient Liaison Officer

Disconsolately she took the fax to show to Davenport.

'Well, we had a punt at it. That's all we can do, isn't it?'
He didn't seem too disappointed.

'I suppose so, yes. The man at Broadmoor told me that
Jarmy hasn't seen a visitor since you were there. Apparently
you are the only one he's ever had. Imagine it, in thirty-seven
years, no one.'

'He saw me for all of twenty minutes. I know I can be bad
company, but to put someone off the whole human race for
the next three and a half decades!'

Glasby didn't laugh. 'I've got a definite location for the photo, Bill. It's a seaside place called Helmswick, in North Norfolk. It's only a few miles from Coltishall. So we've certainly got enough now to go back to Lynette with, don't you think? But unless you talk to him, Tom Lear has got me tied up for the next two days. And Friday's your last day, isn't it? How are we going to handle it?'

'From what you told me about Lynette's behaviour, we absolutely need to let her cool off. She's a very strong-willed woman, as you know, so we need to handle her very carefully. So,' he continued, 'there's no need for us to get ourselves in a twist about the next few days. Let's move this along good and carefully. And you don't need to worry about me leaving. I don't want to let this slip through our hands any more than you do. This is my story and I'll stay on it for as long as it takes. You and I will carry on working on this together. Slowly and surely, that's our motto from now on.'

Any slower and she'd be ready to retire, never mind him. She tried a different approach.

'That reminds me, Bill. When I first showed you the photographs of Leonie's things, you said that she'd mentioned to you once that she'd embroidered the cushion herself. That might help to date when she sewed the photo into it. Can you remember when it was? Because then we might be able to find out who her visitors were, just before then, and we might be able to narrow down who could have given it to her. Do you see what I mean? Or should I go back through the interview notes?'

'Hmmm. Yes, I see what you mean. Although it could be a bit of a long shot. I suppose they must have made records of visitors. But whether they would still have them now, I don't know. I can't say I remember exactly when she would have talked to me about it, but why don't you leave it with me, and I'll see if I can find anything.'

Glasby hid her frustration behind a weak smile.

'Now, maybe you can give me some advice. They told me to look for a leaving present, something they can give me at the do on Friday. Do you think that an old man like me would look stupid on a mountain bike?'

She could have wept.

* * *

The answer machine was flashing when Glasby got in: there was a message. She told herself that she was being silly but quickened her step towards it anyway.

All that was recorded was a few moments of silence and the click of a receiver being replaced. It spooked her a bit, alone in the flat, although really she had always felt pretty safe there. Security was one thing that Hutley had done well. It was the main reason she'd moved there, after the burglary at the house she had shared with Helen and the medics. The street was well lit and always busy, the front door had expensive Banham locks and special bolts on the hinges and all of the windows were lockable.

Hutley had squeezed one other flat on to her floor, whose door was opposite hers. There was an oldish man there but although she'd heard noises occasionally, she'd only seen him once briefly since she had moved in. But there was an Indian family living above the shop next door who always seemed to be around. They were all very friendly: husband, wife and the serious-faced little boy who helped out in the shop after school. She was sure they would be helpful if she ever needed anything.

Glasby flicked through the TV channels without finding anything worth watching. Then she tried to read a novel which she had started a couple of weeks ago, sitting up in bed swaddled in her duvet. At the time it had seemed very promising. It was weighty, which she liked, with a dense plot, based on a reworking of a Victorian thriller. But she had more or less lost track of the story. She couldn't remember who was supposed to be related to whom. If she was going to make any sense of it, she would have to start back at the beginning. She wasn't sure that she could be bothered.

Her mobile rang in the kitchen. Braving the cold, she grabbed it and jumped back on to the bed, covering herself with the duvet again. The caller's number wasn't displayed.

'Hello?'

'Hello, Alison? This is John Redgrave. We met at Simon and Kate's, remember? How are you?'

Glasby hadn't really expected him to ring, not so soon, anyway. She was rather pleased that he had.

'Are you still working with Bill Davenport, on the Dellar case? I was looking through his book again yesterday, you know, *Children Carried Away*. It's pretty cool to be working with him, isn't it?'

'It's great, yes. What did you make of the book?' Glasby asked, remembering just too late that they'd already talked about it.

'I think it's excellent, of course. He was really rigorous in his methods, and sensitive as well. He's obviously very good at getting close to people and making them want to open up to him. It's a real talent. And the fact that he's the only person that Dellar would ever give up anything to, that's amazing really. She wouldn't say a dicky to the police, as I'm sure you know, and yet she talked to him.'

'Yes, he really built up a relationship with her. But he's not one of those fuzzy liberal types; he's not under any illusions about her, you know. It wasn't like she pulled the wool over his eyes.'

'No, I'm sure you're right. He seems very clear in his thinking. Although there was one thing that got me. You know the Jarmy interview?'

'Yes,' Glasby replied. 'Why?'

'Did you get the feeling that Jarmy only saw Davenport so that he could find out whether Leonie really had confessed to the murders? When you've been a copper for a while, you learn a thing or two about villains. The trouble is, if you're not careful it makes you cynical. But we see a lot of nasty types, and you learn to see right through them. To me, it jumped out, reading the interview. It wasn't Davenport questioning Jarmy. It was the other way round.'

'Oh, you think so?' Glasby replied, cautiously, not wanting to tell Redgrave that she'd had exactly the same thought.

'I did, yes, although it doesn't seem to have occurred to Davenport. To be fair, he wrote the book in the early seventies, didn't he? He wasn't to know that Jarmy would go for all those years since then without seeing another visitor.'

Glasby was startled. 'John, how did you know that? That Jarmy hasn't had any other visitors after Davenport?'

Redgrave was embarrassed. 'I was going to tell you but it slipped out before I could. I hope you don't think that I'm interfering, Alison. I certainly wasn't intending to meddle in your business. But after I read the Jarmy interview, I got curious, as I said. So I called Broadmoor this morning – I suppose you know that's where Jarmy's still kept. Oh, of course you do, it was in your article, wasn't it? I thought that was very good, by the way. I noticed that they used Bill Davenport's name mostly, but I'm sure that you actually wrote it, didn't you?'

She couldn't resist the flattery. 'Well, not really. Bill and I wrote it together, as a collaboration. Thank you.' She paused. 'But you were saying, you called Broadmoor?' She didn't know whether to be pleased or angry.

There was an awkward silence, which he broke. 'Well, yes, but if you're not doing anything, perhaps we could talk it over some more on Wednesday evening? Face to face, I mean. I've got the evening free, and if you're not too busy, would you like to meet up?'

'OK,' she replied, more convinced this time. 'What did you have in mind?'

'You said that you live in Stockwell, didn't you? I'll be at New Scotland Yard, in Victoria. I ought to finish by about eight. There's quite a nice Chinese in the old County Hall building, on the South Bank. Right by the London Eye, do you know where I mean? I could book a table there for eight thirty, if that would be convenient for you?'

'OK, that's a good idea, thank you. See you then.'

They both rang off, happy not to have hit any other conversational bumps in the road.

Glasby lay for a long while afterwards, her forehead creased in thought, staring at her bedroom ceiling, near zero temperatures and stomach problems forgotten.

Either the murder squad was seriously underemployed, or by sheer coincidence John was conducting his own investigations into Brian Jarmy, or – and she was pretty sure that this was the most likely hypothesis – he was rather keen on her.

She didn't really know how she felt about that. The last thing she wanted was to have Kate and Simon mixed up in her private life. Given that every word she said would go back to Simon to be analyzed and approved of – or not – there was absolutely no way that she intended to tell Kate anything. In fact, the more she thought it through, the more she regretted agreeing to see John again.

Then she remembered what he had said about Jarmy manipulating Davenport. It must be true. She and John had both independently reached the same conclusion. So Jarmy needed to be sure about Dellar's confession. Why? Simply to know that she had betrayed whatever weird understanding it was that they had forged, never to talk to anyone about what they had done?

She had the horrible sense of missing something, something important, but she had no idea what. Eventually she started to doubt herself. Maybe Bill was right: it was ludicrous to suppose that Jarmy might have been thinking about an appeal against his murder convictions.

Thinking about Davenport, though, there was something strange about his attitude as well. To start off with she had thought that his heart wasn't really in it. Which was a huge disappointment, but understandable enough. Probably he was a bit past it, like people said.

But it wasn't as simple as that. It was almost as if the more she found out, the more he wanted to slow her down. He seemed, well, relieved when he heard that she had to work on other things. And what was he up to with that ridiculous story line that Daniels had come up with? You could read on Davenport's face that he knew that it was a lot of nonsense, but he positively encouraged Daniels to spend the *Herald*'s money buying the story and made sure that it got into the paper.

Was Davenport somehow just trying to protect his own reputation? Or was there something else going on, something he was holding out on her? What had he said when she called him from Coltishall on Friday: 'There are things you don't know about Lynette.' Whatever these 'things' were, he wasn't in a hurry to tell her about them, was he?

What *was* Davenport's role in the case? How involved had he got? Could it have been him that had smuggled in the photo to Leonie?

She slept badly that night, troubled by dreams of Bill Davenport laughing at her, and her father's voice in her head, sounding only too familiar: 'You've always been the same, Alison: trying a bit too hard to be clever.'

*The child was frightened, lying in the dark, listening –
but what was it? Quick, let's get under the sheet.
Trembling, but it was a hot summer night, so sweating
as well. What was that noise? Please God, take me in
your care, keep me safe and hear my prayer. Not again
not again not again not again. If I close my eyes it will
go away. If I promise to be good nothing will happen.*

Eleven

Glasby was still in the shower when the doorbell rang, at two minutes past seven. 'Damn!' she cursed, fumbling for a towel and then her dressing gown.

She ran for the door, the morning air icy against her wet skin.

'Hello love, I'm Wayne. About yer boiler.' He was very fat, blue cotton overalls straining to hold his gut in. One of the buttons had lost the struggle and gone missing, an expanse of flesh showing through the gap it had left. He had a large shaved head, a large toothy smile and a large 'CFC' tattoo on the back of his right hand.

'Coupler's gone again, I bet,' he said. 'I told the guv'nor it would, I told 'im it'd need a new part, but he would 'ave it that I 'ad to refit the old 'un.

'I'm sorry, love,' he added, sympathetically. 'You'll catch yer death standing there like that. You go and get some clothes on, and I'll open the old girl up, and we'll see if we can get 'er working right away.'

Grateful for the opportunity to escape, Glasby hurried back into the bathroom. She emerged fully dressed though still shivering with cold, to see Wayne replacing the front of the boiler. After a few moments it was fired up and some heat started to circulate around the flat for the first time in days. They each had a quick mug of tea as Glasby stood pressed against the sitting room radiator, soaking up the warmth.

By twenty past she was on her way out, realizing as she got on the Tube that she had completely forgotten about breakfast. She was in the office not much after eight, with a buttered roll from the sandwich shop and a conspiratorial look on her face.

Glasby walked down the stairs to a corridor lined with framed reproductions of old *Herald* front pages. Past 'Peace with Honour?', 'Victory in Europe' and 'Long Live the Queen', until she reached 'Leonie: The Truth at Last'.

Making sure that no one was paying any attention to her – not difficult at that hour, since the office was largely deserted – she surreptitiously turned the handle of the door opposite. Great! Working as she did in an open-plan area, she had no idea whether the executives' offices were locked overnight. If they were, the cleaners must open them up early in the morning, and then leave them unlocked. She was pretty sure that Davenport wouldn't be in before nine thirty.

She saw immediately that he had put away all of the papers she had been working on. He must have done it late yesterday. So much for 'leave it to me to go through things', then.

Unless he had taken some of the papers home with him. She started an anxious search for the Leonie Dellar file.

Damn! She couldn't remember the order. Think, come on!

Why hadn't she paid more attention before and memorized what was in which box? The trouble was, before she had had Davenport's instructions to guide her. This time she was having to rely on her memory from the week before. And all the bloody boxes looked the same: large, battered and covered in dust.

That was it – the dust! The ones she had been working on would be cleaner than the others, if only because she had unintentionally been using her suit as a J-Cloth on them. It was definitely the left-hand cupboard, and she was almost certain that it was the left hand pile as well. But they all looked as mucky as each other.

No, it was the middle pile, those three almost at the bottom. Now she saw them, she recognized the printing on one of them and a large brass staple in another. She made a careful mental note of which box was on top of which.

It took her ten minutes to extricate them, being as careful as she could to disturb as little as possible. She had better leave a good fifteen minutes to put the boxes back in order. And probably ten minutes to get the papers back into the boxes in the right order first. Say half an hour in total to be safe, so she had forty-five minutes, max, to work in. If only she could remember which papers were in which box.

After a few moments' rapid searching she realized that her

first choice was wrong. There were police reports, press releases, a huge bundle of files marked 'Background Research' which she hadn't seen before and regretted not having time to look at now.

She found it in the second box, a thick dark blue file with 'Leonie Dellar' written on the front in Davenport's distinctive rounded hand. There was an awful lot of material. She would have to concentrate ferociously to find it. If it was even there to be found.

There didn't seem to be any better method than to begin at the beginning. She tipped the papers from the file on to the floor, sat next to them, started to read.

Despite her pledge to focus solely on the job at hand she couldn't resist lingering again for a moment over the first interview, the one that had caused (or so she had now convinced herself) Brian Jarmy to summon Davenport for his debriefing. Here it was, the crucial passage:

> 'You're right, Mr Davenport. If I want people to listen
> to me, I have to talk. So now I'm going to say what
> they've all been asking me. Are you sure that tape recorder
> is working?'
> 'Quite sure, yes.'
> 'This is my confession. We did it. We killed them.
> Brian and me. All four. Kevin Yallop, Matthew Starling,
> Donna Bacon and Michael Summer. Brian did most of
> it. But I helped. I'm guilty too. I helped him catch them.
> I suppose I told myself that he wasn't going to kill them.'

It was a straightforward, unequivocal confession. Maybe a slight attempt at mitigation at the end, but nothing that would have saved her from a mandatory life sentence for murder. Or from the gallows, if it had been a few years earlier. What was it that Jarmy had been so interested in? There must be something.

She made herself get back on plan. There were reams of notes, with Dellar doing most of the talking, as you would expect. Dellar talking about her health, shortness of breath, chest pains, a diagnosis of angina. Different medical regimes, diets. Prison food, exercise. Education programmes. Her cell. Other prisoners, coming and going. One or two of them almost as notorious as Dellar herself. Comments about the different governors, other prison staff. A couple of references to Mr Dack, whose bending of the prison rules had started Glasby on the search.

And there it was. What a shame she hadn't started at the end. 10th March 1992, at the end of a long and not very interesting discussion of prison educational policies:

> To be honest, Mr Davenport, I don't think they've got any better over the years. The teachers they had back in the seventies were as good as any of them now. Embroidery was the very first course I did, right when they transferred me here after the trial. I always liked needlework as a girl. But I never really thought I had an aptitude for it. Mrs Tweed, she was called, we all thought it was a very suitable name. I embroidered a cushion cover, I worked like crazy at it. I suppose it helped me through the first few weeks, the first Christmas and New Year. I've still got it now after all this time.

Glasby clenched her fist in triumph like a golfer who has holed a thirty-foot putt, breathed in and exhaled a deep sigh of relief. Then she tensed, frozen to the spot, footsteps in the corridor outside the prelude to the door handle turning, the door opening. He must have come in early!

'Bill, I . . . Oh, good morning, um, Alison, isn't it? Still working on the Dellar papers? Well, if you think you can find the time, I suppose. Tom has talked to you about the dating series, hasn't he? Very good, very good. It should be just the thing for you. Anyway, if you see Bill, tell him to give me a tinkle, will you?'

'Yes, of course, Mr Ellington. And thank you. I've really enjoyed working with Bill.'

'Mark, please, not "Mr Ellington".' He smiled down at her, and she smiled back, uncertain what more she was supposed to say. *Go, please go, now!* she thought. He did.

Feeling shaken, she checked her watch. Ten to nine. She scribbled a note as an aide-memoire: '10.3.92, "embroidered a cushion cover, helped me through the first few weeks, the first Xmas and NY. I've still got it now, after all these years."'

She started to replace the papers in the file, careful to get them back in chronological order. Then the file back in the box, between two manila wallets of papers as before.

She checked her watch again. It was still not quite nine. There was time to look for one more thing. More files, more papers, then after a few minutes she made a second aide-memoire.

By twenty past nine all of the files were back in their boxes, the boxes were back in their piles and the chair which she had used to stand on was back by the desk. A quick glance up and down the corridor; there was no one in sight.

Glasby arrived back at her desk just before Lear, resplendent in bright yellow shirt and braces decorated with little pound signs.

'Morning, Tom,' she greeted him, with something approaching genuine warmth. 'I've started to get my thoughts together on the series. I'm just about to make a start on the research now. I'll put together an outline after that, OK?'

'Yes, um, OK,' he replied, a little taken aback by her enthusiasm. She was a strange girl, not bad looking in a boyish sort of way, and quite a good figure as well, but really moody. Obviously she needed a boyfriend, or something. 'OK, let me know if you want anything. Hand on the tiller, you know.'

'Thank you. I'll tell you if I do.' He took the hint and left her to it.

Quickly she typed out a fax. It was short; it only took a couple of minutes. Before printing it she paused and added a few words. Making sure that no one was looking over her shoulder, she keyed in the number for Broadmoor Special Hospital. Once the fax had gone through, she took it from the machine and stuffed it into her pocket.

Returning to her desk, she gritted her teeth and settled down to two days of unmitigated boredom.

About the same time Davenport arrived in his office, took off his raincoat and began his familiar morning routine of filling the coffee machine, something that he wasn't going to be doing for too much longer. He settled at his desk and looked around the scruffy office with a sense of nostalgia. Even though it was nothing like the old Fleet Street building which they used to call the Ship, sometimes he felt that more of his life was here, in this office, than at home. His eye passed the photo of him with Grand National winner Red Rum; another of him with the cats; and the cupboard doors which as usual bulged open sufficiently wide to see the stack of boxes inside.

Strange, there was something about that pile, something not quite as usual. He got up and opened the left-hand door. The middle pile, the one with the Jarmy and Dellar papers – yes. That box, second from the bottom. It should have had a big staple in one corner, squashed almost flat, more than an inch across. But he couldn't see it. Maybe the cleaners had pushed something against it and torn it off? Or maybe – yes! He shoved his hand between the stacks. The box must have been taken out, turned round and put back into the pile with the staple at the *back*. Well, well!

'Alison Glasby. You don't give up, do you?' He went back to his desk and sat thinking, motionless.

After a few minutes his phone rang. 'Bill? Mark here. How are you? Jolly good! I wonder if you have a little time this morning. I just wanted to run some things past you, for my speech. For Friday, your reception, you know. Would you mind?'

'Not at all, Mark,' replied Davenport, wearily.

Actually, Glasby reflected, it hadn't been that bad. She was stretched out on the purple sofa, basking in the heat pumped out by the newly rejuvenated boiler. She certainly wouldn't want to spend the rest of her career on soft stories. Or even the rest of the week, if it came to that. But a series of her own was good going, and it meant that Ellington had definitely noticed her work.

Once she had got started she'd even enjoyed bits of it. She'd decided more or less on the basic themes to cover. She would start with an online agency of which there were loads to choose from. Then she'd go to the other extreme, a very upmarket personalized matchmaking service. Again, there didn't seem to be any shortage of choice. Back to mass market with a basic lonely hearts ad in *Time Out* or one of the nationals, then some sort of speed dating or activity thing and finally Internet chat rooms. She could compare cost, services offered, how much hassle it was, whether or not it felt safe and most of all how likely it was that you'd find anyone. The Leer should be pretty happy with her once she had all the details pinned down.

Pleased with herself, she reached for her novel and started to read. Almost immediately she hit up against the same problem as before; she couldn't remember who was who so the plot just didn't make sense. There was nothing for it. She would have to start again and concentrate more this time.

It was a huge book and a couple of hours later she still hadn't made much of a dent in it. But now she had a grip of the story and had passed the point she had reached before. She was starting to enjoy it again.

Her home phone rang. Exasperated, she reached over to pick it up. If it was another nuisance call, maybe she should tell the operator?

'Ali, hi! It's me.'

Glasby recognized Kate's voice. (She hated it when people said 'It's me' when they phoned you.) Then it struck her; she was due to see Simon's friend John for dinner the next day. Maybe he had told Simon about it, and Kate was phoning for some girls' talk beforehand. Why couldn't people keep their mouths shut!

Luckily it wasn't as bad as she had feared. Kate treated her to several minutes on the topic of a suit she had seen and was thinking of buying. And she wanted her views on whether or not she should change the colour of her hair.

'You know, I've been dark brown since I was seventeen, and I'm bored with it. But maybe highlights would be too tarty. I was thinking of lowlights – what do you think?'

Glasby, who had never dyed her hair except for an experiment with henna in her first year at university, wasn't sure what she thought, but did her best.

'I suppose it would be OK, so long as they weren't, you know, too obvious. Is that what you were thinking?' Apparently it was.

Kate then raised the subject which Glasby strongly suspected was the real reason for her call.

'What did you think of John? We like him. Simon doesn't know him that well, really. They were sort of friends of friends at Reading and he's never kept up with him since. John phoned up earlier to say thank you and he told Simon that he liked you. I don't know about his job, though, what do you think?'

'I don't know. I thought it sounded quite interesting, being a detective.'

'Well, I wouldn't fancy it. Imagine mixing with all those lowlifes every day. And the criminals! Anyway, you didn't say what you thought of him. Do you think he's good-looking?'

'I suppose he was OK. You know,' was as much as Glasby was prepared to give away, although she had decided that she did, in fact. He seemed to be a man with strong opinions and if the tinges of grey around his sideburns and the lines on his forehead made him look a bit old, they also gave him an air of authority which suited him well.

'Yes, I know what you mean. Quite a nice guy, though. Simon and he are going to try to keep in touch now, so maybe you'll see him again. If you'd like to, of course?'

'Of course,' said Glasby, neutrally. The good news was that John clearly hadn't said anything about meeting up with her. That was definitely a point in his favour. And the fact that he wasn't really a friend of Simon's didn't hurt either. No way did she want Kate matchmaking for her.

'By the way, did I mention that Simon's thinking of going for a head of year post?'

She hadn't, but did, and the conversation returned to safer ground. Before they finished, Glasby even remembered to thank her for the other night.

'Not at all, Ali. And don't worry! We'll find a boyfriend for you eventually.'

Why Kate thought that this was her mission in life was beyond Glasby. Her parents were as bad. Her mother regularly asked, 'Have you met anyone nice yet, dear?' which translated as: 'When are you going to get married like everyone else's daughters?' and her father dropped heavy-handed jokes about having to put money by for her wedding: 'Although I can treat it as a long-term investment, the progress that you're making!'

It wasn't as if any of the men she met were particularly interesting. Except maybe John. He had obviously realized that she wouldn't want other people gossiping about her. Probably he felt the same way himself. She could imagine that he was a private person. And with a job like his, he must know how to keep his mouth shut.

He must be good, as well, or he wouldn't be in the murder

squad. And what he had said about Brian Jarmy, manipulating Davenport. He really was very perceptive. If only she had a team to work with, like he'd described. All she had was a half-hearted Bill Davenport and her own efforts.

She realized that she was really looking forward to seeing John again. Probably she should make an effort. She would get home from work early, change her work clothes and make herself look nice. Treat it like a date, in fact!

Well, why not? It had been a long time since she'd done anything like that. She had only really had two proper boyfriends. And the first one hardly counted.

It was conventional for girls to lose their virginity before going to university. She had reached the end of the sixth form at school without even getting close.

One night in the summer holiday, after an evening out drinking in Norwich, she had caught the last bus back with Tom Bailey, a boy whose parents lived just around the corner from hers. There was a short cut on the walk home from the bus stop through the churchyard. He put his arm around her in the dark. He wanted to kiss her. She let him. They stood entwined as he tried to find a way under her top and then her skirt. She was too drunk to feel much, but sober enough to decide that it was time to get it over with.

It didn't last long, didn't hurt (contrary to what some people had said), and wasn't particularly enjoyable. They finished the walk home arm in arm and he kissed her again before she went in to her parents' house. Thankfully they were watching TV, so she shouted 'goodnight' and went straight upstairs.

The next day she was pleased with herself for having done it, until she remembered that they hadn't used any contraception. She knew that she should do something about it. But what? If she went to the doctor, her mother would want to know why. Anyway, talking to Dr Carter, who'd known her since she was a small child, would be more than she could bear. (She knew that there was a clinic in the city; they'd been told about it at school in social studies, amid much sniggering and knowing looks. But imagine, someone seeing her in there!)

So she did nothing except wait, hope, and tell herself she would never do it again if things worked out OK. She was lucky; they did.

For the rest of the summer, Tom mooned around after her, in love. She liked him, and it made her feel a bit guilty that he was upset, but he was *so* embarrassing. He phoned her almost every day. 'Why don't you invite him round, dear? He's a very nice boy,' said her mother, making things worse, as usual.

Even if a conversation began OK you knew it was going to get all heavy and serious. He would say something complimentary but it always had an accusation hiding behind it, like 'I fancy you,' which meant 'I fancy you and you don't fancy me even though you led me on.' She wouldn't know what to say, so generally said nothing, or just 'thank you' in a weak tone of voice, as if he was a shopkeeper who'd just given her the correct change. From there it was generally straightforward self-pity and recriminations, until the next call, when it would start all over again.

Sometimes he would just hang up without saying anything, which was even more embarrassing. Why couldn't he leave her alone?

Luckily he went off to art school in September. She bumped into him occasionally if they were both back home during the holidays, but he had obviously got over his obsession.

The only time she had actually been in love was in her second year at Leicester. He was a philosophy student called Lester, and the pun on his name seemed to cause everyone enormous amusement. He sang in a rock band called Mainline and took lots of illicit drugs. Most people she knew thought he was weird. He was a mature student, eight years older than her, and not even she thought that he was good-looking: no taller than her, a little overweight, with unkempt curly dark hair, staring eyes and a large fleshy nose. He was permanently skint.

He had opinions on most subjects, but most of all music. Whatever she liked turned out to be commercialized and sold out, although complete junk like Abba or Kylie was apparently OK, in a knowing sort of way, of course. They went to see things together occasionally but she gave up after he walked out from Radiohead (the tickets had cost her a bomb) because they showed too much respect for their instruments.

But like her he was very bookish. He seemed to have read everything she had and much more, and he understood people so much better than she did, in books and real life. Most of all, he wrote himself, compulsively – generally songs, sometimes several a day, but also poetry or snatches of short stories. He had neither the attention span nor the discipline for anything longer.

Lester didn't have the discipline for a relationship either. He would turn up several hours late for a date with her, or not at all. The reason for his absence – it was never an excuse; somehow he didn't seem to need one – was usually to do with writing or singing something, but increasingly seemed to Glasby to be connected to drugs.

Sometimes he would say to her, 'Try this, Ali. It'll make you feel different. Forget you're Alison Glasby for the evening.' He would give her a joint, a line of white powder or on one occasion a small pill which he told her was Ecstasy. But she didn't see the point in any of them. She didn't like smoking, and once when she tried to eat some cannabis it made her feel sick. Cocaine gave her a headache and made her nervous, and the Ecstasy didn't really do anything for her at all.

Lester taught her to enjoy sex for the first time. By her standards he was an experienced lover, gentle and sensuous when the mood took him. They used to make love often, sometimes in the morning or the middle of the day. Occasionally she even missed a lecture for his sake (Lester hardly paid attention to his course, whether he was with her or not).

But after a few months he drifted away from her, gradually. She missed their discussions and the physical contact, but she had no idea how to get him back. She put her energy into her English course instead. She finished with a First. He was expelled at the end of the year, having not bothered to sit a single exam. Even after they stopped going out together she was fond of him so she was hurt when she found out that he'd left the city without saying goodbye to her.

All of that was several years ago and Glasby had grown up a lot since. If other people wanted to measure her by whether or not she had a boyfriend, that was their business. She had more important things to think about.

Still, an evening with John Redgrave promised to be interesting. And if things worked out as she was hoping, he might eventually be very useful to her.

Yes, she would make a bit of an effort tomorrow. It wouldn't kill her. And it might even give her some ideas for her series. It was all fitting together quite nicely.

In the meantime, the flat was warm and the sofa was comfortable. She turned back to her book. It really was very good, quite ingenious. She decided to take notes as she went along; that way, she wouldn't lose track of the plot again.

*The child was frightened, lying in the dark, listening –
but what was it? Trembling, but it was a hot summer
night, so sweating as well. Quick, let's get under the
sheet. What was that noise? Please God, take me in your
care, keep me safe and hear my prayer. Not again not
again not again not again. If I close my eyes it will go
away. If I promise to be good nothing will happen. It
can't. It can't.*

Twelve

G lasby slept well, woken only by the alarm at quarter past seven. She immediately realized that it was cold, very cold.

She dragged herself out of bed, threw on her dressing gown as quickly as possible and stomped into the kitchen. The boiler certainly wasn't on. She tried to remember how you set the timer and fumbled with a few buttons. No, the heating had been set to come on at half past six, so that wasn't it. And it wasn't the thermostat either, because that had been all right the night before.

She turned on the gas rings in the kitchen, put the kettle on and switched on her mobile phone. Without any hope at all she rang Robin Hutley, cursing herself for not having taken Wayne the plumber's number the day before.

'Hello? Oh it's you, Alison. Good morning. To what do I owe the pleasure?'

He sounded unenthusiastic to be talking to her but she could hardly blame him as she felt the same way herself.

'It's the boiler again. I've no heating this morning and it's absolutely freezing. It worked OK yesterday after your plumber came round, but it's just the same as it was before now. Completely dead.'

'Have you tried the thermostat, dear? Or the timer?'

Tersely, Glasby told him that she had already checked both; it was definitely the boiler.

'I expect that it's just the pilot light. Why don't you try to relight it?' He explained to her how to do it.

After ten minutes poking around in the innards of the boiler, during which she gashed her right hand, she called him back. Even with the gas rings fully on she was unbelievably cold.

'It definitely won't start.'

'I think you're in luck, dear. Wayne's working near you today. Let me see if I can get him. I'll call you back.'

Blood was trickling down her arm and on to the sleeve of her dressing gown. She realized that her hand hurt a lot and went into the bathroom. It was glacial in there. She had to stand for quite a while with the back of her hand held under the cold tap, which didn't do anything for her mood. She couldn't find any plasters but eventually the bleeding stopped.

She made a mug of tea and took it back to bed, huddled under the duvet listening to the morning news. The phone rang; she had forgotten to bring it with her, so she had to get out of bed again.

'Hello, love,' said a familiar voice. 'It's Wayne. It's never gone again, 'as it? Oh no! Listen, I'm just down the road from you. If you 'ang about, I'll be there soon as I can. 'Alf an hour, if we're lucky.'

She threw on the nearest clothes she could find, trying to avoid any contact with the back of her right hand, and put the kettle on to wait for him.

He turned up at half past nine after several more phone calls complete with long explanations and apologies. Glasby had to suffer the indignity of calling Tom Lear to explain that she would be late.

'Oh. There isn't anyone else at home who could stay in, then?'

'No,' Glasby said through gritted teeth, not trusting herself to say more.

'Well, you will get that outline moving, won't you? You should put in a fair bit of detail on the first article as well. You haven't forgotten it?'

Of course she hadn't bloody forgotten!

Wayne had to go off to get another part while she waited at home draining the system for him. This involved standing around shivering, watching a bowl slowly fill up with muddy brown water, switching it for an empty replacement, then starting again.

She got to the office at half past eleven.

Mike Marshall saw her arrive. 'Are you OK, Ali? What on earth have you done to your hand? Have you been in a fight?'

Glasby explained. 'And now I've got to get this research put together for some articles on different dating agencies. You know, lonely hearts, dinner clubs, online dating and chat rooms, that sort of thing. Ellington asked me to do a series of five, which is good I suppose. But Lear wants to see a detailed outline for all five, by tomorrow.'

Marshall was amused. 'Dating? Ellington's picked you?'

'Why not?'

'Oh, nothing. Just that it's – well, anyway, you're going to be sweating it to get it done for tomorrow. If you need any help, let me know. And you ought to get a plaster on that cut. It looks like it might even need stitches. Hey, you know what, you could call your series "Date-a-base". Get it?'

She got down to work, trying to ignore Serena's interminable phone calls in the background. How could one person talk to so many about so little?

It took a hell of a long time, just getting the basic information about which companies were offering what. There were hundreds of them, if not thousands. You'd think that if there were so many desperate singles around, they'd start bumping into each other without any help from anyone else. Even she'd managed that, with John . . . sort of, anyway. Lunchtime came and went without her noticing.

Every couple of hours the Leer would appear, hassling to see if she had anything to show him yet. 'I'm working on the first one now. Different online dating agencies.' She'd registered for three and was putting together a personal profile for each one, with different age, looks and expectations. 'I'll have something good,' she promised him. 'Funny and poignant. Just wait.'

Her phone rang. It was a disquietingly enthusiastic man from a speed dating agency called (unpromisingly in Glasby's view) 'A Beautiful Stranger', with whom she had registered a little earlier.

'We saw you'd just climbed on board with us. That's fantastic! We just wanted to make sure you knew about this month's special event – it's called "Dating on Thin Ice"! It's going to be just fantastic!'

Glasby already had the feeling that she knew more than she wanted to, but professional diligence required her to ask for more details.

'Three minutes, on the rink, arm in arm – it's a totally flirt-friendly environment.' He was actually laughing with the sheer enjoyment of it all. 'The whistle blows, and it's cheerio Charles, hello Harry! Fantastic, isn't it?'

Somehow Glasby's reaction must not have struck quite the right tone because for the first time a note of concern crept into Captain Fantastic's voice. 'Of course at the end of the day, what you get is what you give, you see my point? If it's not flirting, it's not working, that's what we say! Think about that, won't you?'

Glasby promised that she would and was rewarded by one last 'fantastic' before she was able to get off the phone.

The least welcome interruption of the day, predictably, was from Mr Journalism himself, Jack Daniels. 'Ali, hi, did you see the piece?' He had obviously decided that a man of his attainments could afford to be generous. 'I thought that they worked well together, your and Bill's backgrounder with my exclusive. Didn't you?'

Glasby confined herself to a noncommittal grunt, barely looking up from her papers.

'Anyway, Mark Ellington was very high on the story. He wants me to carry on working at the police. And to push a bit more with the Bacons to see if they'll confirm it. Bill's not too hot on it, me taking another poke at Lynette Bacon but – you know, what has to be, has to be.'

Glasby still had the bruises from her encounter with Lynette. If Daniels was going to try to push her around, then good luck to him. She smiled sweetly and looked back at her screen. He took the hint. She did her best to put all thoughts of the Dellar case to one side.

Marshall brought her a banana and a cup of coffee about three. Later, he appeared at her desk waving two pieces of paper.

'Fax, for you,' he said, looking at her curiously. She snatched it from his hand and read it eagerly:

Dear Ms Glasby,

We refer to your request made earlier today by telephone to the undersigned, for fully supervised restricted public access to Patient Mr Brian Jarmy. Your request has been approved by Mr Jarmy's patient supervisor.

Mr Jarmy has also indicated that he wishes your request to be granted. An appointment has been made per your request for 2 p.m. on Friday, —November. If this is not convenient, would you kindly telephone the undersigned for an alternative time.

It is important that you make yourself available for security clearance at least one hour before the time of your appointment.

Patient/public interactions are strictly subject to guidelines and regulations issued by the management of the special hospital. A summary of these is attached. Kindly note that any infraction of these regulations may lead to immediate cancellation of access, and/or criminal prosecution against you.

Yours sincerely
Roy Allen
Public/Patient Liaison Officer

'Ali, what on earth are you up to?' asked Marshall. 'You're going to see Brian Jarmy?'

'Shh,' she silenced him, looking around. Serena had left and there was nobody else within earshot. 'Mike, I can't explain now. But it's absolutely essential, really essential, that you don't mention this to anyone. Literally anyone. I'll explain it to you as soon as I can.'

'You mean that Lear doesn't know that you're doing this?' She avoided his eye and gave no answer. 'Hold on, when you say "anyone", do you mean that Davenport doesn't know either?'

'Mike, please don't ask. You don't want to know. The less I say, the better it is for both of us. Do you understand?'

'Ali, how the hell you've managed to get Brian Jarmy to agree to see you, I have no idea. But if you're going behind Bill Davenport's back, you're taking a big risk. If he finds out, you'll lose your job. You do realize that?'

'He won't find out. Will he, Mike? And then neither of us will be in any trouble. Will we?'

'What do you mean, *neither* of us? It's got nothing to do with me!'

'Yeah, and all I'm saying is, let's keep it that way, OK?'

Marshall went off, looking unhappy.

She put the fax away in her bag, her heart racing. She was going to be the first person in thirty-seven years to get in to see Brian Jarmy. And it would be this week. Her, Alison Glasby. It would be a huge exclusive!

There was no time even to think about it now. She had to

get back to work. By the time she was through, Ellington would have her marked down as a real all-rounder; hard *and* soft stories, whatever was called for.

Some time later her phone rang.

'Alison, John Redgrave. I'm really sorry, I'm running late – I'm still at the Yard. Something came up this afternoon and I got stuck with it. But I'll definitely be done in half an hour. I'll be fifteen minutes late, no more, but I am sorry.'

'Don't worry,' she started to say, and glanced at her watch. Damn! It was nearly quarter to eight. She wouldn't get to Westminster before half past at the earliest.

'John, I'm so sorry. I'm still at work myself, I've had a nightmare of a day. I had no idea it was so late, or I would have left, but I was trying to get something done, in time for tomorrow. I hate being late,' she finished, lamely.

'Bad day? What happened?' he asked, sounding sympathetic.

She started to tell him, but he interrupted.

'I'll tell you what, instead of talking now and staying at work even later, why don't we get to the restaurant? That's what we said we'd do, isn't it?'

Glasby was hungry, having had almost nothing to eat since breakfast. And she was tired. And, she admitted to herself, it would be nice to see John.

'OK then, very good. You call me when you're halfway, and I'll make sure that I'm at the restaurant first. I don't like to keep a lady waiting! I'll give them a bell now and tell them to change the booking.'

As she got on to the Docklands Light Railway she remembered that she had intended to go home to change first and put some make-up on. She was wearing jeans, trainers and a jumper under a black puffa jacket. Not exactly Paris Hilton, but it would have to do.

She reached in her bag for the fax from Roy Allen. She pulled it from her bag, read the first page quickly again – Jarmy really had agreed to see her! – and started the second page.

It was in small type, smothered in threats of criminal prosecution. Most of it wasn't relevant to her. She had no intention of smuggling in illegal substances or weapons, helping a patient to escape or in any way compromising the security of Broadmoor

Special Hospital. Neither did she have a problem in being barred from any physical contact whatsoever with Jarmy.

Her visit would be supervised. This meant that a patient officer (aka 'prison guard', presumably) would be present at all times. The conversation would be recorded, and an official transcript would be produced. She might if she wished apply for a copy of the transcript, which would be made available at the discretion of the management of the special hospital. But it would remain the copyright of the management, and could not be quoted from without their permission. In fact, she would not be permitted to quote anything that was said to her, or even to refer to the fact of her visit, without prior consent.

In other words, off the record. As in OFF THE RECORD. Big time. So much for her chances of an exclusive. Well, if the whole thing went wrong she'd lose her job anyway, so she might as well go to prison while she was at it.

But although she tried not to, Glasby was beginning to feel very nervous about the whole thing. A picture of an angry Davenport came to her mind, then a sinister, leering Brian Jarmy, grabbing her and slashing at her throat. She realized that she was sweating under her jumper.

Redgrave, as good as his word, was already at the restaurant when she arrived. He waved to her from the table as she was taking off her coat, stood up and made to shake her hand. Then he noticed the deep cut across the back of it.

'You've been in the wars, haven't you? How did that happen?'

She told him, at more length than she intended. It was so nice to have some sympathy from someone.

'Let me have a squint at it then. It doesn't look too good. Don't worry, I'm not making a pass. They do teach us first aid, you know.'

A little embarrassed, she let him take her right hand in his.

'Have you had anyone look at this?'

'No, I haven't had time. I meant to get a plaster, but I forgot.'

'It looks to me as if it needs more than a plaster. It doesn't look too clever at all. Look, we'll have dinner, and then I'm taking you to A and E at St Thomas's Hospital. I think it needs stitching. Unless you'd rather go there now?'

'John, I'm absolutely starving.' And she was, almost to the point of feeling dizzy. She told herself very firmly to watch her alcohol intake. There was no way that she wanted a repeat of that ghastly episode with Daniels, when she'd behaved like a student at Freshers' Week.

'Do you really think that I need someone to look at my hand?'

'Yes,' he said firmly. 'You're a silly girl, leaving it like that. But if you're hungry, let's order right away.' Mercifully, the food started coming very quickly and Glasby relaxed a bit.

'What made you take up policing, John?'

'What's this, interview technique?' he laughed. 'No, I suppose I just wanted something to *do*. After all that sitting around talking about nothing at university, I mean, yapping on about things that don't mean anything to anybody. People think that it's all chasing round in cars with the siren on, or trudging round the streets, but it's a proper career now. It's not bad money either, not when you go in as a graduate. And doing what I do, you have to use your loaf. There aren't many mugs in the CID. If I say so myself,' he added, smiling.

The letter from Broadmoor was still troubling Glasby. She couldn't get it off her mind and decided to go to the Ladies just to have some time to think. He stood up as she left the table and again as she came back. It was kind of nice, but a bit embarrassing too; she hoped that no one would think that they were on a date.

'John, have you ever had anything to do with a special hospital? Like Broadmoor?'

'No, they haven't caught up with me yet.' Glasby wasn't smiling, so he quickly added, 'Sorry, just kidding. I've never been to Broadmoor. When I was a probationer, in Nottingham, they took us to Rampton as part of our induction. Have you heard of it?'

'No. What is it?'

'It's another special hospital. The equivalent of Broadmoor. There are three of them in the country, I think. Broadmoor is the original one and it's the one that everyone's heard of. But they all basically do the same job.'

'What was it like, going to Rampton?'

'It was frightening, to be honest. I'd never been inside a prison then, but even compared to a prison special unit it's a really tense environment in there. The security levels, well, before you actually get to where the patients are, they're quite incredible. It's very high tech, Big Brother's watching you constantly you know, there are cameras everywhere.'

That sounded good to Glasby. 'So you're not in any danger then? When you were visiting, I mean?'

'No, I don't suppose so.'

'But what sort of people did you see there – the patients, I mean?'

'Well, the patients are there because they're ill, not because they are criminals. I'll never forget, I saw one old lady, they said had been there years, and I swear her face was dark green! It was some weird combination of drugs that they had her on, apparently. But they're all there for a bloody good reason, which nearly always involves major league violence. They told us that you shouldn't stigmatize them. They could just be ordinary mental patients who the system couldn't cope with. Maybe they attacked a nurse, or set fire to the ward, something like that. But some of them, Jesus! In Broadmoor, they've got people like the Yorkshire Ripper, one of the Krays was there, Brian Jarmy, of course. Not the sort of person you'd want to meet.'

At this, Glasby's face fell.

'Alison, what's the matter? What did I say? Do you have to go to Broadmoor for some reason?'

She didn't reply.

'Don't tell me that you're going to see Brian Jarmy!'

She looked around. There was a group of Americans, probably businessman staying at the hotel next door. One of them had his hands up inside his shirt, pretending they were breasts, and they were all laughing loudly. Certainly they weren't paying attention to what she and John were saying. A couple sat across from them, holding hands and admiring the view of Big Ben from the restaurant window.

'John, do you remember the other evening, you said if I wanted to discuss anything with you, privately, that we could do that?'

'Yes, of course I do.'

'Well, there is something. Nobody knows about this. Originally I was working with Bill Davenport. But now –' she hesitated, reluctant to say the words out loud – 'now, I don't know if I can trust him any more. Please may I explain? I know that we don't know each other very well. But I can't talk to anybody at work about it, and I would really value your advice. You see, I think, that is, I'm almost certain –' she hesitated again, then continued – 'almost certain that there's something funny about the Jarmy and Dellar case.'

She started talking. He was a good listener when he put his mind to it. She talked a lot, and ended up saying some things that she hadn't intended to tell him.

'So now you understand why I'd want to see Jarmy, don't you? And say, hypothetically, say that he agreed to do it. That's what I was thinking about. Just hypothetically, of course.'

Redgrave looked at her very hard and very seriously. 'So how does all this fit in with the other story that the *Herald* had in it? The one about two of the murders, you know, one of the boys and Donna Bacon, being all down to Dellar, and the police not commenting? What's behind that?'

Glasby shook her head. 'I don't know, is the honest answer. If you ask me, I think that story is a load of BS and I think that Davenport thinks that too.' Then they talked some more.

Eventually he said, 'Alison, you must get that hand seen to. Come on, I'll take you to St Thomas's now. My car's outside, up the steps.'

There was a little argument over the bill, Redgrave insisting that he should pay.

'Thank you, John, but it would be better if we split it. I'd prefer that, please.' Glasby liked him, but she hated feeling beholden; she wasn't his girlfriend, after all. But he absolutely wouldn't have it. He just handed some notes over to the waitress and refused to discuss it further.

As they walked into the Accident and Emergency department Glasby saw a sign: 'Estimated Waiting Time – 4 hours'. Redgrave walked up to the reception desk and spoke for a moment with the nurse. Glasby saw her laughing at something he had said. Then they both turned to look at her and he waved her over. 'This cubicle. The doctor will be here in a couple of minutes. Shall I wait with you?'

'But I thought it said four hours?'

'Perk of the job. You must have heard all the stories about policemen and nurses. If there's one thing a copper knows, it's the inside of A and E.'

Twenty-five minutes and three stitches later they drew up outside her flat.

'Alison, no bullshitting. When are you seeing Jarmy?' His voice was quiet and confident. She couldn't think of anything to say, except the truth.

'Friday this week. I've got to be there at one. That's what I'm worried about. No one else knows about it, John. Not even Bill Davenport.'

'Friday! Jesus, you don't hang around, do you? Listen, Alison, I don't want you to feel that we're overdoing it, but I think I could get the day off on Friday. I could work a bit longer on Saturday instead. I don't have anything planned for then. If you want, I could drive you down to Broadmoor. It shouldn't take too long. I'd wait outside of course – I don't think that Jarmy will be too keen if I turn up as well. Unless, of course, you'd rather go alone.'

Glasby didn't know what to say but she felt a huge wave of relief wash over her. Some support would be great.

'Are you sure that you don't have more important things to do?' He assured her not.

'Well, thank you, John. It's very kind of you. It would be nice to have some company, I suppose. And it might be very useful to be able to talk about whatever Jarmy says, on the way home. If you don't mind, that is.'

'No, I offered, remember? So I don't mind. It would really be nice to see you again. And I'm sure it will be interesting, of course. I'll call you tomorrow to confirm, but let's say for the moment that I'll pick you up at your flat at half eleven. OK?'

'Yes, that would be great. Thank you again. And thank you for taking me to the hospital. Bye.' She opened the car door.

He leaned across quickly towards the passenger seat, reaching over for her arm. But she was already out of the car and closing the door.

'Goodnight, then,' he said to himself. What a strange girl! You couldn't really call her a hot date, could you? He had tried really hard, and she sounded grateful enough, but she didn't offer so much as a goodnight kiss. Still, Friday would be another chance. Maybe she'd be a bit more relaxed, and then who knew? There was something about her . . . He could imagine her as one of those women who were parachuted into

France during the war to operate wirelesses for the Resistance. She had guts, all right, there was no doubt about that.

Glasby got to bed but not to sleep. Her head was full of everything that had to be done in the next two days. Just the dating agencies stuff would have been enough. Lear hadn't been overwhelmed by what she'd shown him so far. She knew that she still had a lot to do to get it into shape, and she hadn't forgotten his comment that her job might depend on it.

She had plenty of unused holiday for the year – in fact she hadn't used any of her allowance – so that wasn't a problem, although Lear would make a fuss about her taking a day at short notice. She would tell him that someone had invited her somewhere for the weekend. That should appeal to his romantic nature.

Mike Marshall was a worry as well. She'd never intended to fall out with him, but he seemed to have taken it that way. Maybe he'd talk to Davenport tomorrow and spill the beans before she saw Jarmy. God! All this, and now Mike peed off with her as well. Perhaps she could make it up with him tomorrow?

If she got through Thursday unscathed, there was then the little matter of a trip to Broadmoor, to see a mass murderer. Jarmy knew that she was on to something, that was obvious, or he'd never have agreed to see her. The question was, what was it?

*The child was frightened, lying in the dark, listening —
but what was it? Quick, let's get under the sheet.
Trembling, but it was a hot summer night, so sweating
as well. What was that noise? Please God, take me in
your care, keep me safe and hear my prayer. Not again
not again not again not again. If I close my eyes it will
go away. If I promise to be good nothing will happen.
It can't. It can't. He's there! Outside the door.*

Thirteen

Glasby was in work the next morning before eight. Her plan was to tell the Leer about her supposed weekend invitation at about four o'clock, by which time she should have her research and an outline of the articles more or less finished. That way he would have no excuse to knock her back.

The hours passed as she worked steadily, trying to keep her mind on that day's task and off the constant chatter of Serena's social life. Mike Marshall was still acting strangely. He was keeping his distance, anyway.

Her head had been aching when she woke up that morning and it hadn't stopped since. In fact, she felt lousy. Maybe she just ate too much the night before or maybe it was all starting to get to her, but she felt really wrung dry.

To make things worse, her hand was throbbing. Every time she used the keyboard on her PC it pulled at the stitches that the doctor had put in. To start off with it was distracting. After the first half-hour it hurt. Why the hell hadn't she remembered to put some aspirin in her bag?

Mike and Serena seemed to be in conversation more than once when she looked up. The first time she was showing him something in one of her glossy magazines. No doubt her or one of her many pals, at a charity ball or a gallery opening, or something like that. It wasn't like Mike to be all that interested, though. Later, they both looked rather serious. Glasby smiled at him but he just gave her a funny look and wandered off.

Lunch was a quick dash to the sandwich shop for an egg sandwich which she hoped might settle her stomach. She had a diet Coke with it for some caffeine, really needing to find some energy from somewhere. There was a huge queue at Boots but she absolutely had to have some painkillers, so there was no choice but to stand in line, shuffling impatiently from one foot to the other. The aspirin seemed to help the pain in her hand a little, although they did nothing for her head.

As she was finishing the sandwich Davenport appeared at her desk. Her heart sank. Marshall must have said something to him. She stiffened, preparing herself for a confrontation.

'Hello, Alison. You don't look too bright! What happened to your hand?'

She explained. 'Dear oh dear! It looks very painful. And you've had to have stitches as well?'

'Yes, I, um, I went to St Thomas's A and E last night.'

'Terrible place, isn't it? I had to go there myself a few years ago. Very foolishly, I hit my thumb with a hammer when I was trying to put a fence up in the garden. It was incredibly painful, they had to take the nail right off. Did you have to wait for hours?'

'Yes,' Glasby lied, not wanting to say anything about friendly policemen.

'Well, I'm sure you're busy so I won't keep you. I just wanted to make sure that you got this in good time.'

He handed her a rectangle of white card, embossed with gold lettering. Her attendance was requested to celebrate the career at Herald Newspapers of Bill Davenport. Reception and party at the Claverdon Hotel. Friday, — November. Reception at 7 p.m. for 7.30 p.m. Carriages at midnight. Dress: black tie.

'You know how slowly information travels around a news-paper office. So perhaps you'll forgive the hand delivery.'

'Thank you,' she said. 'I wasn't . . . I mean, I'm very pleased to have been invited. It's very kind of you. Thank you very much.' Her face bright red, she stared hard down at her desk, hoping that he wouldn't notice anything.

After he had left, she mulled it over. Obviously she was a late addition to the guest list, and Davenport had made it clear that it was his initiative, which was very nice of him.

Or was it? Was he making a point to her, a small sign of what his patronage could bring? Pointing out what she stood to lose if she crossed him?

Her headache was getting worse and she felt sick and shaky. She had to stop worrying about things and just do what she had to do.

The rest of the day was gruelling, but ultimately successful.

Tom Lear was ungracious about her work but he didn't criticize it much, so presumably she'd done OK.

She had decided to wait until it was finished before she broached her holiday request. Lear hesitated but perhaps catching the look in her eye, he signed the form without comment.

Marshall was definitely avoiding her. Glasby knew it was her fault and she ought to mend fences with him but it was just one thing too many to cope with.

John Redgrave called just before she was about to leave, to confirm the arrangements for the next day: 'Half eleven, on the dot, outside your flat. See you then. You won't be late, will you?' He seemed a bit short with her but perhaps he was just tired. He couldn't be feeling worse than her.

All Glasby could find in the flat for dinner was an elderly fish cake and some baked beans. She sat slumped on the sofa munching it, feeling dazed. A good ten minutes went by before she could bring herself to move.

Then she shook herself awake and reached for her copy of *Children Carried Away*. She was about to follow in Bill Davenport's footsteps, thirty-seven years on. He wouldn't have been that much older than her when he interviewed Brian Jarmy, and if he could do it, so could she. She started to read:

> Broadmoor – a name most of us have heard, but very few know a great deal about this most infamous establishment for the criminally insane. The name itself is misleading, conjuring up an image of a distant windswept setting, a forbidding institution rising above peat bogs and heather.
>
> A gentle rise of land above the town of Crowthorne in Berkshire is in fact the home of Broadmoor, as pleasant a part of the Home Counties landscape as you could wish to see. Pleasant, that is, if it wasn't for the massive redbrick boundary wall which encircles what is now properly know as Broadmoor Special Hospital.
>
> Notice the use of the word 'hospital'. Broadmoor is not a prison and most of those incarcerated in it have not been found guilty of any crime. A minority of those held are indeed convicted criminals, transferred from ordinary prisons having been found to be of unsound mind during

their sentences. Most were declared insane – under the strict requirements of the law in such matters – at the time of their trial, and so were never convicted.

No one would wish to see those suffering from severe mental illness punished in the same way as common criminals, so it is without doubt right that these unfortunates are not made to take their place in the prison system. But this in no way diminishes the terrible misdeeds that some of them have perpetrated.

Broadmoor holds men who have killed their parents, their wives, their lovers and sometimes – perhaps most terrifyingly – perfect strangers. Some do not just kill, but torture sadistically as well. There are women held there – kept in segregation from the male inmates except under the strictest supervision – and many of them too are killers, whose victims may have been their husbands but often, tragically, were their own children.

The authorities are very well aware of the public's need for protection from such dangerous and unpredictable people. A casual visitor to the hospital could not fail to be impressed by the precautions that are taken to guard against possible escapes, the impregnable perimeter wall and the bars visible at every window being only the most obvious measures.

Local residents laugh at the idea that they live in fear of their insane and often homicidal near-neighbours, and Broadmoor's record bears them out; I was informed that there has been no serious breach of security of any kind for many years.

A glance at the architecture reveals the history of the institution. Built by an eminent military architect of the day, Broadmoor received its first inmates in 1863. Then known as 'criminal lunatics', many would have been saved from the gallows only by a finding of insanity. (The same, of course, remained true for the next hundred years, capital punishment having been finally abolished only a few years ago, in 1965).

There are now somewhere under one thousand patients held at the hospital, with around 300 staff to guard and care for them at all times. The most modern methods of psychiatric treatment are available, a far cry from the days when one medical superintendent insisted that each inmate be fed at least fifty pounds of rhubarb each year in the belief that it could help to stabilize their unbalanced minds.

There have been many recent developments in scientists' understanding of the brain. This has allowed for significant advances in the treatment of severe mental disorders both by drugs and other means, such as electro-convulsive therapy. As a result, the use of physical restraints is not as widespread as it once was.

But while the medical care has progressed, the underlying purpose of Broadmoor remains: to ensure that anyone whom insanity has driven to such violent acts will be held within its solid rectangular blocks until such time as the doctors can be sure that he no longer represents a danger to the public.

Judged on this basis, as he will be, we can safely assume that Brian Jarmy will be a resident of Broadmoor for many years to come.

Glasby was happy that she didn't have to set off the next morning until half past eleven. She treated herself to a night in bed with her book and no alarm clock. She could read for a while, go to sleep late, and still have plenty of time to get up at ten, or even half past. On second thoughts, she set the alarm in case she slept really late.

The inevitable happened. She turned the light out at about three, couldn't sleep, gave up trying and read until gone four. The central heating came on at six thirty as usual so when she woke up some time later she had a dry throat and a thick head. She tried to go back to sleep, managed to doze but kept being woken by dreams, a madman chasing her through the streets, into her house, up the stairs, a knife in his hand, catching up with her, plunging it into her, into her stomach.

She woke with a jump, folded in two as a cramp hit her in the stomach. It was nine thirty, but not until a good hour later that she could manage any breakfast.

Even though Glasby was dead on time, Redgrave was already there, looking impatient as a wave of cars and buses folded itself around his car. It was a sports model, low and angular with a long bonnet, silver, which she didn't much like. He pushed opened the door for her from the driver's seat.

'Hi! I'm on time, aren't I?' she greeted him.

'Yes. I was about to call you. But you're right, you're spot on,' he added quickly. 'Very good, for a girl!'

He did a U-turn across two lanes of traffic, attracting some angry hooting to which he paid no attention, and they headed for Vauxhall Bridge. 'All set, are you?' he asked her.

'I think so, yes. I've read up a bit about Broadmoor, and I know what there is to know about Jarmy, of course. I don't know what else I can do.'

'The most important thing, when you're going in against a hard case, is to think yourself on to his wave length. What games is he going to play and how you're going to beat him. Whatever you do, don't play by his rules.'

'What do you mean?' she asked, wishing that he wouldn't get so close to the cars in front of them. He was driving fast as well, jumping from lane to lane. 'We should have plenty of time, by the way.'

He ignored this. 'Well, we've both read the same stuff, haven't we? What did you get out of it?'

'I don't know, John. Why don't you tell me what you mean?'

'What I mean is, when you're going in for an interrogation, you have to read your briefing, talk to anyone who's already gone in against the subject – which in your case is only Davenport – and work out how the subject is going to try to play it. Is he going to say nothing, refuse to talk at all? Is he going to feed you a load of bullshit? Or try and lead you off your main goal by giving you something else? That sort of thing.

'Now in this case, unless he's mellowed, which I doubt, he's going to look to wind you up. That's what he did to Davenport, and he's sure to do the same with you. He thinks he's smarter than the rest of us and he can't let a minute go by without proving it. I reread the Jarmy interview again last night, and he's got two basic techniques. What's the first one?'

John obviously knew what he was talking about, but it would be nice if it felt a bit less like a lecture. Still, she might as well have a go. 'He tried to unsettle Davenport, stare him out, I imagine. He just didn't say anything and made Bill talk instead.'

'Right! It *is* pretty obvious. I never said he was subtle, did I? But it's effective as well. So if you get the silent treatment, what do you do?'

'Wait for him, I suppose.'

'Right again! You're on good form this morning, all right! Just wait him out, stay calm, let it happen. When you're good and ready, talk. If he doesn't answer, just say, "You don't want to say anything then, Mr Jarmy." Not "Brian", by the way. He must be, what, in his mid-sixties?'

'Yes.'

'Better to keep it formal – Mr Jarmy and Miss Glasby. And before you tell me, I know people like to say Ms these days. But he's been in a nuthouse for the last thirty something years, so he won't be up with the latest trends. But anyway. The second thing he'll do is, he'll be obnoxious. He'll do it to upset you, to throw you off your stride. But most of all, he'll do it because he's got to keep proving how clever he is. Having a laugh at you. He'll look for your weak points, so we ought to talk about what they are – *you plonker!*'

This last was aimed at a taxi that had pulled out directly in front of Redgrave, causing him to brake hard. Then without any warning it came to a dead halt to pick up a fare. Glasby was thrown forward against the safety belt. For a second, she thought they were going to crash, her heels braced against the floor of the car.

At least it had avoided a conversation about her weak points. She didn't think she wanted John's views on the subject.

'Let me just think things over for a while, please, John. What you've said is really useful, I'm sure you're right. But I don't want to get too nervous about it. And by the way, you wouldn't mind slowing down just a little, would you?'

He glanced at her. 'Are you a nervous passenger? Don't worry, I know what I'm doing. The Alfa's got ABS as well. It's a braking system, totally failsafe. I guess you're not too used to being driven around, are you?'

'I usually take the Tube, during the week. Or I drive myself. Remember?' It came out a bit more pointed than she had meant.

'Of course I remember. It was our first proper conversation, so I'm not going to forget in a hurry, am I? And I had to start off by apologizing, too!'

They both laughed, the atmosphere easing. They were making much better progress now, through West London and out towards the M4.

'How many cases do you deal with at any one time, John?'

'Oh, it varies, of course. And not all of them are what you'd call active. Upwards of thirty, I suppose.'

'Thirty! How on earth can you keep track of it all? How do you remember all the details, all the different clues?'

He laughed. 'To be fair, we don't spend every day like Sherlock Holmes, you know. A lot of detective work is just basic pack drill, working by the book. Get the team out, talk to the neighbours, did anyone hear anything, known associates, all that sort of thing. What you're doing at the moment, that's top-end stuff.'

'What do you mean?'

'You know, looking through the files, seeing things other people have missed, following up, maybe just on a hunch, working your way down the trail. But' – he emphasized the 'but' – 'there's only one thing that matters in the end: getting a result. If you don't get the result, you might just as well have been doing jigsaw puzzles.'

Food for thought for Glasby, food for thought.

It was one of those English days when the weather might do almost anything. It was cold, but not too cold, windy but sometimes strangely still. Heavy clouds would lift from time to time to reveal brilliant shards of sunlight and then roll back so that the whole sky was a glowing, steely grey. It must have rained heavily in the night because the roads were wet enough to be a mirror, the sun threatening to blind them at times, reflecting off the dense spray at others.

They had expected to see plenty of signs for the special hospital, which was a fair assumption but wrong. Crowthorne was an uninspiring small commuter town, its most notable feature a series of over-engineered traffic-calming schemes. Sleeping policemen, raised crossings and artificial chicanes abounded. It was the sort of place where you would expect that a raised voice would stand out, let alone a large Victorian loony bin. But somehow Broadmoor was nowhere in sight.

First they were fooled by the barbed-wire-topped chain fence of an industrial estate and then, on the other side of town, the gateway of a military school, complete with yellow and black striped antiterrorist shield. But even after they had bumped their way twice up and down the length of the main street, there was no indication at all.

They had no option but to stop and ask the way. Even mentioning the name made Glasby feel as if she was doing something illicit. The old man walking his dog didn't seem to find anything strange about it, though: 'Left at the next mini roundabout, down Lower Broadmoor Road. You can't miss it.'

Which was certainly true. Once they were past the evocatively named Broadmoor Housing Estate (home to workers at the hospital, Glasby assumed – was it because of the stigma of being associated with Broadmoor that even the staff housing was hidden away from the rest of the town?) they drove up a hill and were suddenly overlooked by a massive red brick wall, surrounded by the full panoply of high security. Cameras pointed at every section of the wall and beyond it; banks of floodlights towered above them. It made Marsham House, where Dellar had been incarcerated, look like a holiday camp. Broadmoor might not officially count as a prison but you could not mistake it for anything other than what it was: a place of confinement.

The sign said 'This is a non-smoking hospital', which as John said, seemed a bit tough, if you were banged up for forty years waiting for a fag. Next to it was a sign for the visitors' car park, down in a hollow a little away from the wall. As they cruised towards it a burly man stood staring at them, presumably not a passing maniac but a harmless hospital worker. On the other side was a fenced-in patch of grass; in the middle, a small stone angel. A grave, perhaps?

Getting out of the car, Glasby wished she was somewhere else. She shivered; was there a real chill in the atmosphere, or was it just her imagination? 'Frost pocket,' said John, so he must have felt it too. 'Good luck. I'll be here.' He reached for a newspaper from the back seat.

She went up a long concrete flight of steps, waiting first for a stocky black man to come down. He smiled his thanks to her and she smiled in return. It seemed so mundane, the ordinary courtesies of life going on while just a few metres away creatures prowled, perpetrators of the most terrible crimes.

One of whom she would soon be passing the time of day with. If she could have thought of a reason to turn around and go back, she would. But it was out of the question, with

John waiting to hear how it had all gone. She looked behind
her, down to the car park. He seemed to have his head buried
in the newspaper. Two joggers emerged from a track into the
woods; were they more hospital staff, or did some people just
choose to do laps around the perimeter wall?

The first building she came to was a little canteen provided
for the convenience of visitors. Two old ladies were sitting
inside, one of them knitting. It might have been set up as a
tableau to reassure the nervous first-time visitor; a replica
from the high street in any small town in the country.

The automatic doors swished open as she walked into the
reception area. On either side of her, walled in by bulletproof
glass, were two desks. Behind each were uniformed staff. To
her right, one was labelled 'Official Visitors', the other,
strangely, 'Social Visitors'. She had official permission, so
she assumed that this made her an official visitor. She was
directed to the other desk by a brusque man in blue uniform.

She introduced herself again, this time at the social visitors' counter. 'I'm here to see Brian Jarmy. An inmate.'

'Patient.' The woman behind the desk was in her fifties,
grey bun and motherly faced, but not particularly welcoming
in her manner. 'They're patients here, not inmates. If you'd
like to give me your letter of authorization, and please read
this notice.'

First was a full page of prohibited items. Explosives and
drugs seemed reasonable enough; telephones and cameras
weren't a surprise either – no repeat of the trick she had played
at Marsham House, then. Why DVDs and CDs were banned,
she had no idea; maybe, like pens, pencils and keys, they were
considered potential weapons? She emptied her pockets of all
offensive items and put them into her bag.

'Your passport, please. And please read and sign this form.'
She was to consent to inspection by a passive drugs detec-
tion dog, whatever that was, and a full body search if required.
There were two more pages of regulations, warnings and
waivers. She started to read but, noticing the pen which was
pushed towards her in the metal tray, signed her name anyway.

'Leave your bag on the counter, there. It will be returned
to you with your passport. Walk through the detector and wait
to be called forward.'

There was a loud electronic bleep as she went through the

metal detector. A male voice came through a tannoy in the ceiling above her. 'Do you have a metal belt buckle or watch?' She took off her watch and left it in her bag. This time she passed the test.

'Walk forward to the left-hand door, and wait until it starts to move,' the voice instructed her. Side by side in front of Glasby were two turnstile-like, ceiling-height revolving doors, made from heavy glass. The door started to rotate as she stepped into it, forcing her to shuffle forward. Soon she was completely enclosed, one leaf of the door behind and another in front of her. She felt trapped and momentarily panicky, but a few moments later it released her on the far side of the reception area. She was in Broadmoor.

A blue-uniformed man walked up with clipboard and walkie-talkie. 'Miss Glasby? We have certain standard pre-admission procedures for social visitors. Through this door here, please.' He was very thin and his skin was pale as if he didn't get outside very often.

The room was completely empty except for one table in the middle of the floor. 'Wait here, please.' The man disappeared through a side door without any explanation. He re-emerged side by side with a dog which was all big floppy ears and mournful expression. Glasby smiled; her guard (if that's what he was) did not. The dog walked around her, rubbing against her legs and sniffing noisily.

Apparently she had passed this test as well. The dog was taken away again. This time there was a longer delay. Glasby leant against the wall. The room was windowless, bare except for two cameras mounted above her which were protected by wire cages. Her nerves weren't getting any better. The only noise she could hear was a loud humming; air conditioning, perhaps?

The door opened; not the one the guard had left through, as she had expected, but the one behind her. Her heart jumped.

'Follow me please.' It was a different man, older and more human in his manner, a large brown birthmark covering half his forehead. 'Is this your first time here? I expect it's a bit daunting, is it?' She was happy to admit that it was. 'I'm going to take you to the secure patient/public holding room, but first of all we have to clear security. It's the same sort of procedure that you went through before, nothing to worry about.'

She glanced up as something caught her eye and realized it was another camera. They reached what looked like two metal lift doors. Her companion punched in a numerical code and they opened, to reveal an identical pair of doors, set back a couple of metres from the first. She followed him in, trying not to feel claustrophobic as the doors closed behind them.

'2715, requesting clearance,' her companion spoke into his walkie-talkie. The inevitable camera looked down on them. Nothing happened. Glasby became aware of the sound of her own heart. Surely it wasn't usually that loud?

The doors in front of her opened to another cream painted corridor. Mr 2715 pressed some buttons next to one of the doors to her right. 'Please step inside. You shouldn't have to wait too long.' The door closed behind her, the lock clicking back into place. She heard his footsteps moving away from her down the corridor. Somewhere in the distance someone was screaming.

*The child was frightened, lying in the dark, listening —
but what was it? Quick, let's get under the sheet.
Trembling, but it was a hot summer night, so sweating
as well. What was that noise? Please God, take me in
your care, keep me safe and hear my prayer. Not again
not again not again not again. If I close my eyes it will
go away. If I promise to be good nothing will happen.
It can't. It can't. He's there! Outside the door.*

Fourteen

An age went by. Left with nothing to do except worry, Glasby paced around the dreary little room, then sat but couldn't sit still, wriggling her bottom on the moulded plastic chair, shuffling it from side to side, rocking back and forth on its metal legs. She caught herself chewing at a fingernail, something she hadn't done in years, and snatched her hand angrily away from her mouth.

All she had to do was to make a confident start, then it would flow. Stand up, shake hands, then – no, no contact allowed, so we can't shake hands. Stay sitting down? No, that way he might be standing over her. So stand up, smile, and sit down at the same time as he does. 'Good afternoon, Mr Jarmy.' Don't thank him. But be polite. 'Good afternoon, Mr Jarmy, I'm very pleased you were able to see me.'

She realized that she was talking out loud and stopped, feeling stupid, and sat down again. And then the door opened. There was no phalanx of burly guards, no grim-faced doctors. Instead, she was faced by a mild-faced little man with hair so blond and fine you could almost see through it, and pink eyelids like a rabbit. He had on a tweed sports jacket, a bit like Davenport's but neater, and grey flannels, a collar and tie. He was young looking for his age, and about as far as you could imagine from what she'd expected Brian Jarmy to be like.

Startled out of her plan, she jumped to her feet, almost tipping the chair over behind her. Holding out her hand, 'Good afternoon. I'm . . . I'm very pleased that you were able to see me.'

'Oh! Not at all. It's my pleasure, of course, Ms Glasby. Actually, it's normal procedure, you see, once admissions and clearances have approved you, responsibility passes to me for the remainder of your time at the hospital. As the officer responsible for patient/public liaison, you see.'

Bright red with embarrassment, Glasby could feel the beads of sweat on her forehead. 'Of course, Mr Allen. But I'm glad to be able to meet you, to thank you in person for your assistance. I mean, without your assistance, I wouldn't have been able to be here, that's what I meant.' Shut up, idiot!

'That's very kind of you, Ms Glasby,' the little man replied, seriously. 'But I have just followed normal procedures. Perhaps,' he conceded, 'a little expedited at your request. But quite in order.'

There was a pause. Glasby couldn't think of anything at all to say. Her mind was a complete blank. The weather? Don't be ridiculous. Ask him about himself.

'How long—' she started, at the same time as he said, 'Are you—' They both stopped.

'I'm sorry. I was just asking you, are you ready to see Mr Jarmy now? You see, his patient supervisor has told me that everything is in order, which means that they are ready for you. Unless you had any questions of me?'

Glasby assured him that she was quite ready and he led her further down the corridor and round a corner. The cream wall continued, as devoid of decoration as before. Allen knocked on a heavy wooden door and waited as footsteps approached from the other side. Glasby's stomach suddenly felt very empty. The door opened.

A burly young man with unkempt black hair and a goatee beard stood inside, wearing a dark blue uniform, the top a sort of cross between a medical tunic and a prison officer's jacket. Behind him was a room empty of furniture except for a single table, large and square, and three chairs, made from the same moulded plastic as in the waiting room where Glasby had come from. On the far side of the table, unblinking and staring straight at her, was an elderly man, his cheeks sunken, straggly long hair yellowed with age.

'My name is Jenkins,' said the owner of the goatee. 'I am Mr Jarmy's patient supervisor. I will supervise your meeting with Mr Jarmy at all times. Please follow my instructions carefully.' He had the trace of an accent, West Country or something like it.

'OK,' said Glasby, her voice choked, heart racing so fast she could feel its beat inside her head. Her legs felt weak. She badly needed to sit down.

'Mr Allen will collect you at the end of the meeting. Until then you are my responsibility.' Behind her Roy Allen left the room and closed the door. A click signalled the repositioning of the electronic locking devices.

'Please sit down, on this chair here–' motioning her to the chair on the near side of the table, opposite the old man. 'At no time must there be any physical interaction between yourself and Mr Jarmy.' She walked towards the table, a sudden pang of pain from the cut on her right hand making her notice how tightly her fists were clenched. Jarmy, remaining seated, continued to look straight into her eyes.

Now that she was closer she saw how emaciated he was, stretched and angular over a long frame. His head and neck were bony, thin shoulders inside a baggy khaki cotton smock. There were wisps of beard around his jaw.

'Please do not place your hands or arms on the table. Sit down, please.' She sat, smiled at the unsmiling man across the table from her, turned to Jenkins and watched him sit at right angles to them both. Not knowing what to say, she said nothing, Jenkins' presence relieving her from having to take the initiative. Jarmy was also silent, and although she kept her eyes away from him she could feel his drilling into her.

The table was about two metres across, wide enough that there was no possibility of casual physical contact. It was topped in grey Formica and was bare except for a large recording device. Jenkins reached across and pressed a switch. A red light came on and two cassette tapes started to turn.

'Friday, – November, 200–. Broadmoor Special Hospital, public access visit. The time is –' he consulted a watch decorated with an incongruous Donald Duck figure – '2.47 p.m. Present are Patient Supervisor Jenkins, patient Brian Jarmy, Ms Alison Glasby.'

Any moment now and she would have to speak. Her throat felt tight, as if someone was squeezing their hands around it. As she shifted uneasily on the plastic chair she realized that it was bolted to the ground. Glancing down, she saw that the table too had been fixed to the floor. A steel frame held the tape machine to the table top.

'This meeting has been approved as lasting until four p.m. at

the latest,' said Jenkins. 'Of course, either of you may end it at
any time. If you want to do that, just tell me. Then you –'
gesturing with his head at Jarmy – 'will remain seated, while
Ms Glasby will leave the room. Please start.'

There was a silence, uncomfortable for Glasby, though
Jarmy seemed untroubled. She cleared her throat, swallowed.
He continued to stare straight at her.

'Thank you . . .' she began, and stopped. 'I'm pleased that
we were able to see each other, especially at such short notice.'
He said nothing.

Mindful of John's advice, neither did she. Beat him at his
own game, that's what John had told her. And he was right;
eventually Jarmy spoke. His voice was thin like him, almost
a wheeze, as if it had emerged from a little-used dusty place.

'Where's the great Mr Davenport? Why has he sent his girl,
instead of coming round himself?'

Determined not to be riled, she cleared her throat before
speaking, trying to settle herself down. 'Bill Davenport
couldn't be here, so he asked me to come instead, to talk
about some issues with you.'

But instead of asking what these 'issues' were, as she had
hoped, Jarmy lapsed back into silence, looking thoughtful
now, stroking an eyebrow with his right index finger. She
noticed for the first time how old he looked, much older than
his sixty-six years. His nails were long, curling over the end
of his fingers. There were deep wrinkle lines on his forehead,
reminding her of a photograph of Samuel Beckett which she
used to have on her wall when she was a student.

'Mr Davenport couldn't be here.' He broke the silence after
a full minute. 'Mr Davenport couldn't be here, but you particularly asked for this time. He doesn't know you're here, does
he?'

She felt the blood rush to her face. Two angry red circles
spread across her cheeks. Damn! How could he have guessed
that? 'Bill was intending to come, of course. But something
came up, at the last moment. He's really busy. He's retiring
soon, very soon, so that's why he's so busy. He was really
disappointed not to be able to come, but he wanted me to
come instead, so that I can tell him about it when I'm back
in London.'

She stopped herself, painfully aware of how weak it sounded

and made herself look up at Jarmy. He had resumed his stare but now there was a little half smile on his face.

'I didn't like Mr Davenport much anyway. I bet he gets on your nerves, doesn't he, with all that pious stuff he comes out with. We made his fortune for him, Leonie and me, and he never even said so much as a thank you, not to me, anyway. So I don't blame you. Stick it to him when you can.'

Don't rise to it. Don't rise to it! She took a deep breath, determined to start again and stop him from taking control.

'I'm sure you want to know what I came here to ask you about.'

He ignored this. 'You'll have read all about me. You've talked about me with your Mr Davenport, prepared yourself thoroughly like a good girl. So you know all there is to know, don't you? Mr Davenport, the great authority, who knows everything about the evil Mr Jarmy. But if you ask Mr Jarmy about Mr Davenport, he knows the one and only thing worth knowing about him. He's a jack-arse!'

At the last word, he screwed up his face and jerked his head forward at her. It was his first sign of any emotion. But immediately he took on his former expression, half watchful, half sneering. He seemed both at ease and poised, like an animal at the hunt, ready to strike.

She didn't know what to say, not wanting to antagonize him by disagreeing. It didn't seem to matter anyway; Jarmy continued: 'Davenport was an idiot, but a useful idiot. We all used him, even little Leonie. And she was never the brightest penny in the piggy bank – so what does that make him?' A pause. 'And now you're using him too. Are you a useful idiot, Miss Glasby? Or are you just the normal kind?'

Glasby felt the blood come back to her face. Don't let him get to you!

She said nothing, so he changed tack. 'How old are you?'

'What's that got to do with it? I'm twenty-five.'

'Very young, to be cheating on your boss. What do you think of him?'

'I think he's a very fine journalist. And a very decent man, of course. He's had a wonderful career, everyone really respects him. And I think that Leonie Dellar liked him too.'

'Are you doing it with him? Keeping him happy? You get the story, and he gets a bit of the other, is that the deal?'

Glasby went bright red again. Jenkins came to her rescue. 'Mr Jarmy, I explained the rules to you. If necessary, I'll terminate this meeting now. If I do, you'll go straight on review.'

'You don't seem the type, no,' Jarmy retreated. 'So you're a clever young girl, very ambitious, and you've seen how exploiting the sordid appetites of the public helped the oh-so-respected Mr Davenport. And now that he's going to be out of the picture, because he's *had* his career, as you said, you want to make sure that it's your turn next. So here you are, visiting the monster yourself. Do you know what they call me?'

'No,' said Glasby, relieved that he had stopped talking about her.

'I am a psychopath.' A chill went through her: sitting here, opposite him, in this freaky place, only a metre or two away from him.

'I have a behavioural disorder resulting in an inability to form personal relationships and an indifference to my obligations to society, often manifested by antisocial behaviour such as acts of violence, sexual perversion, etcetera. Isn't that right, Mr Jenkins?'

'That's your diagnosis.'

'And what's the cure, Mr Jenkins?'

'That's for the doctor to discuss. You know that as well as I do.'

'Mr Jenkins is too modest –' turning back to Glasby – '*he* knows perfectly well. There *is* no cure. Are you married? No ring. Don't you even have a boyfriend?'

'I don't think that's your business. Do you want to discuss my letter, what I wrote in it, or not?'

'Psychopaths are often characterized by above average intelligence. They can be organized, determined and resourceful. They are often successful in a working environment. The lack of social distractions, not having the conventional concerns and moral qualms, it's a great advantage, I expect you'd agree, in all sort of environments, like a competitive newspaper office, for example.' There was a smile on his face now, smiling as he looked directly at her again. 'Do you have a close relationship with your parents, Miss Glasby? Any brothers or sisters?'

'No,' she said, breathing hard. 'No brothers or sisters. Why?'

'Not many friends either? Not much of a social life?'

She tried but failed to control her voice, echoing in the almost empty room, 'I didn't come here so that you could play games with me. If that's all you want, you can find someone else to mess around with. I wrote to you, I said there was something, something important to talk to you about. If you don't want to, I'm wasting my time!'

His expression didn't change for a moment. 'Relax. Relax. I don't see very many people, you know. It's good for me to get to know you a little. I like to know what I'm dealing with. Now, what did you want to talk about?'

Glasby controlled herself. 'Mr Jarmy, when I wrote to the liaison office, I asked them to pass on to you what was in my letter. Did you see it?'

'Mr Jenkins told me. Very efficient is Mr Jenkins. It's a privilege to be supervised by him.' Jenkins ignored this. '"All I want is to discuss Leonie Dellar's confession. I have no need to discuss anything else." Isn't that it?'

'Yes. And that's why you agreed to see me.'

The smile had gone from Jarmy's face now. 'And why would that make me want to see you?'

'The same reason as you wanted to see Bill Davenport. Back in 1970. Because you want to find out what I know.'

'And what *do* you know, Miss Glasby?'

'You agreed to see Bill because you wanted to be sure what exactly Leonie Dellar had confessed to. You didn't know that she was going to confess, and when you heard that she had, there was something about it, something specifically about what she said, that you wanted to be sure about.' She paused, looked up, but Jarmy's face gave no clues away at all. He simply sat, waiting for her to continue.

'Is there something about Donna Bacon, Mr Jarmy? Some connection between her and Leonie and you?'

Now he was smiling, not the mocking smile of before, but something more real, almost as if he approved of her. 'Donna Bacon? What about her?'

'I don't know. There's some connection between her and Leonie, or you. I'm not sure what it is, although I'm getting closer. There's something special about her death, and that's what you wanted to hear about from Davenport. You needed to know exactly what Leonie had said to him.'

The smile had gone again. 'Well, I hope you enjoy your game. It must give you something to fill your time with, mustn't it? All those evenings at home, when the phone doesn't ring?'

Glasby flared up. 'You don't have to insult me! You asked me what I knew, and I've told you. And I'm right, I can tell that I am! You know I am! You think you're so much cleverer than me, don't you? Well you're stuck in here, and—'

Jenkins interrupted, getting out of his seat. 'I think it's time this meeting came to an end. Miss Glasby, I'm going to page Mr Allen now. Remain in your seat, and do not get up until I tell you to.'

'You're going to need to grow a thicker skin, Miss Glasby,' Jarmy sneered. 'A young girl like you, you're going to have to swallow a lot to get all those things that you want so much. What is it, money, power? Or do you just want everyone to understand how clever you are?'

Glasby stared miserably down at her knees but there was no stopping Jarmy.

'That's it, isn't it? No one appreciates you for what you are, do they? That's what you need. Well, if you want to get on, you need to learn a bit more about how to handle people. You could do a lot of things, such a lot of things, if you can just manage that.'

Careers advice, from a child murderer! Furious, she tried to control her breathing and calm herself down.

'You know a little more than you want to let on, don't you, trying to be a bit crafty. Well, good for you! You've a look of Leonie about you, you know. She wasn't a woman of the world, no sophistication, not very advanced in her thinking. But . . .'

There was a knock on the heavy wooden door.

Jarmy leaned forwards over the table, ignoring the restraining arm on his shoulder from Jenkins, hissing at her, 'Keep it inside you, girl. Don't give it away.'

'Please go to the door now, Ms Glasby, and wait for it to open.' As she got up, Jenkins positioned himself between the table and the door, leaving Jarmy seated on the far side. She walked away, the bitter taste of failure in her mouth. He had given her nothing! She bit her bottom lip, hard. Whatever happened, she mustn't cry. Roy Allen was standing in the doorway, waiting for her.

'Miss Glasby –' she turned, looked back at Jarmy, waited

for a last insult – 'little Leonie, she was never the same after
her first ice cream.'

Allen took her by the arm, ushered her out of the room,
the door closing behind her as the locks slipped into place.
Ice cream! What the hell did he mean? She hardly noticed
Allen as he led her back down the gloomy corridors to the
holding room.

By the time she was back in John Redgrave's car she was
starting to wonder whether Jarmy had just decided to have a
final joke at her expense. He had treated her like a kid, wound
her up and watched her run around in circles like a kitten
chasing its own tail. She'd risked her job – for that!

'How did it go, love?' She didn't even register Redgrave's
endearment. He glanced at her face, set and grim. 'I'm sure
it must have been tough, it would have been for anyone. Why
not start at the beginning? Not many people have done what
you have, you know. Tell me about it. Was Broadmoor what
we'd expected?'

She didn't want to talk but made herself and, having started,
began to feel better for it.

'Well, you were right about the security. It was nearly three
by the time they let me in to see him. It took ages. They
checked me for drugs, took my passport, I had to fill in forms
– oh, and I had to sign an undertaking of confidentiality. I'm
not supposed to tell anyone that I've even been there.'

'I don't think you should worry about that too much. You
obviously can't publish anything about it, but you already
knew that, didn't you?'

'Yes . . . not that there's anything much to write about,
anyway. He wouldn't tell me anything.'

'Just having been there, and seeing him, that's quite something, isn't it, quite a coup in itself? If you were allowed to
write it, I mean.'

'But I didn't go there just to get the bloody T-shirt! Anyway,
I'm not allowed to write about it, I told you, so what's the
point? I mean, I know I'm on the right track, but I needed
something from him. Some sort of clue, and all he wanted to
do was play these obnoxious little games with me. He's so
full of himself – I could kill him!'

'You might have a bit of competition there. Why not try to
calm down a bit, take a deep breath and tell me about it.'

'All right. But don't patronize me! I'm not a kid.'

He looked across at her, then back at the road. There was a moment's silence as he swung the Alfa round a corner and on the slip road to the dual carriageway. Then he spoke carefully, patient and measured as if he was addressing a fractious child. 'Alison, you've had a very tough day. You're a young woman, you're not very experienced, and just having done what you've done is a great achievement. You know that I think you're right, you are on to something. But if you want to take it further, you've got to calm down and think things through properly. I told you that Jarmy would try to wind you up and it looks like he succeeded. That's to be expected. Even detectives, men with a lot of years' experience at dealing with villains, everyone lets it get to them sometimes. But it's over now, and now's the time to take stock. Debrief, let's see what you've got, and then we can plan the next move.'

Glasby felt put down but knew that he was right. She swallowed hard and tried to catch her breath. 'I'm sorry, John. I really appreciate your help.'

'Not a problem. Let's hear what you've got.'

'OK. The first thing was, he said that I'd gone to see him behind Davenport's back.'

'Phew. That was pretty smart of him, wasn't it? How did he reckon that?'

'Obvious, really, I suppose. Because I'd asked for today particularly, and I said in my letter to the hospital that Davenport couldn't make it. He said it didn't add up – and he's right, of course. He said he didn't like Davenport, called him an idiot.' She stopped, remembering.

'He did say one thing though, listen. He called him a jack-arse, whatever that means, and an idiot, but then he said he was a *useful* idiot. He said, "We all used him, even Leonie." What did he mean by that?'

'Well, we already know that Jarmy manipulated him, don't we? I told you, it was really obvious, as soon as you thought about it.'

'Yes,' she said, impatiently, 'but I didn't mean that. What I meant is, he said, "We *all* used him." He didn't say "I", or even "both of us". He said "all, even Leonie". In other words, *he* used him, which we both knew, *she* used him, and other people as well.'

'How did Dellar use him? She didn't get anything out of it, did she? She died in prison, for God's sake.'

'No, but she told him things when she wanted to, and then he wrote about them in the paper. She confessed to him, she told him about Kevin Yallop's body. She wasn't trying to get anything out of it like that, anyway. She never even applied for parole.'

'What, then? What's your point?'

'I don't know.' She felt deflated again. Something was there, hidden just under the surface, but as soon as it started to appear it was gone again. 'I just don't know.' To her horror, she felt tears welling up. She screwed up her face fiercely, hoping that he wouldn't notice.

'Hey, hey, don't worry. You poor thing. Don't get upset.' He took his left hand from the wheel and squeezed her shoulder. She was furious with herself – and with him. The last thing she wanted was sympathy. Why the hell couldn't he see that?

'I'm not upset. Just . . . just frustrated, that's all. Let me carry on. We can come back to the first point later.'

'OK, but you shouldn't be so hard on yourself. Girls are allowed to have a cry sometimes, you know.'

'I'm not a bloody girl! I'm a woman, and a professional, like you.'

'OK, OK! Sorry I spoke! Jesus, there's no need to take it out on me!' He put his hand firmly back on the wheel. 'Go on, then. Let's hear it.'

'When I talked to him about Donna Bacon, I could tell that I was on the right track. There's definitely something that he knows.'

'Why? What did he say about her?'

'He didn't really *say* anything. I asked him if there was anything special about Donna and Leonie, some connection. I didn't mention the photo, like we said. And he said, "What about Donna?" It was the way he looked, he was smiling, not sneering like he was the rest of the time, but smiling as if we both knew something, like we were sharing a secret together.'

'But he didn't say anything at all?'

'No. He just started to get nasty, more and more, he said horrible things about me, to try to upset me.'

'As I told you he would. What sort of things?'

'Well . . . It doesn't matter. Personal things. Just to be abusive.' She felt her eyes getting hot with tears again but swallowed hard and kept talking.

'Right at the end, just as I was leaving, he said this really strange thing. He said, "Leonie was never the same, after her first ice cream." It was the last thing, they were taking me out of the door so I couldn't even ask him what he meant.'

'Ice cream? Are you sure he wasn't just having a laugh?'

'No. I'm positive. It means something. But I've no idea what, no idea at all.'

She sat deep in thought but completely perplexed as they got closer to London, the Friday afternoon traffic beginning to get heavier. The sun had disappeared and the sky was grey again. John's driving had been a bit calmer on the way back, at any rate. She looked at her watch: five fifteen. If she got home in twenty minutes, she'd have another twenty to change, and then she should be in time to get to the Claverdon. Where, of course, she would have to face Davenport. Still, he'd have loads of people around him, so she probably wouldn't have to talk to him much.

'You've got to talk to Davenport,' said John, inopportunely. She started.

'Why? You mean tell him about today?'

'Yes, of course you must. You've got as far as you can. There's a time to run with the ball yourself, and a time when you have to play as part of the team. You won't get on if you always try to be a one-man band. If you're right, you know, that this ice cream thing means something, you need his help. There's no one else, is there?'

'But if I tell him what I've done I'm going to be in real trouble. He could get me fired, John.'

'Maybe he could, but he won't. You've broken the rules, but you've got a result. How can they fire you? They don't want you going talking to anyone else, do they? Surely that's the one thing they've always got to worry about, isn't it – the competition?'

'I suppose so, yes. But—'

'So he may get the hump, but he'll get over it. They'll want you on the case, not working for the opposition. Call him on Monday morning. Don't wait; the longer you leave it, the worse it looks. Do it at the first opportunity, you know, then it will look better.'

'I could tell him tonight, actually. At his reception. I'm supposed to be there in a couple of hours.'

'Tonight? You didn't tell me you were tied up. I thought, you know, we'd go out, have a drink or two and a bite to eat, and try to get to know each other a bit better . . . '

'I can't, not tonight. I'm sorry, John. I didn't think. I mean, you didn't say anything, did you? Or I'd have told you.'

'Oh.' A silence filled the car, which Glasby eventually broke.

'It's a work thing, John. He's my boss. He invited me. I can't just not go. If I wasn't busy already, of course I'd have dinner with you, to say thank you for driving me. It's very kind of you. But you did offer; I didn't ask you.'

'You're right, I did. But I thought that we might spend a bit more *personal* time together. Not just work. Like I said, get to know each other. I mean, I'm very happy to help you when I can, but you have to relax a bit as well, don't you?'

'Of course, yes. You've been really kind. I really value your advice, I really do.'

'Well, if you can't make it tonight, why don't we meet up tomorrow evening instead?'

'OK, thanks. I'll call you during the day. I'd really like to see you again.' She hoped that it sounded genuine. At the very least, Redgrave deserved that.

If she was being honest, right at that moment Glasby wasn't sure if she meant it or not. But then, she had a lot of other things on her mind.

The child was frightened, lying in the dark, listening –
but what was it? Quick, let's get under the sheet.
Trembling, but it was a hot summer night, so sweating
as well. What was that noise? Please God, take me in
your care, keep me safe and hear my prayer. Not again
not again not again not again. If I close my eyes it will
go away. If I promise to be good nothing will happen.
It can't. It can't. He's there! Outside the door. Why won't
someone help me?

Fifteen

She was home, and it was still only five thirty. Alison Glasby stood in her kitchen, thinking. How on earth was she going to tell Davenport? Then she ran into the sitting room, reached for the phone book and dialled a number, making sure to ring 141 first so that the call could not be traced. She spoke for a couple of minutes, put down the receiver and started to organize some clothes to change into for the evening. She realized that other than Davenport, she would probably hardly know anyone at the reception. Except for her new friend Mark Ellington – oh, and the Leer, of course.

Her mobile phone rang.

'Hello? Yes, I'm Alison Glasby. Oh . . . Hold on one moment, please.' She pressed a button on the handset. 'Did you say that you're with the *Chronicle*?'

'Yes, that's right. Paul Lewis, I'm on the news team.'

'How did you get my number?'

'Someone at your office gave it to me.'

'Oh, did they? What can I do for you?'

'I'm covering the Dellar and Jarmy story. I know that you're working with Bill, Davenport. I saw your piece last weekend. It was very good.'

'Thanks.'

'We're on to a lead about one of the victims. A connection with Leonie, something new, very confidential. Not that crap the *Herald* ran about the Starling family, something real. It's a big story and we heard that you've got something interesting on it. You *are* on your own, aren't you? You can talk?'

'Yes . . .' said Glasby, sounding uncertain.

'We should get together, Alison, privately, I mean. And we need to do it quickly, this evening or over the weekend. We could make you a great offer. I know that you've been doing some very good work, and the *Chronicle*'s very interested in you, to take you on, I mean, in the newsroom. We're always looking for really good people, people who can work a story well. If you bring what you've got on Leonie over to us, I can guarantee you a good job, a great salary – now, I mean. You could start next week. You don't have to decide anything this instant, of course, so let's meet up, and we'll talk it over.'

'I'm sorry, you . . . you mean you want me to take the Dellar story, what I know, and write it for the *Chronicle* instead of the *Herald*?' Her voice was shaking.

'All I'm saying is, let's talk. We could have lunch, tomorrow if you're free, and if you like what you hear, and you will, I guarantee you, then you can make a decision, I mean. OK?'

'But I'm working for the *Herald*. I'm working with Bill, as a team. I can't just walk away.'

'Alison, I've been round the block a few times, you know. I used to be on the *Herald* myself once, so I know them there. If you stay, what do you think you're going to get? "Good show, old sport" from Mark Ellington and a byline so your parents can see your name in the paper? I'm not suggesting anything that someone else wouldn't jump at, you do know that?'

'Thank you, Paul. It's very kind of you. But I don't think it's the right way to do things. Thank you anyway.'

'Alison, listen, here's my mobile number.' She wrote it down. 'Call me any time over the weekend. Think it over. Don't talk to anyone about it, obviously, but think it over, that's all I'm saying. I mean, do you really want Bill to get all the credit?'

Hands trembling, she went into the kitchen for a glass of water, gulped at it and went back into the other room. She dialled Davenport's mobile.

He answered on the first ring. 'Oh, hello Alison.' He sounded surprised. 'You're coming along to the Claverdon, I hope?'

'Yes, thank you. But I need to talk to you, urgently. About Dellar, I mean. There's two things that have happened today, and you really need to hear about them.'

A short silence. 'Do you want to tell me what?'

'Bill, I did something, maybe you'll be angry, but there was a reason, I'll explain it when we talk. I went to see Brian Jarmy.'

'Brian Jarmy! How the hell . . . ?'

'Yes, Jarmy. In Broadmoor.'

'I know where he is, for Pete's sake. He's been there for thirty bloody years. But how the hell did you get in to see him? And why didn't you tell me about it before you did it? Jesus Christ, Alison!'

'I'll explain everything, Bill. I never thought he'd see me, but I was always going to tell you if he did. But something else has happened, just now. I got a call from someone called Paul Lewis.'

'Paul Lewis? On the *Chronicle*?'

'Yes, that's right. You know him, then?'

'He used to work for me once, donkey's years ago. What did he want?'

'He knows that we've got something on Dellar. Something about a connection between her and one of the victims, although he didn't say which one, so maybe he doesn't know that. He wants me to go and work for him. Immediately. I told him no, of course. But it sounds like they're on to it. I recorded the call, Bill.'

'You did what? How did you do that?'

'It's easy, on my mobile. You just press a button and it does it. I can play it all to you.'

'Where are you? Are you in the office still?'

'No, I'm at home. I took the day as holiday. So I could see Jarmy. I just got back and Lewis called me.'

'Does he know that you went to see Jarmy?'

'He didn't say anything about it, no, so I don't think that he does.'

'So no one else knows? Apart from the people at Broadmoor, of course.'

She hesitated. 'No Bill, no one else knows. Except . . . except a friend of mine, a CID guy, he drove me there.'

'CID? What have you told them about all this?'

'He's just a friend, Bill. I mean he took me there because he, well, he likes me. It's nothing to do with his work.'

'Hmmm.' He paused, breathed in and exhaled noisily. 'You're at home, you said. It's Stockwell, isn't it? How soon can you be at the Claverdon? I'm there now.'

'Twenty or thirty minutes, I suppose, if I'm lucky. With getting a taxi, I mean. Do you want me to come over straight away?'

'Yes. We need to talk, you're right. The paper's got me a

room here for the night. The room number is twelve eleven. Did you get that, one two one one? Come up as soon as you get here and we can talk before the ruddy speeches start.'

Glasby ripped off her socks, trousers and top, leaving them in a heap in the bedroom. She dragged the only black dress that she owned out of the wardrobe and pulled on a pair of tights and some horrible court shoes from Marks & Spencer which Kate had made her buy for the interview when she went to the *Herald*. After a quick dash into the bathroom to wash her face she added the bare minimum of make-up to her lips and eyes and pulled a brush through her hair. Her black velvet jacket would go OK and she had a bag that would do, but no coat.

It was a good job that it wasn't raining. She managed to stuff phone, wallet, keys and a few other necessities into the bag and dashed downstairs to look for a taxi.

It *was* raining. Hard. Damn! Glasby bolted back upstairs. Unused to heels, she stumbled and nearly fell headlong into the front door, steadying herself on the door post and banging her wrist in the process. Her hand started to hurt again. She found an umbrella in the kitchen.

Her luck was in. As she raced across the street, dodging the rush-hour traffic, she saw the orange glow of a taxi's light no more than a couple of hundred metres off, heading in her direction. She stepped into the street, waving her umbrella and it pulled in for her. Two middle-aged men in raincoats ran across the street. One opened the door behind the driver while the other leant down to talk to him. 'Hey!' Glasby shouted. 'It's my taxi. He was stopping for me. Weren't you?'

'Sorry, mate, but she's right. You'll 'ave to wait. There'll be another one, soon, know what I mean? Where you goin', love?'

'Claverdon, please, the Claverdon hotel.'

'Very nice too,' the cabbie said, reaching back to open the door for her. ''Op in, then.'

Central London can be a nightmare, and on a Friday evening it is often much worse than that. Although the Claverdon was no more than three miles from Glasby's flat, she would have to reckon on thirty minutes, and if she was unlucky it might have been more like an hour. But sometimes, just sometimes,

St Christopher appears to guide the fractious traveller. Traffic lights turn green, buses wait obediently before pulling out, yellow boxes are scrupulously observed so that busy road junctions flow smoothly. In eleven minutes precisely she was deposited outside the Claverdon, under the capacious umbrella of a solicitous doorman.

The Claverdon is one of London's grander hotels. Glasby had passed it before, set back on its own little side street off Piccadilly, but she had never gone inside. In fact she had never been to any five-star hotel before. A few days ago she may well have felt nervous, going through the swing doors so smartly held open for her, across the opulently carpeted lobby and up to the marbled reception desk. But after the day that she'd had? She just wondered briefly if anyone had ever been before to Broadmoor and the Claverdon in one afternoon, and smiled to herself.

'I've come to see someone who's staying at the hotel, please. Mr Davenport, William Davenport. He told me to meet him in his room.' It suddenly occurred to her that this statement was open to misinterpretation. 'We're colleagues, we have some business to discuss. Before his reception here, with the *Herald* newspaper.'

Whatever the silver-haired man behind the reception desk thought of this, his face betrayed nothing except a suave concern to be of service. 'Of course, madam. Mr Davenport, yes. Allow me to call him for you. Who may I announce you as, please?'

'My name is Miss Glasby. Alison, Alison Glasby.' She was starting to feel a little awkward in such splendidly unfamiliar surroundings.

'Miss Glasby is here for you, sir. Yes of course, sir. It's my pleasure, thank you. Miss Glasby, the lift is just to your right. Mr Davenport is in room twelve eleven, if you ask for the twelfth floor, it will be to your left as you step out from the lift. I hope you enjoy your evening with us, madam.'

As she went up in the mirrored lift, surrounded by polished brass and accompanied by a uniformed operator, Glasby wondered whether for some people life was always like this.

Bill Davenport was feeling old. Mark Ellington could be faulted for many things, but meanness was not one of them.

Putting him up at the hotel was a very decent gesture. It had been presented to him as a surprise, with the room already booked, so there was really no chance to turn it down. In truth he would have preferred his own bed for the night.

But here he was, a small figure in the high-ceilinged and even more highly decorated room, French polish on every surface and none of his usual heaps of books and papers to obscure them. They'd consulted him on every detail of the arrangements for tonight and then ignored everything he had said. In the end, he had tried digging his heels in on one thing only: 'I am not dressing up like a bloody wine waiter.' They had agreed, of course, but after all it *is* the Claverdon, and . . .

So now Davenport was squeezed into a dinner jacket which he had last used several years before. The tie had been a long struggle: fight to the death between man and bat, he thought, watching himself in a mirror, which was hardly more shiny than the hugely ornate wardrobe it was set into. The bat had won and now had a strangle hold around his neck, held in place by a strange metal contraption.

He had just called for a scotch and ginger on room service when Glasby's call had come. Listening with incredulity, then horror, he had done his best to stay calm. He thought that he had succeeded, more or less, in running her out of steam. What the blazes was she doing, slipping off to see Jarmy behind his back (although he had to admit, he might have done the same in her place)? But as to how she had got Jarmy to speak to her, never mind what he had told her when she did, he would just have to wait to find out.

At least he'd had a chance to collect his thoughts and decide how to keep this under control. Get it *back* under control, rather. And this time keep it there. From now on, young Alison was going to stay firmly in his sight.

Someone had talked to Paul Lewis, no doubt about that. Lewis would certainly know more than he was letting on, but if he was so keen to get hold of Glasby he couldn't have all that much. There was only one explanation; someone inside the *Herald* had sold them out. The girl obviously knew something that she didn't want to say. You could tell that from the way she'd answered his question.

Now Lewis had the scent he'd stay on it, spending to smooth

the way whenever he needed to. Davenport was going to have
to move fast. He was damned if he was going to see everything
go up in smoke now, taking his reputation with it.

Propped up with cushions on a huge overstuffed chair,
sipping at his Glenmorangie, waiting for her to arrive, feeling
old – but not too old, Goddamn it! He knew exactly what had
to be done – barring any new revelations from Glasby.

There was a rather tentative knock at the door. It was Glasby,
sooner than he had expected, looking very young in a black
jacket and dress. 'You were quick! Come in. You look very
nice.'

Glasby thanked him and looked around the amazing room.
It was like something out of an old film. It should have been
David Niven greeting her, not Bill Davenport, although even
he looked rather elegant in his black tie and DJ, quite a change
from the usual scruffy jacket and trousers he wore at work.
'It's a bit different from the office, isn't it?' he said, echoing
her thoughts. The oversized bed with its brightly veneered
headboard and brass light fittings dominated the room and
made her uneasy. Not that Davenport had ever given her any
reason, but you didn't really expect to be having a crunch
meeting with your boss in his bedroom.

'Sit down, won't you?' He pointed her towards an armchair,
the pair of the one he had been sitting on and separated from
it by a small burr walnut writing desk. 'What would you like
to drink?' He picked up the phone to ask room service to
bring her a pot of tea.

He'd never really noticed before but she was actually quite
a good-looking girl. Maybe he was old-fashioned, but he'd
never met a woman who didn't look better in a dress. She
had nice slim legs and a lot of character in her face.

He glanced at himself in the wardrobe mirror. He was
compact, with what was still a pretty good head of hair and
a firm enough jaw for his age. Not too much of a paunch
either. He held himself straighter; he looked distinguished,
even, in his DJ. And old enough to be her father, if not her
grandfather, he reminded himself.

'I've got forty-five minutes, Alison. You've got some things
to say to me, and there's something I need to talk to you about
as well. But I think that you should start. Why don't you tell

me what you found in my office, on Tuesday?' Her face was a picture, guilt and embarrassment burning out of every pore. 'You put one of the boxes back the wrong way,' he helped her. 'Don't worry. You did it because you didn't know if you could trust me. I understand why you felt like that.'

She started to stumble out an apology but he stopped her. 'Let's skip that. We're a team now, and it looks like we've got some opposition. It's time to put our cards on the table, both of us. Go on, if you're sitting comfortably, why don't you begin?'

'The first thing,' Glasby told him, 'was the cushion, I mean when it was that Leonie made it. I looked through your old interview notes. I'm sorry, I haven't got my notes with me, but sometime, about 1982 I think it was, she talked to you about how she'd done embroidery classes at Marsham House and made the cushion, just a few weeks after they first put her there. In other words the photo of Lynette and Donna must have been sewn into the cushion then, and then it stayed there all that time until she tore it out just as she was dying.'

Now she was into her stride. 'I can't see how she could have brought it with her – they'd have found it, wouldn't they? So I think someone smuggled it into the prison for her, a visitor almost certainly, soon after they transferred her there. That would mean, in late sixty-nine or early seventy.'

Davenport didn't seem convinced. 'Why would anyone do that?' he asked. 'And who would have had the photo, anyway? You're not suggesting that Dellar and Jarmy had an accomplice are you, someone who was never caught?'

'I hadn't thought about that. I don't know who brought it in. But I bet Lynette Bacon does, or she knows something, anyway. She must have known about the photo, who took it, and I bet she knows who gave it to Dellar. And why.'

A Filipino man from room service arrived and fussed around pouring tea. Davenport sat further back in his chair and took a deeper sip of his whisky and ginger. He was thinking, hard.

'You said that was the first thing which you found in my papers? Was there something else?' Remembering his reaction to her suggestion that Jarmy had manipulated him, she hesitated. 'It was to do with when Lynette found out that you were going to write your book.'

'What about it?'

'Nothing, really. I thought that it might mean something, but then I thought I was wrong. So that was it, until today.'

'Hmmm.' He waited to give her another chance but she showed no sign of having anything more to say. 'Let's talk about Jarmy then. First, however did you do it? What did you say to him to get him to see you?'

She handed him her letter to Broadmoor. 'I sent this, on Tuesday. I'm sorry. I didn't think you'd let me do it if I told you.'

He read it, lips tight:

Dear Mr Allen,

I would be grateful if you would be so kind as to repeat my request to visit Mr Brian Jarmy. Please note that this request relates to myself only, as Mr William Davenport will not be available.

Would you please ask the patient supervisor, when passing the request to Mr Jarmy, to include an explanation for the request as follows: 'I only want to discuss Leonie Dellar's confession. I have no need to discuss anything else.' It is essential that these exact words are passed to Mr Jarmy, as I feel that he may then be prepared to allow the visit.

Would you also kindly advise if it would be possible for the visit to take place on Friday of this week, the – November.

As you know, I can be reached by phone or fax at the above numbers.

Yours sincerely
Alison Glasby

Davenport sat back in the armchair, his brain racing but outwardly calm. 'Leonie's confession. What do you mean? What were you thinking?'

'Can I tell you later, Bill? When you've heard what happened, I mean?'

'OK. It's your story. But we haven't too much time, so don't take too long. Tell me.'

'Jarmy saw me. He was really obnoxious. Like he was with you – worse, really. But he did say something, right at the end, and I don't understand it. But I'm sure it means something, something important.'

'OK.' He was getting impatient now. 'What was it?'

'He said that Leonie was never the same after she had her first ice cream.'

'And what on earth is that supposed to mean?'

'I don't know. But don't you think it means something? You know, he kept playing stupid games with me. Like he did when you saw him. But they weren't riddles, like this. He thinks he's really clever, but he's not subtle, just rude. I'm sure he was telling me something.'

'So, he was setting us a test, you mean? You could well be right.' He stopped, and nodded his head a couple of times. 'I think you are. We'll come back to it. Tell me about the *Chronicle* first.'

'It was when I got back home. Paul Lewis called on my mobile, and I told you, I recorded it. Listen.' She reached in her bag and played through the whole conversation. Davenport listened without a word, impassive at first but becoming more and more agitated.

'Who's told them? Who is it?' He looked hard at her.

'It could have been Dack, the prison officer. Or anyone else at the prison. Or the IT bloke who downloaded the photos on to your PC. You know, when I first showed them to you, on my phone.'

'No. If that was it, Paul would have the photo. Or know about it, anyway. He'd have run the story without risking tipping you off. And I can't imagine any technician knowing what the photos meant. Who have you told? There must be someone.' Davenport turned to face her.

'No one, really,' replied Glasby, trying not to sound defensive.

'Alison, this isn't the time to play games. Who is it? What about this policeman boyfriend of yours? Who is he?'

'I already told you, Bill. He's just a friend, not my boyfriend. His name is John Redgrave, and he's a sergeant on the murder squad at Scotland Yard.'

'Murder squad? Interesting friends you have! Who does he work for, Henry Dunne?'

'I don't know, I haven't asked him. But he's a really decent guy. And . . . well, he's rather keen on me I think.' Strangely, it felt rather good to Glasby to be saying this. 'He's the last person to start trying to sell our story to another newspaper, honestly Bill.'

'Well, someone has, haven't they?' Davenport was grim-faced. 'Alison, I know that this sort of thing goes on, just like Paul Lewis told you. But he didn't tell you how he would feel about working with someone who would sell out her own colleagues, did he? If you'd have taken his offer, how long do you think you would have lasted on the *Chronicle*?'

He had some more of the whisky. She glanced at her tea, untouched and getting cold. 'Let's forget about Mr Lewis,' he continued, to her relief. 'Whatever happened, it's done now. There's a lesson in all of this for both of us. It all came about because of lack of trust.'

He paused. Glasby kept quiet, having no idea what she could say.

'You were right to think that there was something which I hadn't told you about. There was. It was a confidence, a very serious one, and not mine to break, but it's too late for that now. If we're going to work together, we've got to do it as a team. No secrets from now on, none at all. Do you agree?' He looked across to her, questioningly.

'Of course, Bill. I've told you everything that I know. I really have,' she protested.

'All right; now it's my turn, then. Lynette Bacon asked to see me once, a long time ago. It was sometime in early 1970. We went for a drive, parked up, and then we talked in my car. We did that a few times afterwards but this was the first time. You won't have seen any notes on it because there aren't any.'

He talked to Glasby as if it was all still fresh in his mind. There was a gale which had come straight from Siberia whistling down the east coast that day. He was expecting another request to drop his plans for the book, tears, maybe even threats, but Lynette was calm enough. She had waited until he had parked, down a country lane with grass pushing through great cracks in the tarmac, the engine left running to give the heater of his Triumph a chance against the wind.

Straight away she'd told him that she had changed her mind and promised to do everything she could to help him. 'I know you'll treat us proper, like you told me.' Then she said she needed some help from him. 'This is secret, isn't it?' He promised her that it was. 'I want to look in her eyes. Dellar. I want to ask her where our Donna is. Me and Mum, we want her back, to treat her right. Bury her, you know, do it right. I want to see Dellar, if they'll let me. But I don't want all them journalists round ours again. Can you help me, Bill? Mum don't even know about this, and she mustn't neither. Can you do it, without them all finding out?'

'So I did,' Davenport told the astonished Glasby. 'I went to see Adam Mullins, the chief superintendent in charge at the time. He was sure it wouldn't do any good. And as it turned out he was right, of course. But he didn't have it in him to say no, so he arranged it through the governor at Marsham House.'

'How did you get her in there? Surely half the prison would have known about it? I can't believe that it never came out in public!'

'It was quite a little performance.' He smiled, even at this distance proud of what had happened that day. 'I picked her up from home just as I had the time before. I think her mother was glad for her to get out of the house for a few hours. Patricia wasn't a healthy woman, even then. She got a lot worse later; Lynette gave up her job to look after her, but at that time she could look after herself. I drove Lynette to Norwich, to Adam Mullins' house. He borrowed a WPC's uniform, he told them it was for his daughter for a fancy-dress party, I think. Then they drove up to Marsham House, and the governor got them in to see Leonie, just Mullins with a new WPC. I don't suppose anyone thought anything of it. Then she got changed back at Mullins' house and I took her back home. Lynette's a brave woman, you know. And tough, as you found out for yourself.'

'Yes,' agreed Glasby, remembering the marks Lynette had left on her shoulders. 'But Dellar didn't tell her anything, then?'

'No. But it was a hell of a thing for a girl her age to do. Just think, going to see the monster who had butchered your little sister. And not telling a soul about it. Imagine what character it takes to do that and not say a word, all these years.' He turned to face Glasby again. 'The governor died years ago. So there's only Adam Mullins, and me. And now you. You can understand why I didn't want to tell you, can't you? You have it on the same trust that I did. Do you understand?'

'Of course, yes,' Glasby reassured him. Then, thinking again, 'Do you know what happened, what was said?'

'No. I told Lynette I wasn't going to ask her. She could tell me as much or as little as she wanted. We never talked about it.'

'And Mullins? Did you talk to him?'

'Yes. He saw Leonie first, and broke the news to her, who it was that wanted to see her. When she agreed to do it, he stood outside the room and left them on their own. It was what they both asked him to do, apparently. Lynette told him that Leonie had agreed to think about it, and that was all. Nothing more.'

'So . . . so Lynette *could* have given the photo to Leonie then. That must be it!' Glasby was triumphant.

'Possibly, yes,' Davenport agreed. 'Although I'm not sure I know why she should have wanted to. But I agree that she could have done it then, yes. I'd had the same thought myself, of course.'

He got out of the chair and stood looking down at her. 'I've got to be downstairs in five minutes – I think they'll notice if I'm not there, don't you? So what were you getting at in the message you sent Jarmy? Were you trying to get him to say something about Leonie's confession?'

'I don't know,' was the response he got. 'I just thought, the way he kept on at it when you got in to see him, that he must think there was something strange about it. But I don't know what.'

It was pretty clear that she was holding back on him, but there was no time to push her further now. 'Then we've still got Jarmy's little riddle to solve, and we need to talk to Lynette, before young Mr Lewis gets any further down the line.' (And, he thought, before the *Chronicle*'s enticements got too much for an ambitious young woman to resist.) 'I'll go up to Norfolk tomorrow. If Paul Lewis is on the scent, we've no time to waste. Are you going to come with me?'

'Yes, Bill. Yes, of course. But don't we need to do some work on this ice cream thing first?'

'We do, you're right. There's nothing I can do tonight, I'm afraid – I'm otherwise engaged. But if you want to go back to the files, my office key is here. I'll call old Dave and tell him I've given it to you. Not,' he grinned, 'that you seem to mind letting yourself in, anyway.'

'I did say sorry.' Glasby was embarrassed again.

'I'm teasing you, ignore me. Did you get any lunch, what with charging off to Broadmoor?'

'Not really, no.' She'd been running on adrenalin, and wasn't hungry.

'Come downstairs, and listen to the speeches. There's Mark and then me, and one of us will be very brief, I promise you. See if you can guess which one. Grab yourself some food, and then hotfoot it to the office. I'll get out as soon as I can, about one, I should guess. Call me.' He paused. 'I don't know where you'll find it, but I bet it's there somewhere. We're looking for a Bacon connection, so you need to check everything you can find on the family. And you might try the background files. Have you seen them?'

She had. They were huge. 'If you get done before we can talk, go home – Dave will get you a cab – and leave me a message to phone you. And don't record the call, if you don't mind.'

They went down together in the beautiful lift, Glasby praying that no one would see them – what would they think? They were directed to the rear of the hotel lobby, a sign next to the ballroom saying 'Herald Newspapers'. There were two girls checking invitations on the door and with them a harassed-looking Mark Ellington.

'Bill, there you are. We thought you'd gone AWOL. Should have known that you'd turn up with a young lady for company!' Glasby, mortified, was very glad when Ellington hustled Davenport away.

The room was huge, crystal chandeliers and heavy drape curtains everywhere. There must have been 500 people but she recognized no one. She did, however, spot a very tempting looking buffet at one side. Refusing champagne in favour of an orange juice she headed for the food as Ellington began to speak.

'Thank you, ladies and gentlemen. I've had the enormous pleasure and privilege of being able to invite you here tonight to honour, to celebrate, the career of the great Bill Davenport.' Applause. Glasby had a large prawn in one hand and so didn't join in. 'Now Bill is a man of many marvellous qualities, but he would agree that punctuality has never been one of them. So I shouldn't have been surprised to see him arrive a little late tonight. With a beautiful young woman on his arm, of course.' Laughter.

The whole room turned as one and stared at Glasby. In her

mind only, luckily. She munched grimly on her prawn and reached for another.

'Alison!' she heard a familiar voice behind her. Of course Serena *would* be here. 'You look lovely!'

Compared with Serena, who seemed more at home in a party frock than an office, she felt cheap, shuffling awkwardly from side to side in her unfashionable shoes. Whatever was glittering in Serena's ears would probably pay Glasby's rent for the next few years. 'You look very nice too, Serena,' she managed, surreptitiously putting the remains of the second prawn back on the table.

'Thank you. But you really do, Alison. You have such a good figure, really gamine, so all you need is a simple little dress and you're a revelation. Whereas I have to paint myself up like a trollop just to look half as good. You're so lucky.'

Glasby, as surprised as she was flattered, was no better at receiving compliments than she was at giving them and had no idea what to say. She just stood and stared self-consciously at the other woman, who smiled benignly at her.

Serena moved closer. 'What's eating Mike Marshall?' she whispered, stagily. 'He's been snapping at everyone all day, and you know what a dear he always is. He practically bit my head off when I mentioned your name.'

There was nothing that Glasby could say to that either, but a stern-looking elderly lady saved her, swivelling round and frowning at them. They stopped talking and turned back to Ellington's speech.

'As you all know, Bill has been with the *Herald* since the ark. 1962, to be precise. But he was already a seasoned hack when he joined us, after four years with the *Eastern Daily News* in Norwich.'

The *EDN*? Davenport had never told her that he'd lived in Norwich! Why hadn't he mentioned it? It was before the murders, before Dellar or Jarmy were even living in the city. Although neither of them were that far away. And neither were the Bacons. Lynette would have been . . . Glasby worked it out; nine or ten when Davenport started there, thirteen when he moved to London. And Donna Bacon was born . . . while he was there, in 1962.

Donna was a small child, with blonde hair just like Bill's . . . No, this was getting silly! She could hardly imagine

Davenport and Patricia Bacon having a love child after a passionate affair. And it wasn't as if he would have been the only fair-haired man in Norfolk – if it came to that, Brian Jarmy had blond hair as well. Forget about it.

Looking around, Glasby saw that Serena had wandered off in the company of a tall elderly man. She concentrated on the buffet, applauded first Ellington and then Bill, and made her escape as soon as she was able.

*The child was frightened, lying in the dark, listening –
but what was it? Quick, let's get under the sheet.
Trembling, but it was a hot summer night, so sweating
as well. What was that noise? Please God, take me in
your care, keep me safe and hear my prayer. Not again
not again not again not again. If I close my eyes it will
go away. If I promise to be good nothing will happen.
It can't. It can't. He's there! Outside the door. Why won't
someone help me? It's not my fault, I didn't do anything
wrong.*

Sixteen

The Claverdon eased its guest's exit with just as much civility as it had welcomed her in. A taxi leapt forward, beckoned into action by the top-hatted doorman who guided her by umbrella to its waiting door, enquired of her destination so that he could instruct the driver, and bade her goodnight. Unsure whether she was supposed to tip, Glasby decided against.

An orange light came on in front of her as they turned right into Piccadilly, heading east. 'You did want the Isle of Dogs, did you, madam?' asked the taxi driver through the intercom.

'That's right. The *Daily Herald* building. Telegraph Lane. Do you know it?'

'Telegraph Lane? That's one o' them new ones, isn't it? Past Canary Wharf?'

Glasby had never had to find the office by road before, let alone on a filthy dark night like tonight. But a quick look by the driver at a screen by his side was enough to get them there without any help from her.

Taxis were getting to be an expensive habit. It was a good job that she had plenty of cash on her. She supposed that Tom Lear would sign off her expenses. She would have to ask Davenport to talk to him if there was a problem.

It was a weird feeling, walking through the empty corridor along the executive floor, surrounded by silent terminals and empty offices. Everyone else was enjoying themselves at the Claverdon; and here she was, sitting on the floor surrounded by dusty old papers.

Glasby was feeling a bit light-headed. An inane old song kept going round her head: 'You scream, I scream, we all scream for ice cream.' It wasn't getting her much further – looking for a wild goose in a haystack, or something like that.

She had already been through Davenport's Leonie interview

notes twice, the second time painstakingly. She hadn't been looking for the same thing then, but even so, she was sure she would have remembered anything about ice cream. And if Jarmy had been telling her what she thought he had, there had to be not only an ice cream reference, but also a connection of some sort to the Bacons.

That made the Lynette notes another possible source. But Glasby had been through them before as well. Any Leonie reference, other than the obvious ones, would have leapt off the page at her.

There was only one thing left: background research, where Davenport had told her to look. It didn't take her long to find it; she was becoming quite an expert. 'And, Alison Glasby, your specialist subject is . . . the boxes and papers in Bill Davenport's office, 1969 to 20—.' (*Mastermind* had been her father's favourite quiz show, but she couldn't remember the name of the old man who used to host it.)

The trouble with background research was it wasn't really an 'it' at all. Davenport's system had let her down for the first time. There were more than twenty files in bundles held together with large decaying rubber bands and in one case, for some reason, a length of bright pink ribbon. Most of the files were a mess, basically just a jumble of old papers. A lot of it was handwritten – thank God he always seemed to write neatly. But there were typed pages in amongst them, and some of them were covered in his writing as well.

There was nothing for it. She was going to have to read the lot.

Glasby had decided to do it in two stages. First, anything with any reference to Dellar (which was a heck of a lot) or the Bacons was put to one side. In the process, whatever order there was in the files was destroyed but that was tough luck. Once she had done that, she would go through every piece of paper in her pile, meticulously. If it was there, she'd find it.

And she did. In March 1970, Bill had talked to a Colin Brighty, who lived in School Street, Coltishall. His occupation was listed as 'farm contractor', but whatever that involved seemed to allow him plenty of time in the village pub. Most likely he was related to Mrs Brighty in the post office. Mr Brighty had known the Bacon family well, and Davenport had got him talking about them:

'So John was quite a regular, then. Not Patricia?'

'No, not her. They used to be down here, when they was courting, but not after. He wouldn't have had it, I don't reckon. Wouldn't have thought it right, you know. But John, he were a good old boy, he were, he liked his pint.'

'Did he drink a lot, or just the odd pint?'

'You're asking now! No, not the odd pint, not him. He could put 'em back, he could, and no mistaking. A great talker he were as well, once he'd had a few.'

'But it wasn't a problem? It didn't stop him working, or anything like that?'

'Well, it weren't the drink what killed him, was it? That was a heart attack, and no wonder, either. You know what I mean, with what them bastards done to his poor little Donna. But as for work, he never had much luck, really. He were always on the lookout, driving, labouring, help with the picking, strawberries, raspberries, you know. Nothing regular, like.'

'Did he never have a regular job?'

'Not that I remember, he didn't – no, I'm telling you wrong. That must be ten years ago, though, he used to drive an ice cream van. He went all over, not round our way but some of them other places. Stalham, up the coast round Helmswick, Cromer I think. That weren't his van, of course. He done it for two or three years, I think, that's right. That's the only steady work I can remember him doing.'

Glasby leapt to Davenport's terminal. She fumbled with shaking fingers to change the log-on to her name, drumming her foot impatiently while the PC did its warm-up routine.

On the network at last, she went to the same map page that she'd used before. Just as she'd thought! If that was John Bacon's ice cream round, he would almost have *had* to go through North Walsham, where Leonie Dellar was living. She would have been a little girl, somewhere around eleven or a bit younger. Very much ice cream-buying age. This must be it.

What it meant was another matter. But before she stopped to think it through, Glasby felt duty-bound to go through the rest of the bundle. It was only eleven thirty, after all.

It was after one in the morning by the time she got home, dialling Davenport's number as she went through the door. He sounded drunk and she could hear someone singing *Yellow Submarine* in the background. 'Hold on a tick, Alison. Rory! Give me two minutes. Now, what have we got?'

He sobered up fast when she told him. 'OK. Well done. Is seven thirty too early for you? Good. Come over to my house then. We'll drive up in both cars. We'll need them once we get there.' He gave her the address.

'By the way, Bill, I messed up the background papers a bit. I'm sorry, but it was the only way I could work it.'

'Not to worry. You can easily sort them out again later.'

Thanks a lot, Bill.

She was in bed the second she got home but she just could not sleep. There was something, something she'd seen, that meant something. It was there, just out of reach. Exhausted, she gave up trying and eventually dropped off. She kept dreaming the same stupid dream: the photo of Prince Charles and Lady Di, and Diana was talking, telling her something, something important. But however hard she tried, she couldn't quite hear what it was.

It was seven thirty on a freezing cold late November morning and the only sign of life from the address Bill had given her was a black and white cat craning its head around the curtain to peer at her out of a French window. And, his mobile was switched off. And, it was absolutely throwing down with rain. All this on three hours' sleep. Oh, and she hadn't had time even for a cup of tea.

A black taxi pulled around the corner of the narrow little street and a cheerful sounding Davenport emerged. 'Morning!' he shouted from across the road. At the sound of his voice the cat disappeared and there was the noise of carpet being scratched from inside the house.

'I expect you want some breakfast, don't you?' he said as he pushed open the front door.

'Well . . .' Glasby began, before she realized that he was talking to the cat, which seemed to be trying to trip him up. A second cat, almost identical to the first, had appeared from somewhere. They both seemed extremely affectionate, although they weren't paying much attention to her.

'Don't stand in the doorway, come on in,' he invited her. 'Let's have a cup of tea before we get going, and we'll plan out the day. I'll feed the livestock, and would you like a bit of toast?'

Sitting in a battered leather armchair, trying to fend off a cat with one hand and eating toast and jam – home-made, surely – with the other, the day was certainly starting to look up.

The plan was that they would drive up to Norwich, each taking a car so that they could split up when they got there. Davenport, who of course had his overnight bag permanently packed and whose only domestic concern seemed to be organizing cat feeding for the weekend, would phone ahead and book rooms at a hotel he liked in the city, and they would meet there. Then he would go off to track down Mr Brighty.

'If I need to, I can ask Joyce in the post office. She's a niece, I think. But if Colin Brighty's still in one piece, odds on he'll be in the local.'

Remembering her earlier encounter with Joyce Brighty, Glasby readily agreed to leave him to it. She had every intention of confronting Lynette Bacon again before the weekend was over and that was quite daunting enough, even with Bill alongside her this time. There was no point in going looking for trouble when you didn't have to, was there?

They were in Norwich by late morning. It looked like the east coast had the best of the weather, a beautiful crisp day just made for Londoners to get out of the city.

Davenport's hotel turned out to be the White Hart, an ageing institution often used by Glasby's parents on Saturday shopping outings, not so much for the quality of its hospitality as because you could leave your car there, sneak out and enjoy free parking for the rest of the day. It felt very grown up, driving in behind him into the hotel car park, walking through the beamed reception area and checking in for her first proper business trip.

After a rapid cup of coffee in front of a huge fire which filled the air around them with the smell of wood smoke, Davenport departed to look for Mr Brighty. Glasby was left on her own with an hour to kill and possibly a lot more. She felt self-conscious in the hotel lounge, slowly filling up with Saturday shoppers, elderly couples, a couple of families with

small children and a group of middle-aged ladies enthusias-
tically comparing their morning's purchases.

Why she suddenly felt so unsure of herself she had no idea,
but for whatever reason she quickly finished her coffee and
went to pay, discovering that Davenport had already put the
drinks on to his room bill. But in her room, with a choice
between a lumpy armchair or stretching out on the chintz
bedspread, she felt even more alone.

She was never exactly a friendless child. Private, yes, never
the centre of attention, but not by any means a loner. That
she gave of herself so little meant that she had a certain rarity
value amongst the other girls (there were no boys at her
school). So she tended to be welcomed into conversations,
asked for her opinion, and invited to parties or pubs. But she
never felt part of anything in the same way that the others
seemed to, the easy exchange of intimacies, plans, conspira-
cies and occasionally vicious little feuds. She would be asked
along, but as an afterthought, her company enjoyed but easily
forgotten.

Back in Norwich with time on her hands for the first time in
years, she thought of looking someone or other up. In a fit of
efficiency a few weekends ago she had copied her address book
into her phone, so contacting people wouldn't be a problem.

Glasby even got as far as dialling an old friend's number
before changing her mind. Instead she lay down on the bed
to think things through, maybe read for a while, and . . . Damn!
The last thing she should be doing was falling asleep. She
splashed cold water on to her face, and decided that if she
couldn't stay awake indoors, she'd better go out for a walk.

In one direction was the cathedral, towering against the
bright blue sky, and a pleasant walk down to the river, past
an old pub in which she had once been spectacularly sick
after too much cider. Some boys emerged through the gate-
house to the Cathedral Close wearing blue school blazers, the
same uniform that Tom Bailey used to have. One of them
even looked a little like him.

Glasby decided to go the other way, up a steeply cobbled
hill and through an alleyway to the main shopping streets.
When she was younger there had been a large second-hand
bookstall amongst the striped canvasses of the marketplace.
She fancied a look at whether it was still there.

But she took a wrong turn along the way – how could she get lost, in Norwich? – and found herself in a dark side street, an old church set back amongst deserted office buildings. A man walked past, huddled in an oversized grey coat, staring at her. Uncomfortable in the empty street, she quickened her pace. There were footsteps behind her, then she jumped as a hand touched her shoulder. 'Alison, Alison Glasby?'

'You need Alka-Seltzer,' trilled the car radio. Davenport hit the off button irritably. He had woken with an unnaturally clear head, the type which only a hangover and too little sleep can produce. Caffeine and his natural good humour had kept him going. That and the release of finally *doing* something. But he wasn't as young as he used to be, and although it was barely lunchtime it had been a long day already. What he needed was some decent grub. And absolutely no alcohol.

The Rose and Crown was warm and welcoming, the saloon bar much as he remembered it, and thank God there was no juke box. He didn't recognize the barmaid but she knew her regulars well enough. 'Old Col? He'll be along. Give him another ten or twenty minutes.' Davenport chose a seat with a view of the doorway and settled down behind a large plate of sausages and mash and a pint, forgetting that he'd only just taken the pledge of abstinence. Soon he was feeling much better.

The bar gradually filled up, mostly youngsters, the occasional older man but none that he recognized. He started to wonder if he would know Brighty when he saw him. It had been years, after all, so he asked the barmaid to point him out when he came in. 'He's just here now, see – the old gent with the tash.'

Davenport needn't have worried. Some things don't change much and Colin Brighty was one of them. He had a huge beer gut, a shock of grey hair under a flat cap, a splendidly bristling moustache and a cigarette sticking out from underneath it.

Apparently Davenport hadn't changed much either because before he had said a word, Brighty waved his stick in greeting. 'Bless me!' he wheezed. 'Bill Davenport! Didn't reckon on seeing you down here. Are you all right, boy?'

He accepted the offer of a pint with aplomb. With the help of his stick and a leather-jacketed local who seemed to be called Gub, Brighty lowered himself into a seat across from Davenport. 'I saw you was in the paper Saturday last. What you doing round here then? You aren't never taking a holiday on the Broads, are you?' – accompanied by a dig in Davenport's ribs and a deep chuckle which quickly turned into a long series of wheezing coughs and snorts. They both took some time to get their breath back.

'No, I'm not here on holiday,' Davenport admitted. 'Although it's very nice to be here again. A bit different from London.'

'I ain't never been up there, and never wanted to, neither. It's all right for all them young people, discos and such like. No good for an old boy like me, is it?'

'Well, I'm a bit of an old boy myself these days, you know,' replied Davenport.

Both men lifted their glasses, Davenport sipping rather gingerly while Brighty knocked his back with relish, pausing only to wipe his moustache clean of foam, and lit himself another cigarette. They chatted for a while about the weather, the price of beer (as Brighty waved his arm at 'my little beauty' behind the bar to get a refill), the fickleness of racehorses and eventually, steered a little by Davenport, to family and then village affairs.

'So she's not been too well, then?' he asked. 'I'm sorry to hear that. Lynette's looking after her, though?'

'Oh ar, she's a good old girl, Lynette. You couldn't want for a better girl. She ain't half got a temper on her, mind. Bit like her dad, that way.'

'Hmmm. I remember you talking to me about John Bacon. He was a friend of yours, wasn't he?'

'Well,' said the old man carefully, 'he weren't what I'd call a friend exactly. I knew him well enough, of course. Me and Patricia and him, we was all at the school together. When that used to be in the village, before they closed it. They have to do that with everything, now. That's the same with the hospital, you know.'

Davenport listened patiently to a list of complaints about the way things were nowadays, and agreed that everything was changed, just for the sake of it, and not for the better, neither.

Then: 'I don't know about you, but I'm feeling a bit thirsty today. Would you . . . ?'

'Don't mind if I do, thank you,' was the predictable response. Davenport did the honours; a half for him, and another pint for Mr Brighty.

'As you were saying, Colin, I'd heard that John Bacon wasn't an easy character. It can't have been a bed of roses for Patricia, I suppose?'

'I don't suppose it was, no. Mind, things was different in them days. Not like now, with them women's libbers. Men was men, in the house. Not that I'd go along with any rough stuff, you know.'

'He used to knock her about, then?'

Mr Brighty leant forwards, his voice dropping to a low rumble. 'I knowed Patricia since she were a little girl. And I seen her sometimes, marked up, and once I seen him, and I said to him, you want to try someone your own size, boy.' He chuckled again and wheezed some more, which was the cue for another cigarette. 'You'd never think it to see me now, but I used to be able to take care of myself, you know. He didn't want to know.'

'Mr Bacon used to drive an ice cream van once, didn't he?'

'Right you are, that's years ago that was. Harvey's, he drove for, Harvey's of Wroxham. Hell of a long time ago.'

'Why did he give the job up?'

'I couldn't rightly tell you. To tell the truth, I think they give him the sack. I remember once, he were in here, one over the eight, cursing and swearing about old Mr Harvey. Listening to some young girls – not that that were the word he used, mind – instead of to him, a grown man. I remember it because old Dusty – you remember him, Dusty Miller. Or maybe he was before your time, he used to be landlord in here. Anyway, Dusty threw him out, on account of his language. He was a stickler, was Dusty. There was one time, a long time ago . . .'

Davenport was starting to fade. He'd only actually drunk about a pint, but maybe it hadn't been such a good idea. He let the conversation drift, edged it back to John Bacon a couple of times, but it looked as if he'd got all he was going to get. One last thing was worth a try, though.

'You mentioned Mr Harvey. He ran the business, I suppose. Is he still alive?'

'Joe Harvey? Yes, he's still here. As much as any of us are.'

More wheezing. 'He's in a home. Masons'. Over at Lamas. Now then, it don't do to go thirsty, do it? Do you want another one?'

Davenport declined gracefully and, as they say in the tabloids, made his excuses and left.

Glasby would never have recognized him, not in a hundred years. At first she had thought that Paul Lewis, the *Chronicle* man, must have been tailing her and Davenport. But it was her ex-boyfriend, Lester. He was wearing some trendy rimless glasses which suited him, putting his nose into perspective with the rest of his features. He had lost weight and the curls had gone, replaced by a skull shaved almost clean and long sideburns which made his face look thinner.

She had gawped at him like a fool when he said hello. 'Don't you recognize me? Lester. For God's sake, Ali, what have you been smoking? Lester! Lester Dolland. I thought I was the one with the memory problems!'

'Lester,' she had squeaked. 'What . . . what on earth are you doing here?'

'I live here. Just round the corner, in fact. I moved up a couple of years ago. I still can't get used to how cold it is up here. We've set up a community publishers. We get funding from the European Commission. How about you? Don't tell me you've moved back home?'

'Home?' She had still felt completely witless. 'Oh, no. Of course, you wouldn't know. My parents don't live here any more. They moved, ages ago. I live in London. I'm just up here for a day or two. Working. I'm a journalist.'

'Trust you to be working at the weekend! Although, to be fair,' he had grinned, 'I've just come from the office myself.' He'd put his hand on her arm. 'Why are we standing here on the street corner? It's so cool to see you again! You've got time for lunch, haven't you? Come round to mine – it's just down the road. It's such a far-out place to live, we love it.'

Glasby had wondered who Lester meant by 'we'. Probably he was set up with some intellectual alternative-culture type, baking their own bread and having loads of sex. Not that there was any reason why she should care. It had been five years, after all.

It didn't feel like that. They were on each other's wavelength immediately. He'd read the novel she had been struggling through, of course, and nearly blurted out the ending before he realized that she hadn't finished it yet. And although he hadn't seen her in ages, his intuition on Kate was dead on. 'Don't tell me. I bet that she's coupled up, playing house, and slowly turning into her mother?' And it took them all of ten minutes before the usual argument about music started. ('Coldplay? They're all right, I guess, if you like your angst sliced up and nicely packaged for you. Dashboard Confessional are ten times more real.' She'd never heard of them.)

His flat really was cool. It was in an old mill overlooking the River Wensum, bare floorboards and bricks. A bit poky for two, but really light so it seemed bigger, and so quiet. 'It's housing association. Alex got it, and then he needed someone to share with, so I got the other room. He's registered disabled, although no way would you know it. He's as blind as the proverbial church mouse, though.'

'I thought church mice were poor, not blind,' she objected, literal as ever.

'You're probably right. Unless there's three of them, of course.' They both giggled. 'He's away at the moment. It's a shame, I'd love you to meet him. We're setting up a talking book project and he's down in London, fundraising for it. But very thoughtfully before he left he made tons of soup. So you won't have to suffer my cooking.'

The soup was stone cold before she had finished it, they were talking so much. He seemed to know loads of people in Norwich, far more than she ever had. And they all seemed to have really interesting lives: writers, a jazz poet (whatever that was), people from the art school down the road. No mention of any girlfriends, though. It was such a nice feeling, really being at ease with someone. Maybe . . .

She jumped up to get her bag, hearing her phone. It was Davenport.

'John Bacon used to beat Patricia up. He had a nasty temper, apparently. And –' he couldn't resist the pause for dramatic effect – 'it sounds as if he lost his job because of something that happened with some young girls.'

'No! Oh my God, I don't believe it! What did Brighty say?'

Davenport told her, more or less verbatim. 'Of course it

was off the record, as you'd expect, and completely uncon-
firmed at the moment. So now we need to see this Joe Harvey,
if he's not too gaga to talk to us, and see if it really was how
Colin Brighty told it. We can meet up outside the home. Lamas
is only a tiny place, I think, so it shouldn't be hard to find.'

He was right. The Royal Norfolk Masonic Home was
signposted in suitably majestic purple, from the beginning
of the lane which led from Coltishall to the hamlet of Lamas.
And it lived up to its billing: a gorgeous red-brick Georgian
pile, thirty or forty bedrooms, with stepped lawns to the
front and natural woodlands all around. She found Davenport
standing next to his car in the visitors' parking area, located
discreetly around the side of the home. He was looking a
bit frayed around the edges.

'Well, you can't sit in a pub and not have a pint, can you?'
he said, defensively. 'Come on, let's see what Harvey's got
to tell us, and then you can let a poor old chap have a bit
of shut-eye. Me, I mean, not him. Remember, I'm supposed
to be out to grass now. You might at least let me rest in
peace.'

Davenport had already worked his charm on the uniformed
nurse on reception and Mr Harvey was prepared to receive
them. They were ushered briskly down an over-heated corridor,
carpeted in lush blue and gold and lined with framed photographs, mostly elderly men in what Glasby presumed was
Masonic regalia. 'Joe Harvey's ninety-two, yes,' their escort
told them. 'He's still in perfect health, though. He really is
as bright as a button.'

She stopped at a heavy oak-panelled door. A brass plaque
announced 'Visiting Suite'. 'Joe,' the nurse shouted. 'Your
visitors. Mr Davenport, and, um . . .'

'Alison Glasby,' she said.

'What did you say, my dear?'

'This is Miss Gatsby,' the nurse bellowed, even louder than
before.

'Thank you, Marjorie. Can I offer you some tea? You wouldn't
mind, would you, dear?' Marjorie said that she wouldn't, and
disappeared through a door at the side of the room.

Joe Harvey was a lean old gentleman in a tweed suit, collar
and tie. His moustache was only marginally less impressive
than Colin Brighty's and he had a fine head of perfectly white

hair. Glasby tried very hard not to look at his glass eye, which was staring disconcertingly straight at her.

'You'll have to forgive me, I'm a little hard of hearing,' he told them, unnecessarily. 'I've seen you in the newspapers, haven't I? Bill Davenport, that's it, isn't it? What can I do to help you? Are you both journalists?'

'That's right, Mr Harvey. Miss Glasby and I are with the *Herald*.'

'A very good newspaper. But I don't think we'll have many stories for you at the home. We lead a quiet life here, don't we, Marjorie?' The nurse bustled around, handing out tea and biscuits.

'I saw your story in the paper the other day, didn't I? Leonie Dellar? I remember her uncle, you know, Fred Dellar. I used to go and watch him, down at Carrow Road. "Demon Dellar", they called him. He was the fastest thing on two legs. They had a good team in those days. Still,' he stopped himself, 'you haven't come all the way from Fleet Street just to listen to an old man reminiscing about football, have you?'

'There was something we wanted to ask you about, you're right,' agreed Davenport. 'This is a lovely cup of tea by the way. There's nothing like it, is there?' He raised his voice a little more. 'It was John Bacon we wanted to talk about. He used to work for you. Back in the late fifties. I don't know if you remember him, do you?'

'Oh yes, I remember him, of course I do. It was his daughter that they did away with, wasn't it? And he passed away during the trial. That was a terrible business. But I don't know that there's anything that I can tell you.'

'I think that there is, actually. The thing is, he was a bit of a problem, John Bacon, wasn't he? When he was working for you, selling ice cream, I mean. Would he have had a regular round?'

'Oh yes. I always gave the drivers their own round. That way, they could get to know their customers and how long they ought to be spending in each place, and so on and suchlike.'

'And his round was in the Stalham area? And did it also cover North Walsham?'

'Now why would you need to know all of this, Mr Davenport? I don't think I want to see my name in your newspaper, you know.'

'Mr Harvey, you have my apologies. I should have made it clear from the start that this is a private conversation, in the strictest of confidence. We wouldn't dream of mentioning your name or using anything that you've told us in the newspaper. Isn't that right, Alison?'

'Of course,' she agreed, wondering whether Davenport really had to accept so easily that everything that Mr Harvey said would be off the record. At this rate, they might not be left with much of a story at the end of it.

'You have our word, Mr Harvey,' Davenport continued. 'As I say, there's no question of anything that you tell us appearing in print, without your express permission. This is just to confirm some information, things that we have heard from other places. But we always try to find the most reliable person. So as to make sure that what we've heard is right. I'm sure you understand that.'

Joe Harvey nodded and shifted his position so as to sit up a little straighter. Even his glass eye seemed to Glasby to be shining a little more intensely than before. 'Now that that's understood, of course I'm happy to help you if I can.'

'Mr Bacon's ice cream round, you were saying,' Davenport prompted him.

'Oh yes. Well, it was Stalham, as you say, and Walsham. Up to Helmswick, and he would have had the east side of Cromer as well. We used to split Cromer into two, or else in the summer, there'd be too much for one van to cover. That was about it. He worked for me for about two, maybe three years.'

'But you had to ask him to leave eventually.' It was a statement, not a question. Glasby, who was practically hopping out of her chair, tried hard to look calm and professional.

'I did, yes.' The old man's head dropped a little, as if he was suddenly weary. 'You are very well informed, Mr Davenport. A credit to Fleet Street.'

'Mr Harvey, I wouldn't ask you this if it wasn't important.' Somehow Davenport managed to let his voice drop while maintaining its volume. 'I don't like to speak ill of the dead any more than you do. I hope that you'll understand that we can't explain to you at the moment why we're asking this. It would be breaking a confidence, you see. But I need to hear from you, why you had to stop Mr Bacon from working for you.'

'I often used to think it would come to this.' A silence filled the room. Somewhere in the garden a blackbird started to chirrup a warning to another bird. Mr Harvey made up his mind.

'I'm not going to give you any names. Perhaps you know them already, but I don't want to hear about it if you do. One of the girls I know for a fact is still alive. She's a married lady – a grandmother, now I think of it. I was told, told about certain activities of John Bacon's, by a very respectable lady. She came to see me, confidentially.' He hesitated again. Glasby bit into her bottom lip, so hard that she could taste the blood. 'Today they would call him a paedophile. We didn't have a name for it in those days, did we? Now, I think I've said enough, don't you? And I mustn't keep you any longer.'

They left him with profound thanks and renewed promises of confidentiality from Davenport. As she walked out of the room Glasby glanced back over her shoulder. Mr Harvey was sitting a little less upright than before, one eye closed in tiredness or contemplation. The other was wide open, looking straight through her.

A line from a book came back to her, something by Rebecca West. 'An open door in a mean house that lets out the smell of cooking cabbage, and the screams of children.'

*The child was frightened, lying in the dark, listening –
but what was it? Quick, let's get under the sheet.
Trembling, but it was a hot summer night, so sweating
as well. What was that noise? Please God, take me in
your care, keep me safe and hear my prayer. Not again
not again not again not again. If I close my eyes it will
go away. If I promise to be good nothing will happen.
It can't. It can't. He's there! Outside the door. Why won't
someone help me? It's not my fault, I didn't do anything
wrong. Please! Please don't let him touch me.*

Seventeen

They'd been sitting in his old hatchback, shaded from the low winter sun by the trunk of a massive old oak, a study in contrasts.

'So will you call Lynette, or do you think it would be better to turn up without warning them first?'

Davenport hadn't answered. His thoughts had drifted a long way away, decades back in fact. He'd been sitting in his car then as well, next to a girl, younger than the one he was with now. Lynette Bacon, a girl who had lost her sister and her father a matter of weeks before. Who needed help, needed him and trusted him.

And now this.

'Bill,' Glasby had insisted. 'Those girls John Bacon was doing it to, one of them must have been Leonie. That's what Jarmy was telling me, wasn't it? When he said that thing about her and ice cream.'

More silence. Then, 'It might be. We don't know that, but it might have been.'

'It must have been! And, if he was abusing other girls, he may have been doing it to his own daughters as well.'

'We don't know that!' Davenport, who had spoken much more sharply than he intended, lowered his voice again. 'I'm sorry, but these are such shocking things, such a tragedy even to think about, we have to be very careful what we say, even to each other.'

'But you agree that we have to find out? From Lynette, I mean. That's why I asked if you were going to call her.'

So that was what he was doing now, shut in the car for privacy while she paced around. Why was it taking so long? What was he saying that he didn't want her to hear? Through the window he looked agitated and defensive. At one point his voice was raised, and she heard him say, 'We've got to, damn it! Don't you see?'

He put his phone away but instead of telling her what had happened he just sat where he was, staring at nothing. Glasby was starting to worry. She'd been right, proved right, more despite Davenport than anything else, and here he was behaving oddly again. What was going on between him and Lynette Bacon?

Eventually he got out of the car. 'She'll see us. We can go round to the house now. Patricia is in hospital again, so Lynette's there alone. Patricia's quite bad this time, from the sound of it. But Lynette wants to talk to me first, on my own.'

'What does she want to talk about?' Glasby didn't like the sound of that at all. What were they going to do, cook up another cover story to fob her off with?

'I don't know, Alison.' He sounded tired, really tired. 'It's taken me all this time to persuade her to see us at all. To see you, to be honest. You shouldn't take it personally but you know, she doesn't like to talk to the press, at the best of times.'

'And this isn't the best of times? Because it's me, you mean?'

'Probably, yes,' he admitted. 'You have to understand, from her point of view. She had Jack Daniels pestering her again yesterday as well, which probably didn't help much. Although it sounds like she gave him pretty short shrift. Let me speak to her, and then we can all talk together, I'm sure. OK?'

'What are you going to talk about? Without me there, I mean?'

He snapped at her. 'Alison, I told you, don't make it personal. Wait outside the house for me, in your car. I'll come out, or call you. As soon as I can.' Before she could answer he wheeled around and was back in his car and away, sending gravel spinning as he raced down the driveway.

The door of number 51, Recreation Road opened for the second time. This time a man came out. He was scrawny, shaven-headed, and wearing jeans that were too big for him with just a string vest on top. His chest and arms were covered in tattoos. Like the children a moment ago, he walked to the gate and stared at her as she sat in the car. Glasby glanced up, met his gaze and looked away quickly, but not before checking that the driver's door next to her was locked. The man stood picking his nose, then spat on the pavement in her direction and sauntered back past the rusting piles of metal in the front yard. Glasby heard the door slam shut.

Almost immediately it opened again. The woman was so fat that she had to turn at an angle to fit through the doorway. She wobbled purposefully towards the Punto and rapped a pudgy fist against the car window.

'You from Social Services?' she demanded.

'No!' replied Glasby, startled.

'Then what you doing round 'ere? Sittin'?'

Glasby's phone rang. It was Davenport, at last.

'Lynette's ready to see you now. Come on in,' he said. Glasby opened the car door and shoved past the woman, muttering 'excuse me' on the way.

Glasby had had warmer welcomes. 'You'd better come in,' Lynette greeted her, with a sour look on her face. She looked older than Glasby remembered, as if she hadn't been sleeping properly.

'I'm sorry to hear your mother's not been well,' Glasby tried, but was rewarded with nothing more than a grunt. Without a word, Lynette led her down the passage and past the flimsily patched door to the now familiar sitting room, through the same cabbagy smell as before.

Without her mother there Lynette seemed to be economizing on electricity. Neither of the two fires was on and instead a clinging dampness hung in the room. Davenport, who seemed to have regained his usual relaxed air, was sitting on one of the chairs next to the fireplace. Rather alarmingly, the other was draped in Mrs Bacon's pink blanket with her slippers poking out from underneath it, as if their owner had metamorphosed into an armchair since Glasby's last visit.

It was Davenport, not Lynette, who invited her to sit down. Not wanting to move Mrs Bacon's things, she went back to the same uncomfortable corner of the pvc-covered sofa. Lynette sat at the other end, staring down steadily at the threadbare carpet in front of her. It looked as if Glasby was going to be spared ordeal by tea, anyway.

'Alison, Lynette and I are sorry to have kept you waiting like that, but we needed to do some talking. I've explained to her some of what we've been doing, and why. She understands that we're among friends here. So she feels that it's time to explain some things to you.' He paused. If this was supposed to be Lynette's cue, she didn't take it. The room was tense. A woman was shouting somewhere in the distance; number 51, presumably.

'Lynette understands that whatever's said in this room, stays between us three. There are some . . .' he hesitated, uncharacteristically unsure of himself, then started again. 'Lynette has every right to talk, or *not* to talk, about very private, personal . . . Alison, you know, very *painful* things. So Lynette, we're both very grateful to you.'

Again, neither woman said a word. Glasby was dismayed that yet another conversation was going to be off the record, but there was nothing that she could do about it. Lynette was motionless, head still down. Looking around the room, Glasby's eye rested on the photo of Charles and Diana, then the picture next to it of Patricia and Lynette Bacon, then back to Charles and Diana. Something slipped into place in her mind.

Davenport was forced to try again. 'Lynette, there was something you were going to say to Alison.'

At last she began to speak, her eyes still fixed firmly on the carpet, her shoulders stiff. 'I'm sorry.' She was so quiet that Glasby had to strain to catch her words. 'I'm sorry, for getting angry with you, the other day. Only me and Mum, we was shocked, by that photograph. And I can't have Mum being upset by no one. I won't have it!' Some of the usual strength was back in her voice, but she was looking anywhere but at Glasby.

'You understand that, don't you, Alison?'

'Yes, Bill. I understand, of course.' It all felt like a little play, scripted by Davenport for her benefit. What had he prepared for the next scene?

'That photo,' Lynette continued, shaking her head, 'Mum hadn't ever seen it before, even. And I hadn't either, not for all them years. So it was a right shock, you with it like a rabbit out of a hat. You could have knocked me down, I was that shook up, I can't tell you.'

Glasby decided that it was time to intervene. 'Can you tell me where the photograph came from? When was it taken?'

Lynette shifted on the sofa and relaxed her shoulders a little. 'Me and Donna, we were at the seaside. It was this little place called Helmswick. I took her, on the bus, just me and her. She was on school holidays, July I think it was, that was a beautiful hot day. There was this man, he was taking pictures and he came up to us, took our photo, then he said we could buy it if we wanted, for a souvenir, but I told him I didn't have no money for souvenirs.' She smiled for the first time, but still wouldn't look at Glasby.

'So he said, "What pretty girls you are!" I think he was a bit sweet on me. He said if I gave him a kiss, he'd give me the photo when it was ready, and he did, 'n all. He gave it to me a few hours later, and I put it in my handbag, in a pocket you could zip up, and I told Donna not to say nothing to Mum or Dad. He wanted to see me that evening, but I told him that we had to catch the bus.'

She hesitated again. Davenport was looking at the wall between the two women. Glasby was about to say something, but Lynette continued. 'When we got home, there was a big bust-up. Dad he was . . . he was shouting, angry at Mum, something she'd done, and he said she didn't ought've, and Donna was crying, and I forgot all about the photo.'

'And then you gave it to Leonie Dellar?'

Silence. From Davenport: 'Lynette?'

She answered, as if every word was scorching her lips. 'Yes. You're right, Miss Glasby. I gave it to Leonie Dellar. Now you know the answer to your little mystery.'

'Why did you give it to her? What made you do that?'

Lynette jumped to her feet. Now she was looking at Glasby all right, eyes blazing, face twisted in anger. 'You come round here, putting on your fake Norwich accent like we don't know you're a spud, you think just because we're common we must be stupid. Keeping asking all them questions, nosing away in things that are best left alone . . .'

'Lynette!' Davenport had both hands on the woman's arms, looking straight into her eyes. She was shaking with rage, and Glasby was shaken too, expecting another outburst, but Davenport radiated confidence. His voice deliberately low, he told Lynette to sit down, calm down, and do her best to explain things. 'You don't mean to upset anyone, do you, Alison?'

'No, of course not, Bill. I just . . .'

'Then that's OK. You can carry on, can't you, Lynette? Tell her about what happened, with Dellar.' Glasby shivered, from relief or from the dank air in the room.

'I wanted to go to ask her what they'd done with Donna.

Where she was, where they'd . . . where they'd put her. So
Mum and me could have her back, give her a proper funeral.
Mum was so upset, and what with Dad gone . . .' She paused,
collected herself, and started again.

'So I asked Bill if he could help me, 'cos I didn't want no
journalists, or them television people making a big song and
dance about it. And he called the policeman, the one in charge,
Mr Mullins. He was a really nice man, everyone said so. And
he said he could get me in, and no one would know anything,
only the governor of the prison where they had her.'

'Marsham House?'

'That's it, yes. Marsham House. Up past King's Lynn, in
Lincolnshire. So Bill took me in his car to Mr Mullins'
house, up in Norwich, and when I got there Mr Mullins had
a uniform for me, with a hat, like I was a policewoman.'
She laughed. 'I wasn't as big then as I am now, but it was
a bit tight on me. Mrs Mullins, his wife, she had to help zip
me up. I was that nervous, but it was funny too, we was
laughing about it.

'Then Mr Mullins and me drove up to the prison, all the
way from Norwich, in his big car. It was really high up, his
car, which was a good job, because the weather was terrible
that day, it was sheeting down the whole time. Then we got
to the jail, and the governor came out to meet us. He was a
little man with grey hair, hardly any taller than me, but he
was really nice too.'

She was speaking quickly now, as if having started, she
wanted to get it over with. 'Mr Mullins went in to see her.
Dellar, I mean. And I waited, in his car, then he came out to
get me, and he told me to go in to see her, and he waited
outside the door, and I went in and I saw her.'

'And that's when you gave her the picture?'

'That's right, yes. You see, when I went to Mr Mullins', I put
my good clothes on and that was my best handbag, the same
bag that's in the photo. So I took it, and when I was waiting
for Mr Mullins in his car, outside the prison, I was fiddling in
the bag, and I found the photo. I'd forgotten it was there. And
I thought it might help to show it to her, so I put it in the jacket
from the policewoman's uniform and then when I saw Dellar I
gave it to her. She must have kept it, all these years. It gave me
such a turn, when you had it the other day, I can't tell you.'

'And your mother didn't know that you went to see Leonie – Dellar, I mean?'

'No. I didn't say nothing to her. Mum was in a really bad way then, what with Dad 'n all. I didn't want to tell her anything.'

'What exactly did you say to Dellar?'

Lynette's shoulders tensed up again, and her voice lowered. 'I already told you. That we wanted to know where Donna was.'

Glasby waited, but Lynette didn't seem to be prepared to add anything. She decided to try a different tack.

'When was it, when you went to the prison?'

Lynette hesitated. Davenport answered for her. 'It was right near the end of January. Dellar had confessed to me, just a few days before. That was why you thought she might tell you where Donna was, wasn't it?'

'Yes, that's right. I didn't remember the date, that's all.' Lynette was talking quickly again now.

'But I remember the day. Like I said, the weather was terrible. We had to start really early so that I could get to Norwich and then Mr Mullins and I went to the prison. And when Bill was driving me to Norwich it was just raining and raining like it wouldn't never stop. All the roads were wet, big puddles everywhere so you couldn't hardly see, I was really scared, it was flooded all over. That was the same all the way up to the prison until we was past Lynn. And then, when I got in, Mum was worried sick about me, because there'd been a big accident just up the road, near Stalham. There was a school bus had crashed, because of the rain I suppose. Three little children died. That was so sad, we were both crying when they showed it on the telly, we just couldn't help thinking about our Donna.'

'When you asked Dellar to tell you about Donna, what did she say?'

Again, a pause. Lynette was back on her guard. 'She didn't say that much. It was only ten minutes or so. She said that mostly he'd done it . . . you know, what they did. I believed her, too. Not like that bullshit that Daniels man keeps going on about. And she didn't really know anything about what had happened to Donna. But maybe he'd said something to her, and she said she would think really hard about it.'

'And you never saw her again? Or heard from her?'

'No.'

'She didn't say sorry, or anything like that?'

Davenport interrupted again. 'Dellar never really apologized for any of it, you know, Alison. I think she regretted what she'd done, quite genuinely. Repented is probably the right word. But saying sorry wasn't her way.'

There was another pause. Glasby took a deep breath and steeled herself.

'Lynette, you still haven't explained to me why you thought that going to see Dellar would do any good. Let alone why you chose to give her a picture of you and your sister. Dellar and Jarmy had murdered her, only a few months before. Your mother had never even seen that photo . . .'

There was a terrible wail, a scream of anguish from deep inside the older woman. She wasn't crying like a woman cries but almost bellowing, like a cow which has woken to find its calf dead beside it, rocking Glasby back as if by the force of her pain. Lynette subsided into sobs, words coming in between them but so incoherent that neither of them could understand her.

Davenport got to his feet, put his arms around Lynette, then turned to Glasby, shot her a furious look and with an angry jerk of his head gestured her out of the room. Burning up with embarrassment and shame she slunk out, banished like a wicked child.

For some reason Glasby thought of John Redgrave. If he was here, would he have approved of her interview technique? Or would he think that all she was doing was tormenting a helpless and traumatized woman who deserved something better? As if in sympathy with Lynette's suffering, a throbbing ache started up from her injured right hand.

But she was only trying to get at the truth. It was her *job* to do that. She wasn't doing anything just for the fun of it. And she hadn't meant to upset Lynette, just get her to stop avoiding the subject. Bill must have told her what they knew about her father, surely. That was why Lynette was talking to her in the first place. So why didn't she stop beating around the bush?

All she could hear from the other room were muffled sobs and the low sound of Davenport's voice, saying something

which she couldn't catch. She looked around the dark hallway.
Ahead of her was the kitchen; she could see an old top-loading
washing machine and a large brown electric cooker. To be
fair, it all looked clean enough, but imagining it as the source
of the stale smell which filled the air around her, she didn't
investigate further.

Across the corridor was a room with a double bed covered
by a pale pink candlewick bedspread. Next to it was a darkly
veneered low cupboard on which two photograph frames were
standing. With a glance behind her – the sitting room door
was still closed – Glasby sneaked past the half open door. She
took a quick look into a full-length built-in wardrobe, the door
painted in peach-coloured emulsion. The clothes inside
confirmed that she was right. This must be Mrs Bacon's
bedroom.

When she looked at the two photos next to the bed she saw
that she'd been right about something else too, something
important. The first was a black and white photograph of a
baby, Donna presumably, the other of Lynette as a young
woman. That was all.

There was a noise from inside the sitting room so Glasby
nipped sharply back into the hall, hoping that she didn't look
guilty. Davenport walked out, his face set. 'Lynette's very
upset, but she's calming down. She's very tough, more than
she damned well should be, but you do realize how difficult
this is for her. Don't you?'

He sounded accusatory but surely it wasn't all her fault?
He had insisted on talking to Lynette first and the whole point
of that was for him to smooth things over so that they could
question her. 'I'm sorry, Bill. But I was trying my best to be
sensitive, you know, let her take her time and everything.' She
leant towards him. 'She does know about what Mr Harvey
said, doesn't she?'

'Yes, of course. That's what we were talking about, before
you came in. I didn't say anything specific, of course. I haven't
said who it was that told us.'

He led her back into the room. Lynette was seated as before,
her eyes red, but otherwise with no sign of emotion on her
face. Her voice, though, was shaking.

'I know what it is you want me to say.' She was talking to
Glasby but looking at Davenport as if for support. 'He told

me. But it isn't easy. I ain't never said anything about it and I wasn't going to, either. Until . . .' She swallowed hard, looked down at her feet.

'It was a long time ago. So don't start asking me what day of the week things happened, or anything like that. I'm not educated like you so maybe I'm just common, and you think I'm stupid. Don't start up with all your questions. All right?'

Glasby was chastened once again. 'Yes, of course. I'm really sorry you were upset, Lynette. I know all this must be really hard for you, all these terrible things with your sister, and your father –' there! It was said – 'and we wouldn't be asking, except . . .' Another pang of self-doubt hit her. Why *was* it so important? Was it really worth all this pain, to get to the truth?

Lynette swallowed hard again, gathered her strength and began. Her tone was monotonous, almost matter of fact really, but there was an edge there too, not far below the surface. 'He started when I was about six. First he used to touch me. I didn't really know better, but I didn't like it. He'd come into my room, and I'd ask, "Where's Mum?" and he'd always say, "Oh, she's busy."'

She paused and Glasby looked at her, worried that she might be about to break down again. But she was just taking her time to find the right words. For the second time, Glasby felt a shiver run down her the back of her neck.

'And then,' Lynette continued, 'one time I asked for Mum, and he got angry. He said that he was my dad, and that I didn't ought to want no one else. And then . . . it got worse. And he told me I mustn't tell no one, or I'd get wrong. I'd be put away, and I wouldn't never see him or Mum again. So I had to let him do what he wanted. Mind you, he never done anything that hurt me. I didn't like it, but I never let on, and the rest of the time, he was all right to me. Him and Mum, well, he used to shout at her a lot of the time, but he never did to me. I was his little princess, that's what he said. He was a good dad, really, he used to buy me things when he had any money, he'd always tell me he loved me, and . . .'

She tailed off into silence again. How could she say that he was a good father? He was a monster, exploiting a young child – his own daughter, for God's sake! Glasby felt sick, just at the thought of it. Why did he have to die, before he could be exposed for what he was, locked up – *strung* up?

And why didn't the mother do anything? How could she just let it happen?

Lynette answered her unspoken question. 'Mum didn't know anything about it. I never said not one single word to her. No one knew. It was just him and me, like he told me. Our little secret, that's what he called it.'

'But eventually, it wasn't just you, was it?' Glasby had almost forgotten Davenport was there, he had been so quiet. He was hunched in the chair by the fireplace, still staring into the mid-distance. It had grown dark while they were sitting there. The chair in which he sat was in the centre of a pool of light from the standard lamp behind it, but Lynette was in semi-darkness. Glasby herself was almost totally obscured, which was fine by her. The airy brightness of Lester's flat was a lifetime away.

'When I was seven, Dad got this job with Harvey's of Wroxham, driving an ice cream van. It was blue with yellow sides, and on the back there was this picture of a girl eating an ice cream and Dad always said it was me. And . . . there were other little girls, who he met. He used to tell me about them, but he always said none of them loved him like I did, that I was the best one of all of them.'

Lynette stopped again, and this time it really did look like she was going to cry. Davenport started to say something, but she silenced him with a shake of her head.

The same unnatural calmness was back in her voice. 'He started telling me about this girl called Leonie. He said she didn't have a dad, and that's why she needed him, like I did. And then he used to talk about her more and more. She lived in Walsham, he said, and her dad was dead, there was just her and her mum, and often her mum weren't there. But he still wanted to do things with me.

'One day he told me that Leonie was his little girl now, like I was. And . . . he never wanted to touch me no more, not after that. I was worried at first, like he didn't love me any more. I never liked it, you understand –' Glasby nodded, not noticing that Lynette still wasn't looking at her – 'but I thought he was going to leave me and go off and be this Leonie's dad instead. But of course he never done that, he just used to tell me about her, what a good girl she was, she had really good manners, like a little lady. And he used to call me his little barrel, 'cos I was a bit fat in them days, and this Leonie was older than me and tall and thin, that's what he said.

'But mostly he was still all right with me, and now I didn't have to do things for him, it was like she was doing all that for me and I still had my dad who told me all his secrets and brought me presents 'n all. I was really happy. He used to talk about taking me to meet her but he never did.

'And then one day he didn't have the van any more and he wouldn't tell me why, but he was really angry. He still never hit me but he used to lose his temper a lot, mostly with Mum, and I saw him beat her quite often, and I'd ask him not to and cry, and he'd get angry and go on out. Mostly he was out, looking for work, Mum said, but I think often he was just out drinking. He used to come home drunk a lot, singing and crashing round the place, and I'd stay in my room. He never used to come in and see me like before. There weren't no more secret talks.

'Then after that there was Donna and I used to spend all the time I could with her. Right from when she was just little, it was like she was my baby. I used to feed her from the bottle, change her and clean her and put her down. She was the sweetest little baby you could imagine, like a little angel, that's what Mum says, and she's right, too.'

Lynette's voice was choked. Her eyes were dry, so far as Glasby could see, but she rubbed at them hard with her hands clenched, like a child. Glasby felt dirty, wanting more than anything to get out of this awful house where such disgusting things had happened. But she was determined to get the whole of the story first.

'That's why you thought that Leonie Dellar might help you? Because you knew what had happened, with your father and her?'

Lynette nodded.

'And you told her that you knew about it, when you saw her in prison?'

Another nod.

'What did she say?'

Davenport interrupted. 'I think she's already told us that, Alison.'

'That's all right,' said Lynette. 'She didn't really say anything. What could she say? There weren't two girls that age in North

Walsham called Leonie, what had no dad and was living just with their mum, were there? So I knew it was her, and she knew I knew. And I told her about Dad and me, sort of, so I wasn't trying to make out like I was better than her or anything. She didn't tell me anything more about what happened to Donna, anyway, like I already said.'

'So if *you* knew who *she* was, did she and Jarmy know who Donna was? That she was the daughter of her . . . of your father, the man who Leonie used to know, I mean?'

'I don't know.' Lynette was beginning to sound agitated again. 'There you go, with all your questions again. There's lots of people called Bacon, round our way. Dad's family come from Hautbois, up the road, and half the village used to be Bacons, when I was little. It's different now, of course, all them people come up from Norwich to live in the country. I ain't got no idea what Leonie and him knew or what they didn't know, do I?'

'No, of course not. I just wondered if you'd have asked her, that's all. I'm sorry. I don't mean to ask too many things. Can I just, um, a couple more, please?' Lynette was silent, which Glasby took to mean that she could carry on.

'Did he ever do anything to Donna?'

'No! I wouldn't never have let him, and he'd have known it. I wasn't ever scared of him, not from when I was six years old. If he'd so much as put one finger on her . . .' Lynette tailed off into silence again.

'The other thing was, you said that your mother didn't know anything, about what your father did to you. And I suppose that she didn't know anything about Leonie and your father, either?'

'No, of course she didn't. Or she'd have said something to me, wouldn't she?'

Glasby looked up at the picture on the wall of Charles and Diana, as if for strength. 'All around the house, there are photos of you, and Donna, and your mother. But why doesn't your mother have a single photograph of your father anywhere? Not even from their wedding day?'

Lynette looked like she wanted to jump up off the sofa. 'That's it, that's enough. You push it you do. Bill, I did what you told me, but that's enough now. Isn't it?'

Davenport got up and put a hand on Glasby's shoulder to

tell her to do the same. 'Alison, we both owe Lynette a lot of thanks. For helping us to understand, and trusting us. And now I think we can agree that it's time we left her in peace.'

'But—'

'No buts. Not this time.' He turned to Lynette, who had remained seated in the gloomy room. 'Do give your mother my best tomorrow, won't you? I'll call you, late morning, to see how things are.'

Before she could do more than mutter her own thanks, Glasby was through the door and back outside on Recreation Road. Two feral looking boys were bouncing a half deflated football off the back of her car. She glowered at them and they stared back insolently. Davenport swished an arm at them as if they were unruly sheep and they scuttled back past the rusting old Ford and disappeared inside.

'I don't know about you, but I need a drink. A large one,' said Davenport. 'Let's meet back up at the White Hart, and we can collect our thoughts. This job,' he added, 'can be hell sometimes. Pure bloody hell.'

*The child was frightened, lying in the dark, listening –
but what was it? Quick, let's get under the sheet.
Trembling, but it was a hot summer night, so sweating
as well. What was that noise? Please God, take me in
your care, keep me safe and hear my prayer. Not again
not again not again not again. If I close my eyes it will
go away. If I promise to be good nothing will happen.
It can't. It can't. He's there! Outside the door. Why won't
someone help me? It's not my fault, I didn't do anything
wrong. Please! Please don't let him touch me. I've got
to find somewhere to hide, somewhere he can't get me.
If I'm really quiet I could get out of the window and he
won't hear nothing.*

Eighteen

The thermometer in her car told her that it was twelve degrees outside, which was unseasonably warm for a winter afternoon in East Anglia, but Glasby couldn't stop shivering. The stale dampness of Lynette's sitting room had wrapped itself around her and not even the best efforts of the Punto's heater could blow it away. She turned it up further and let the driver's window down, leaning half out to take gulps of fresh air as she drove.

Davenport had driven off again like a lunatic so presumably he wasn't feeling great about things either. But it was her fault, not his; it was she who had insisted on dragging them all through the misery and shame that was Lynette's childhood.

Glasby felt unclean and desperate for a shower. She shuddered again. How must it feel, to be mistreated like that? In the very place where you should feel safe? And how could Lynette have been so calm, telling them about how her father abused her, right under her mother's nose?

She imagined John Bacon, huge, covered in hair, smelling of drink and BO, his hands clammy in the night. It made her want to throw up. Maybe this was how it felt, like she did now: sick, and dirty. But she wasn't a victim. She had forced Lynette Bacon to relive it all, for the first time in all those years. Did that make her as bad as the rapist himself?

Well she wasn't doing it just for her own pleasure, was she? Or was she? Were John Bacon's perverted lusts all that much worse than Alison Glasby's almighty ego?

'Shut up!' she screamed at the top of her voice, at no one. Shocked at herself, she fumbled for a CD and with an unsteady hand managed to push it into the slot in the dashboard. Louder and louder: *'You're no angel, yes you've done it again, done it again . . .'* until finally it was loud enough to drown out the thoughts in her brain.

Her head was starting to hurt as much as her stomach, but she didn't turn the volume down all the way back to Norwich.

'Excuse me!' Davenport ordered himself another large scotch and ginger. The first had lasted him all of five minutes. He took a gulp of the second before going back to his table in the corner of the hotel bar. His head was starting to clear.

Spotting a machine he hunted around in his pockets for change and bought himself some cigarettes, something he hadn't done in years. A woman at the next table gave him a disapproving look as he lit up. Why did young people have to be such bloody puritans these days? And so damned sure of themselves?

OK, so when he was young you worked hard and took life seriously. But the War wasn't long over, London was a mess, National Service was in full swing (the fighting in Cyprus was no joke): life *was* serious in those days.

Nowadays as soon as they were out of school they thought they should be running the show. Sure, some of them were smart, but narrow, they had no experience of life, no respect, that's what it came down to. Not for *him* – he didn't care about that. But someone like Lynette. God, what a life she'd had. The hell her father had put her through, her sister dying, then her father, her mother's illness. And she'd never told anyone but him, for all these years, until Glasby had turned up.

After all that he had put her through, Lynette could still find it in her to talk about John Bacon as if she loved him and he loved her, choosing to remember that side of him rather than . . . There was fat chance of little Miss Glasby understanding *that*. Her only regret would be that she wasn't going to be able to trumpet all of this from the front page, with her name prominently attached to it, of course. And that would be tame compared to what the gutter press would have done to Patricia and Lynette.

Not to mention what they would say about a certain Bill Davenport. His reputation, his whole career, founded on a lie. They still might, if it all came out.

What a legacy John Bacon had left. Davenport's memory of him was hazy, a thick-set, gormless-looking man in his thirties or forties, staying in the background behind the teenaged Lynette. And no wonder if he was hiding himself. God only knows what responsibility he bore for warping Leonie Dellar's mind. Maybe if she had never been unlucky enough to have met him, Leonie would have grown up a normal girl. She could now be happily clucking over her grandchildren in some small Norfolk town. Jarmy might never have done anything without Dellar as his accomplice, and those little children would have been spared.

Not to mention Lynette and Patricia, two frightened women growing old together in that sad little house, terrified that their secret – *his* wrongdoings – would come back to haunt them, even all these years later. 'The evil that men do lives on after them.' Too true. Too bloody true.

Compared with that, any concerns he had for himself were pretty unimportant. But one thing everyone knew about Bill Davenport was that he was a fighter, and even if all that was at stake had been his own reputation, he'd be doing everything he could to protect it.

Well, he had done his best, and no more could any man do. (Who the hell was it who said that? He really was starting to feel tired again.) He would have a quiet dinner with Adam and Rita Mullins tonight. All it needed was a few words in Adam's ear and the last piece would be in place. A good dose of flattery and a little surprise for young Wonder Woman tomorrow, then home to the cats and they could all get on with the rest of their lives. And if his didn't involve a certain Miss Glasby for a while, so much the better.

As he took another deep drag he saw Glasby come hurtling in from the direction of the hotel garage and charge up the stairs, pale as a sheet. Maybe this was some sort of sign of a guilty conscience after all?

If so, there was no trace of it a few minutes later. No sooner had she joined him at his table than she was off again.

'It's too much of a coincidence, isn't it?' He didn't know what she was talking about, and he didn't think that he wanted to find out.

'What I mean is, I – I mean, *we* – found the connection, between Jarmy and Dellar and the Bacons. But it's *too* much of a connection now. Of all the children in Norfolk they could have picked on, they just happen to kill the daughter of the man who abused her. It's beyond belief.'

He had carefully constructed a prize for her and it would be ready for presentation in the morning, shiny and gift-wrapped. All he had to do was hold her off until then. But she really was being a pain in the neck.

'You see, Bill, the only thing that would fit is, could they have done it out of revenge? You know, John Bacon raped Leonie, so she came back and took his daughter from him. But I don't see how that fits with the other children they took, not at all. It all sounds a bit far-fetched. What do you think?'

It was too much for Davenport.

'Jesus Christ!' He must have spoken louder than he'd intended. That miserable looking girl at the table in front of them was looking round again with her equally po-faced friends. 'Haven't you had enough for one day? If anything beggars belief it's what we just put that poor woman through. You have to know when to stop, for crying out loud!'

He controlled himself with an effort. 'Look, Alison. I'm sorry. This has been a big strain on both of us. I'm sure you've got friends to see, and I'm having dinner at the Mullins'. When you stop to think about it, you'll realize what a great job you've done. Let's talk about it tomorrow, after breakfast. Ten thirty, say? Go out, have a good time, relax. You deserve it, really you do.'

He gulped down the rest of his scotch and left without even offering to buy her a drink. If he had looked back, he would have seen that she had a thoughtful look on her face. Yes, Alison Glasby was looking thoughtful, and very determined indeed.

Up in her room she sat down on the edge of the bed, still thinking.

And then – John Redgrave! Oh hell, she was supposed to be going out with him, and she hadn't even called him! She grabbed her phone.

'John, hi! Listen, I'm so sorry, I really am. You know we were supposed to see each other this evening?'

'*Supposed* to? You mean you can't make it tonight either?' He sounded annoyed.

'I can't John, no. I'm sorry, honestly. You see, I'm in Norwich, with Bill Davenport. There were some more developments on the Dellar story, after I left you yesterday, and he asked me to come up here with him to work on it today. You see . . .' She tailed off, unsure what to say for the best.

There was a pause. 'Alison, you don't have to give me any reasons. You don't owe me anything for yesterday, really you don't. I offered you a lift down to Broadmoor, and you accepted, and that's it. If you don't want to go out with me again, you don't have to. End of, you know?'

'But John . . .' she started, and then, unaccountably, was in floods of tears. Before she knew it, she was explaining it all to him: John Bacon's ice cream round, old Mr Harvey telling them that Bacon was a paedophile, Bacon abusing Lynette, and Leonie, and that being the connection between them, and more besides.

'You're doing everything right, Alison. And you're spot on, you are going to have another crack at Lynette, she's obviously still holding back on you. The best thing would be if you could work something out on those dates though, first. Anyway, you seriously need to give yourself a break for tonight. Isn't there someone you can go and see, and just take the rest of the day off?'

Thank God he was being nice to her again. 'I didn't tell you yet, but I had the oddest coincidence earlier, I bumped into this guy I used to go out with, from uni. So I said that I might have a drink with him.'

'You did say that this guy, he's an *ex*-boyfriend, right?' Redgrave sounded a bit less happy again, but this time Glasby was, if anything, rather pleased about it.

'Very definitely ex. I promise,' she replied.

'OK, well you go and unwind a bit, and call me any time you want, and we'll see each other as soon as we can.'

The line went dead and she lay for a moment curled on the bed, head in hands. At least there was one person who understood her and realized that she was doing her best. She wasn't feeling well, she'd hadn't slept properly in days and everyone was pissed off with her: Bill, Lynette, Mike Marshall . . .

But it wasn't really in Glasby's nature to indulge in anything for long, including self-pity, and after a few moments the determined look of earlier returned to her face. 'Why not?' she asked herself, and didn't find any answer. Probably nothing would come of it, but everyone seemed to agree about one thing, anyway. She did deserve an evening off.

With a loud sigh she sat up and reached for her phone again. 'Lester? Hi. It looks like I am free tonight, after all . . . No, I'm not that great, to be honest. I didn't realize it was so obvious, though. People keep shouting at me all day, and my head's killing me . . . No, I'd love to see you, really. I've probably just been trying to do too much, but I'll be fine, I just need to chill out a bit. Fifteen minutes? OK, cool.'

The table which Davenport had been sitting at was still free when Glasby went back downstairs. It was so typical of Lester to be late (although to be fair, she was a bit early). She'd had time for a quick change of clothes and freshened herself up a bit and so, to her surprise, had he. He looked like he'd just shaved and he was positively chic in a grey round-neck jumper under a charcoal suit. And he'd been spot on time after all! *And* he'd insisted on getting the drinks, which he was just bringing over now.

'Thanks, Lester.' Redgrave was right, it was exactly what she needed. But before she relaxed too much, there was just one more thing.

'You seem to know half of Norwich, Lester. I don't suppose you know anyone on the *EDN*?'

'I really can't stay, baby, it's cold outside . . .'

'You a Catatonia fan, then?' asked the taxi driver.

'Catatonia?'

'That song. That's Cerys, and that old geezer, Jones, Tom Jones.'

Those few of Davenport's brain cells which were currently functioning struggled to work out what the man was talking about. Song – he'd been singing. Catatonia? God knows what that was supposed to mean. But Tom Jones, he was a singer. He must have done the song – ruined it, probably.

'That song was by Johnny Mercer, originally. A long time ago. You wouldn't remember.'

'When was he, eighties or something?'

Davenport thought about replying but subsided instead into loud hiccups which he tried to disguise as coughs.

The taxi driver gave him a hard look in the rear-view mirror. There were quite enough young lads – and girls – puking up on a Saturday night, without him having this old fart doing it in the back of his car. Better get rid of him quick. He put his foot down, raced round the bend into the evocatively named Tombland, past the flint-covered archways to Cathedral Close and screeched to a halt outside the White Hart.

'All right, steady on! No need to scare the horses! Who'd you think you are, Stirling Moss?' The cab driver didn't have a clue what he was talking about and didn't much care. Stupid old fool should have known better at his age. He wound down the window to get the smell of whisky and fags out of the car.

Davenport lurched in through the hotel lobby and up the big oak staircase. After a lot of fumbling he found the room key – why did jackets always have so many pockets? – and sat down heavily on the side of the bed.

It had been a corker of an evening. Adam was a super chap. You could even forgive him for being a bit of a Tory, he had no side to him at all. As Rita said, becoming a councillor certainly seemed to be keeping him young. And her duck à l'orange! It was the best meal he'd had since . . . well, since Lisbeth's pheasant the other day. She'd put the Claverdon to shame, he'd told her, and he meant it, too.

When they'd found out that it was his first day as a retired gent, Adam had absolutely insisted that they toast it properly with Cragganmore, twenty-odd years old, from Speyside. It had a bit more peat in it than he usually had a taste for, but once you got used to the smokiness, it slipped down beautifully. Maybe they'd had one or two more than was strictly necessary, mind you. What with the sherry before dinner, and then the Bordeaux, and the scotch he'd had at the hotel – *and* the pint and a half at lunchtime. He was going to have a sore head in the morning, all right.

Pulling himself wearily to his feet, he went to draw the curtains. His room looked over the hotel car park and glancing down he saw Glasby's car. She'd parked it on its own, away from all the others, which was quite appropriate really. Talk about the cat that walked by itself. (Not like his pair, who you could bet would be doing their impersonation of the beast with two tails by now, rolled into a single ball of black and white fur.)

She was a strange one, and no two ways about it. You couldn't imagine her having much of a social life, could you? There was nothing wrong with being keen on the job, of course, but she was . . . he searched for the right word. *Driven*, that was it. You could imagine a girl like that as a Red, explaining very logically to some poor sod exactly why he needed to be sent to the camps for re-education. For the greater good, and quite incidentally her own career, of course.

He caught sight of his reflection in the glass of the sash window. 'You're getting old,' he told himself. 'Old and soft. Forty years ago, you'd have been competing with her, and bloody well winning, as well.' He smiled at his own image, a silly old boy with a belly full of booze. He pulled the curtains closed and dumped his jacket on the back of the chair.

There would be time enough in the morning to worry about Miss Alison Glasby.

It had been an awesome evening. Lester was just great, so not like he used to be. He was such a laugh and he knew such weird people. Like those poets who lived in a commune called Elysium, because it was the land of the beloved in Greek myth, except that they all seemed to hate each others' guts. And there was a junkie called Money who painted tourists' portraits on to real five- and ten-pound notes.

When they were at university Lester had been very politically right on, which impressed her at the time and intimidated her a bit as well. But now he was working with all these super correct left-wing types – he claimed that there really was a disabled lesbian mothers' writing group – and all he did was take the piss out of them.

He told her that he'd started writing a new song for her, and sung her the opening lines. 'Walked down the street, and who did I meet? The long lost love that I'd been dreaming of.' Some lads on the next table heard it and cheered and she went a bit pink.

Another change from the old Lester: he was as good as his word. His mate (who introduced himself as Lucky but turned out to be called Paul) turned up as promised, and he was the business. A film reviewer and arts critic on the *Eastern Daily News*, he'd driven them up to his office and showed her how to access the newspaper's archives. They were still on microfiche, but she knew that what she was after would have been front page news, and she pretty much knew the date too, so finding it was no big deal.

January 1970. First of all the 28th. Nothing. She started working back. On the 23rd, there was a huge banner headline: 'At Last, The Truth', and underneath it in only slightly smaller type, 'Dellar Confesses: We Killed Them'. Then, on the 21st, she found it. 'Tragedy on the Roads. Norfolk Children in Horror Crash'. Three children had been killed after a school bus skidded off a flooded road outside Stalham, the afternoon before. The driver was on the critical list in the Norfolk and Norwich Hospital. There was a photo of the bus, on its side in a ditch.

Glasby sat back in the office chair, her eyes closed, seeing everything. It was like a map with all the place names appearing, one by one at her command. Jarmy: 'We all used him.' Lynette: 'We don't want no book.' *Then*, the visit to see Dellar. And *then*, Dellar's carefully phrased confession: 'We killed them, all four.' And not a single photo of John Bacon, anywhere in the house.

Lynette had lied to her again. And not just Lynette. How much did Davenport know? 'We'll work as a team,' he'd said. Yeah, right! Well, he wasn't going to stop her now. She needed one last conversation with Lynette – on the record this time, *her* rules for a change – and she was done. And if Davenport didn't like it, well that was tough, wasn't it?

'Ali. Like, hello! What are you, lost in space? What the hell have you found, anyway?'

She was bursting to tell them, but they'd know soon enough. 'Sorry, Lester, I was just thinking about something. Lucky, you're a star. And Lester, you're . . . a whole solar system. Let me buy you both a drink.'

They never did quite make it to a restaurant, but they seemed to cover most of the rest of Norwich: an old pub down by the river which she used to go to underage; a bar which she didn't know where some friends of Lester were playing jazz; one other bar or maybe more, she couldn't remember very well; then a party where she had been dancing (and when did she last do that?) and someone was fire-eating out of the sitting room window.

And finally, somehow, she was back at Lester's flat and it was just the two of them, and suddenly she was quite sober, so that when he asked if she had any condoms she told him very sharply that there was no way they'd be needing them, and he told her that she should spend the night there anyway, and she had, with them holding each other like . . . Well, if it hadn't have been for her promise to Redgrave, it might just have felt like long-lost lovers.

Glasby had still remembered to set the alarm on her phone. It was dark when she jumped out of Lester's not very comfortable bed and when she whispered goodbye he didn't even stir. She felt guilty as she crept back into the hotel, light-headed from too much drink and excitement and not enough food or sleep, but no one saw her. It took her a while to clear her head, with the help of a cup of tea made with a little carton of UHT milk and some shortbread biscuits, provided, so she read on the card, as a complimentary in-room offering by the hotel to its guests.

But she wanted to catch Lynette before she went out to see her mother or anything, so well before nine o'clock Glasby was on her way.

Davenport had been right about one thing: he had a real thumper of a hangover. Ten on the Richter scale. A dry throat (oh God, he'd smoked the best part of a packet of fags), a filthy headache, the works. He scrabbled around for his watch. It was only eight thirty, too damned early.

He closed his eyes and tried to get back to sleep, but it was hopeless. He started to think that he might as well make the best of it, get up and have a leisurely breakfast. The thought of a huge pot of tea made his mind up. His mouth tasted like a pub ashtray. He swung his legs out from the bedclothes and carefully found his feet.

Outside he heard the sound of a car revving up. Someone was up and about pretty sharpish for a Sunday. He peered out into a gloomy November morning. It was barely any lighter with the curtains open than when they were closed. Looking down, he saw the tail lights of a car as it turned out of the hotel car park. Glasby! Her car was missing.

He groaned. What the hell was she up to now? Of course it was always possible that she was going out for breakfast. Even if her parents didn't live in Norwich any more, she could be seeing an aunt or an uncle, or maybe some cousins her own age or old friends.

Or getting her hang-glider out, ready to join the squadron

of pigs that were about to begin flying past the window. She was up to something, sneaking out early like that. He hadn't been a reporter for close on fifty years without having a pretty advanced nose for trouble and it was twitching right now, like a bloodhound on the trail.

He tried her phone: there was no answer. Bloody irritating girl!

*The child was frightened, lying in the dark, listening –
but what was it? Quick, let's get under the sheet.
Trembling, but it was a hot summer night, so sweating
as well. What was that noise? Please God, take me in
your care, keep me safe and hear my prayer. Not again
not again not again not again. If I close my eyes it will
go away. If I promise to be good nothing will happen.
It can't. It can't. He's there! Outside the door. Why won't
someone help me? It's not my fault, I didn't do anything
wrong. Please! Please don't let him touch me. I've got
to find somewhere to hide, somewhere he can't get me.
If I'm really quiet I could get out of the window and he
won't hear nothing. Sindy, you come with me and we'll
tiptoe like Lynette learned us and then we'll push it open
and—*

Nineteen

'What are you doing here?'

Glasby hadn't expected anything better. 'There's something else that we need to discuss,' she replied, more confidently than she felt. 'It would be better if we did it inside.'

'Where's Bill?' Lynette demanded, not making any move to invite her in. 'He told me that there weren't going to be no more, once we'd done yesterday.' Her hands were covered in flour and she was wearing a striped blue apron.

'Lynette, there's some things that I don't understand from what you said yesterday. What you and Bill said, in fact. I'd like us to have a conversation, just the two of us, and we can straighten everything out. It shouldn't take too long. OK?'

This time she put a hand on the older woman's arm, motioning her into the hallway behind her. Still Lynette did not move, although she did nothing to shake Glasby's hand off her either.

'It would be better if we weren't talking in front of your neighbours, don't you think?' Recreation Road was deserted at this hour on a Sunday morning, but nonetheless this seemed to have the effect that Glasby was hoping for.

'All right then,' Lynette said, ungraciously, turning on her heels and leaving Glasby to follow her down the hall and into the kitchen.

'I'm making a cake for Mum and the nurses. I haven't got long, so say what it is you want to say.' She stood leaning against the wooden work surface, arms folded, jaw thrust forwards. Glasby stood across from her, her back against the washing machine on which stood a large pile of towels and sheets.

'OK, thanks.' She needed a glass of water but it didn't seem like a good idea to ask for one. 'I want to try to keep things in order, so let's start with when Bill told you that he was going to write his book. You weren't happy about it, were you?'

Lynette seemed to relax slightly, her arms dropping to her sides, wiping some of the flour on to her apron. 'Of course I weren't happy. Mum weren't either. People like you, you don't never stop to think about people like us. We're just *stories*, aren't we, something to put in your newspapers so everyone's got something to read about in the morning. They were like bloody vultures, them journalists, and I didn't know anything about Bill then, so I thought he'd be just the same. All we wanted was for everyone to leave us alone, but they wouldn't do it then, and you won't do it now, will you?'

She glared accusingly at Glasby, who was determined not to be intimidated.

'So Bill persuaded you that he would behave responsibly, then? Not take advantage of you, I mean?'

'Yes. What's it to you, anyway? You can ask him about it yourself, can't you?' Almost absentmindedly Lynette picked up something off the work surface and fidgeted with it from hand to hand. Glasby saw that it was a small knife. She swallowed, her mouth even drier now, but carried on.

'So you decided that you could trust Bill, and that's why you asked him to help get you in to see Dellar?'

'Yes.' Lynette sounded suspicious.

'It wasn't long after he'd told you about the book, that you asked him to help you, was it? So you must have decided very quickly that you could trust him.'

'I don't remember how long that was. But I suppose you're right, it wasn't that long. He ain't never given me no reason to regret trusting him, though. He's an honest man, Bill, and a good man too, and I won't hear different from you.' She glared again, the knife gripped in her right hand.

Glasby told herself that there was nothing to be frightened about. Lynette wasn't going to attack her and even if she did Glasby was half her age and several inches taller.

'Bill told you that he was writing the book on the 6th of January. And Dellar confessed on the 22nd. So in between those times, you went to see her.'

'No, I didn't. Me and Bill told you yesterday, it wasn't like that. I went to see her in the prison *after* she confessed, to ask her if she'd help us, once she'd said that she'd done the murders.'

'Oh yes,' said Glasby. 'You said that you couldn't remember

the dates. But you remembered the weather that day, because it was really terrible, and there was that awful coach accident. That's right, isn't it?'

Lynette said nothing, staring at her even more suspiciously.

'I checked yesterday. That accident happened on the 20th of January, not the 27th. It was in the *Eastern Daily News*, I looked. You went to see Dellar, and then two days later she confessed. You didn't decide that you wanted to appeal for her help because she'd confessed; she confessed because of what it was that you said to her.'

'I don't know what you're on about. I'm sick of you, getting on to me like this!' Lynette was holding the knife out in front of her now like a weapon.

Undaunted, Glasby continued. 'You said that you gave Leonie the photo to ask for her help. You thought that she would agree to help you, because of what your father had done to her, because he abused both of you. So you gave her the photo, and she took it, and then she sewed it into a cushion, and kept it until the day she died. And when she was dying the last thing she did was try to reach it. But according to you, she didn't help you at all. You told me that she never said a word to you about what they'd done with Donna.'

'You just tell me straight what you're bloody saying!' Lynette was shouting, her face livid with anger. Glancing to her left, Glasby mentally measured out the distance to the front door, thankful that she not Lynette was standing by the entrance to the kitchen.

She tried to sound calm but she could hear her voice echoing round the room as if someone else was talking, not her. 'Leonie didn't tell you where Donna's body was, because she didn't know. You went to see her as soon as you found out that Bill was writing his book, because you were scared, scared about what he might find out. Leonie didn't know where Donna's body was because she didn't kill her. And neither did Jarmy. You gave her the photo to persuade her to confess. You asked her to cover up what really happened. And that's exactly what she did.'

There was a terrible silence. Lynette's head dropped, all the strength seemingly drained from her shoulders. Glasby pressed on relentlessly, speaking quietly again now, and steadily.

'Who killed your sister, Lynette? Who were you covering up for?'

The knife clattered against the tiled kitchen floor. Lynette made as if to pick it up, bending over slightly, but then straightened and with a wordless scream threw herself across the kitchen at Glasby, hands outstretched, strong fingers reaching for her throat, tightening around her neck.

Davenport crashed in through the door at improbable speed for a man of his age. 'Lynette, no! That isn't the right way!' He pulled at Lynette's wrists, prising her fingers off Glasby's neck, angry red marks left behind them. The younger woman collapsed lifeless on to the cold kitchen floor.

When Glasby came to she was lying on her side on a small single bed. Her head ached like hell and so did her neck. She prodded at it experimentally with her fingers. It felt bruised and sore. Her shoulder hurt as well, though she wasn't sure why.

She could hear voices, one of which she recognized as Davenport's. There was a distant memory of someone bending over her, which must have been him. She could remember Lynette jumping at her, all too vividly. Presumably she was in no danger now?

Bending forward painfully she looked around. She was certainly still in the Bacons' house but not in a room that she had been in before. There was the same cord carpet as in the sitting room and not much furniture. Just the bed, an upright wooden chair next to it on which were hung her jacket and bag, a dark wooden wardrobe and, at the end of the bed, a white painted chest of drawers.

On top was a small doll wearing a white dress. 'They found her Sindy, down by the stream.' This must be Donna's room and that was her doll. Glasby shivered. She was starting to feel sick.

Her phone rang. She found it in her bag. 'Alison? This is Paul, Paul Lewis from the *Chronicle*. Can you talk?'

Talk? Why would she want to talk to him? Things had moved on so far since she'd set him up and he didn't even realize it. It was funny, so funny that she had to stop herself from laughing.

'Hello?'

She realized that he was waiting for her to answer. 'No, no, I can't talk. Sorry.'

He sounded impatient. 'Alison, this won't wait, you know.

It's in your own interest, you know, we really need to have a conversation today.'

'I'm sorry, no,' was all that she could manage.

'Alison, I'm a busy man. There's no way—'

'I said, no!' she shouted at him. 'No! Leave me alone!' She hit the red button on the phone and dropped it on the floor.

Davenport walked in looking at her curiously. 'Alison! It's good to hear you up and about again. You gave me a bit of a fright, you know. Look, Lynette's absolutely mortified, she's so sorry, and she's made you a nice cup of tea to get you back on your feet.'

He held out a large mug of steaming brown liquid. The sickly smell reached Glasby, quickly followed by a wave of nausea as she threw up, all over the horrid brown carpet.

They were back in the sitting room, all three of them in their now customary places. Lynette had made Glasby some dry toast which she'd finished now, slowly sipping at a large glass of tap water. Her neck and shoulder still hurt and she seemed to have fallen on her hand, but the aspirin were helping and her head felt clear again now.

Lynette had apologized so profusely that it was embarrassing, especially as Glasby still had some tough talking to do, and had fussed over her shoulder as well, bruised from where she had fallen on to the kitchen floor. But it really was nothing much to worry about.

'Lynette, and Bill, I know that things happened a bit differently from what you told me yesterday. Dellar said that she murdered Donna but only because of what you said to her, Lynette, and that was why Jarmy was so keen to see you, Bill. He was trying to understand why Leonie had chosen to confess to something which he knew she hadn't done.'

Neither said a word so she kept going. 'And so was I, until I realized that she'd made her confession right after you went to see her. What did you tell her, Lynette, to persuade her to say what she did?'

Still neither she nor Davenport responded, and nor would either of them look at her.

'Lynette! You know who killed your sister and you told Leonie, to persuade her to help you, didn't you? Who were you covering up for?'

Yet more silence. This was it; her last try. 'Why aren't there any pictures of your father in the house, Lynette? He killed Donna, didn't he? You covered up for him, after he killed his own daughter. You knew he did, and so did your mother.'

'You leave Mum out of this! You say what you want to me but don't you go messing with Mum!' Lynette's eyes were blazing and Glasby was starting to worry again.

So apparently was Davenport. 'No one's going to involve Patricia, Lynette, don't worry,' he said quickly.

'Don't worry? I done nothing but worry, ever since *she* walked in through that door. You keep telling me I don't have to worry, and she keeps picking away, nosing into what's not her business, and messing with I don't know what and . . .' She burst into loud sobs, head buried in her chest, shoulders heaving.

'Lynette—' began Davenport, rising from his armchair across the room from her.

'No!' she shouted. He sat down again fast. 'You –' turning to Glasby, her face now streaked with tears – 'you keep going on that you want to know what happened. I'm going to tell you and then I don't ever want to see you again.'

Glasby wished that she'd had a chance to make sure that her phone was recording all this.

'That night,' Lynette began, face to the floor again, 'I wasn't feeling right. It was –' she stopped, glancing at Davenport who was looking away from her, and continued – 'it was my time of the month, and I went to bed early, after tea. I don't know what happened. All I know is, I was asleep and then Mum was making all this noise, screaming and shouting at Dad outside my door, and I run out and Dad had Donna in his arms and her eyes were open but she had all blood on her head and she wasn't alive, she was dead. Her eyes, they were staring right at me. It was horrible.'

None of the three people in the room were looking at each other. Glasby became very conscious of the sound of her own breathing. Lynette paused as if to gather strength, and continued.

'Then Dad ran into his and Mum's room and he come out still holding Donna but he'd covered her with this old blanket. It was blue and it had holes in it and one of her fingers was poking through one of them. And he took her outside and he had this old van for some job he was doing and I heard him go off in it, and then he come back about an hour or something afterwards and he didn't have her no more.

'And when he was gone, Mum was in her room crying, on the bed, and I went into Donna's room and I saw that the window was open wide, and I went to close it and I looked outside and I saw her Sindy, lying on the floor outside the window. So I leant right out and picked her up and put her on Donna's bed.

'When Dad came back I was waiting for him and I asked him what had happened and he swore to me that he never touched her or anything, that it was just an accident, Donna trying to climb out the window and him stopping her, but he kept saying that the coppers'd never listen to no one like him and he'd be put away for ever and it'd kill Mum. He kept looking at me, for help.

'So I made him and Mum sit down and I told them that none of us had seen Donna since tea and that was what we all had to say. I asked Dad what he'd done with her and all he said was, she was somewhere safe and I didn't want to know.

'The next day he was like one of them zombies and Mum couldn't hardly talk. I couldn't sleep so I was up as soon as it was light and I took Sindy and I put her down by the stream. And that's when I saw that she had this blood on her little dress and I wanted to wash it off, but I didn't, of course. And then I called the coppers and I told them Donna had gone and all these police came round, loads of 'em, and they found Sindy and afterwards they gave her back to me. And it was only then that I could clean her up.'

'But—' Glasby started, but Lynette rounded on her.

'Don't you start none of your questions again. All the rest, it was like you been saying. It was me that the police talked to, and they told me that it must have been the same person that took Donna as took them other poor little kids, and then Dellar and Jarmy were on trial and they didn't say nothing. Then Dad died, all of a sudden, and Mum threw out all their wedding photos, but she never said nothing to me and I never have to her. She's heard it told so often now, I reckon she thinks herself that it was Dellar what killed Donna.

'But I was scared the whole time that Dellar or Jarmy would

say something and it'd all come out what had happened and we'd all go to jail. Especially when Bill said that about him writing his book. So I went to ask Dellar if she would help Mum and me, being as Dad was dead anyway and whatever happened that wasn't my fault or Mum's, and Dellar was in for life for them other children anyway. And that's why I gave her the picture, just like I told you before, I just found it when I was waiting for Mr Mullins and her. And she said she'd think about it and she was crying and so was I and she kissed me before I went. Then afterwards, later, she saw Bill and he phoned me after to tell me what had happened, that she'd confessed that they'd killed Donna.' Lynette paused and Glasby waited, but she had reached the end.

Davenport cleared his throat as if he was about to speak but Glasby jumped in first.

'You said that you haven't talked to your mother about what happened, but you must have asked her if she knows where Donna is, what your father did with her?'

'I asked her once, after Dad died, but she didn't tell me nothing,' replied Lynette in a sullen monotone.

'She didn't tell you? You mean she didn't know, or she didn't want to tell you?'

'I told you, she didn't tell me *nothing*. Mum gets in such a state about Donna. She don't know what's going on, always. Sometimes when she's not well, she gets all confused, and she calls me Donna like she thinks Donna's still alive. She doesn't know nothing about nothing and she doesn't need to. Except now you, you're going to put it all in your newspaper, and it'll all be everywhere, and me and Mum, what are they going to do to us . . . ?'

She was crying again, and this time Davenport was on his feet and taking control again.

'Alison, I think that we've heard everything now, don't you agree?'

This time Glasby was as keen as he was to get away.

'OK, then. Alison, could you please give me two minutes with Lynette?'

Surprised and trying hard not to be suspicious, Glasby jumped up and left the sitting room. She wandered down the hall and stood in the doorway to what had been the little girl's room. What had really happened in here? A child abuser with a pretty little daughter, just about the same age as his other daughter had been when he started to attack her? Or maybe he'd been too frightened of Lynette to do anything to Donna and it really was just a tragic accident.

She saw the Sindy doll across the room and walked over to pick her up. 'You know, don't you?' she said. The little doll looked back up at her with wide, sightless eyes. Her white dress was immaculate, spotless. Glasby looked round at the patch near the bed where Lynette had cleaned up after her, the carpet starting to dry. Davenport was calling her from the other room.

'We're not printing that,' he told her. She was sitting on a wooden bench, the pub behind her and the river curving round in front, a beautiful spot in the weak winter sun. Davenport was standing over her, his arms crossed, his voice hard.

'Think of the misery it would cause. The one thing that Patricia Bacon has clung on for all these years is being a victim. Are you prepared to take that away from her? Imagine it, the locals will be blaming her for not stopping her bastard of a husband molesting their kids, and covering up for him afterwards as well. She and Lynette both told lies to the police, they could still be prosecuted. And that's if anyone believes them, that they didn't kill the poor girl themselves. After all, John Bacon's not around to be questioned, is he?'

Glasby was lost for words. 'But Bill, that's not . . . right! You see—'

'Right?' he interrupted. 'Alison, listen. The older you get, the harder it seems to get to decide what's right and what isn't. Sometimes it doesn't seem to matter very much at all any more. What's fair, what's decent, what's kind; those sorts of things are what's worth caring about.'

'Bill, I'm sorry, but you're not being fair to me. You said that we were going to be a team, but we weren't, you just kept lying to me. You knew Lynette had gone to see Leonie before she confessed but you made out that it was the other way round, so you knew all along that she was asking Leonie to cover up, or you must have guessed anyway. Either that or they really did all use you then. Which was it, Bill? Tell me the truth.'

'You've heard the truth, from Lynette. You were determined to get it and you did. You succeeded. What I knew about or didn't know doesn't matter much, does it? What matters now is what we do next. And I'm telling you. We're not publishing it. End of story.'

Glasby was shaking her head, forgetting how much her neck hurt. 'You keep saying that we have to protect the Bacons, but it's your own reputation that you care about. You missed the biggest story of the lot and I've got it. It's my turn now and I'm going to publish!'

She was bright red in the face but as determined as she had ever been in her life. Davenport stared at her, took a deep breath and sat down next to her. His voice was much quieter now, as if he was sorry for her.

'OK, Alison, just stop and think for a moment. You've been very smart to get this far, really you have, but if you think that I missed out on something, well, I think you've missed something yourself. You read all my notes, didn't you? All the interviews with Lynette?'

'You know I did. So what?'

'All those hours of conversations, I expect you thought that a lot of it was boring, right?' Glasby just looked at him. She had no idea what was coming next.

'So what about when I asked Lynette about what happened to Donna?'

'But you never did ask her – what do you mean, Bill?'

'If I had no idea what was going on, if I was just being *used* by everyone like you think, don't you think that I might have asked her some questions? When she asked me to get her in to the prison? After she'd seen Dellar? After Dellar decided to confess to me, two days later? You think that it never occurred to me what was going on, hmmm?

'Alison, you haven't got a story. You've no evidence, nothing at all. All you've got is the photo, and who's going to confirm where you came by that? Your prison officer certainly won't. He'd lose his job and his pension with it. Lynette won't, you can be sure of that. And I won't. You can't prove that Lynette saw Leonie, either. Adam Mullins won't help you and the governor's long dead. And I don't see Jarmy signing affidavits either, or anyone believing him if he did.'

She just about managed not to smile as she played her trump card. 'I've got it all recorded, Bill. Everything that Lynette was saying just now, my phone was set to record.'

Now, to her surprise, it was him that was smiling. For a few seconds, they just looked at each other, almost a grin on his face, a look of complete incomprehension on hers.

'Why are you smiling like that, Bill? I really do have it recorded.'

'I bet you do,' he replied, something like admiration in his voice, 'I bet you do.'

He sat down beside her. 'OK, Alison, you win. You've got your story, if that's what you want. I tried to stop you, but you beat me. You can write it up, it'll be big, really big, and that's one option you have. I'm going to give you another one, and you will choose. I've underestimated you right from the start, but now you can make your choice and if you're the person I think you are, you'll make the right one.'

'What do you mean, Bill? What choice am I supposed to be making?' Glasby was starting to feel a bit suspicious again. What was he up to now?

'I'll explain in a moment. Before I get to that, I want to tell you what happened, my point of view. And you can record that as well if you want, I mean it. But first, I'd just like to know something from you. For my own satisfaction. Paul Lewis – how did all that happen? You called him yourself, didn't you?'

She hesitated, but this time the truth seemed like her only option. 'I did, yes. Anonymously, I mean. I told him a bit about the story, not enough for him to have anything he could use, and I gave him my details. I put a different voice on, and I'm pretty sure that I fooled him as well.'

If she had been concerned at Davenport's reaction she needn't have been. He shook his head as if in wonder and burst out laughing.

'You, Alison, you're quite a girl, you really are.' She looked down, hoping desperately that he wouldn't see the burning red glow that had spread from her hairline to her shoulders.

Then his voice was serious again. 'It was a terrible thing, you know, Alison. Four little children, gone. Every one of them, their whole future, everything they might have achieved, all the other lives that they touched and all those that they could have been a part of. A catastrophe for all the families. But think of Patricia, and most of all think about Lynette, forced to cover up for that evil man, just like she'd been covering up for him ever since she was a tiny child, and she still has to do it, even today.

'It was obvious that there was something wrong about Donna Bacon's death. The more I got to know Lynette, the more it was clear that she knew something. And the more I had the feeling that if I wanted to know what it was, if I was patient, she'd tell me herself.

'So when she asked me to get her in to see Leonie, I had a feeling something was up. I didn't know what, until the famous confession, a couple of days later. Then it was obvious – to me at the time, I mean. How you've pieced it together after all these years is nothing short of a miracle.'

He looked over at her and smiled again.

'So I knew that Dellar had confessed because of something that Lynette had said to her. And so did Adam Mullins, by the way. After that, little by little, she decided that she trusted me, and she told me about . . . about that bastard that she calls "Dad".'

He stopped, but Glasby guessed correctly that this was just a pause to gather his thoughts again.

'I've never known the whole story before, mind you. And although the last thing I want in this world is to see Lynette suffering, I have to admit that I'm enough of a newsman to be glad that I've heard it all now.'

Glasby seized her chance. 'But surely Bill, to be a journalist, you've got to not just *hear* the truth, you've got to write it too?'

Now he was on his feet. 'The truth? What's that got to do with journalism? That load of baloney that got young Daniels' name on the front page, that's journalism! They're called "stories", remember, that's what we get paid to write.

'You, Alison, you are going to have a long and very successful career. But I want you always to remember one thing. Murder isn't just a story. Murder is ugly and brutal and real. If that friend of yours at Scotland Yard is worth half of you, he'll tell you just the same. Every time he appears, every time people like us appear, with our mobile phones and our notepads and our deadlines, someone's life has been taken and everyone else's lives are in pieces. People . . . people like Lynette Bacon.'

He stopped, swallowed hard, and took a breath. He looked down and to his surprise saw that Glasby's eyes were filling with tears. She blinked them back hastily, so he continued.

'That's enough of speeches from me. I never was very good

at them, and that's two in two days now! I told you that I had
another option for you. Here it is.'

Davenport was holding a piece of paper out to her.

'You'd have to write it up your own way of course, but I
expect that Ellington will decide that dating agencies can wait
for a bit once he hears about it.'

She was bewildered. What was he going on about?

'I'm sorry Bill, I . . . what do you mean?'

He grinned at her. 'Blow your nose, wipe your face and
read this.' Glasby found some tissues in her bag and did as
he had told her.

It was a single piece of A4 which looked like it had been
folded and unfolded more than once. Both sides had been written
on, in what Glasby immediately recognized as Bill Davenport's
hand:

EXCLUSIVE: I LOOKED INTO THE EYES
OF MY SISTER'S KILLER
Victim's Teenaged Sister in Secret Prison
Visit to Leonie Dellar
By Alison Glasby
With further reporting from Bill Davenport

Lynette Bacon: 'Mum and I were so desperate to know
what they'd done with our little Donna, I'd have done
anything. So I went secretly to see Leonie Dellar, straight
away after she confessed to the murder.

'Mr Mullins, he was in charge of the murder police,
and he helped me. He and the prison governor were the
only ones who knew. Not even Mum knew I'd done it,
not until now.

'I begged Dellar to help us. She said that Jarmy had
taken Donna's body and she didn't know what he'd
done with it. I believe her, I think she was telling the
truth. I looked right into her eyes and she looked at
mine. I'd have known if she was lying, I'm sure of
that.

'It was January 1970, just a few months after they
took my sister. I was only nineteen. It was the hardest
thing I've ever done in my life. To sit in the same room
as Dellar, just her and me, knowing what they'd done to

Donna and those other poor little kids. But I had to do it, for Donna and for Mum.

'No one can understand the pain that Mum and I go through. There's not a day that we don't think about Donna and what they did with her. If it's true that Jarmy knows where she is, even now he could tell us and save us from more suffering.'

Adam Mullins: 'Of course it wasn't a normal request. But that case touched all of us, all the police that were involved. It was the toughest case any of us ever worked on, before or since. Anything that we could have done for the family, anything at all, well, of course I wanted to help her.

'Lynette Bacon was only a young girl at the time. It wasn't just her sister's murder, either. Her father died, right in the middle of Jarmy and Dellar's trial. The stress that victims' families go through, it's shocking how easily people forget that.

'Lynette was one of the bravest people I've ever known, to do a thing like that for her sister.

'It was important to keep it out of the press. They would have been all over it, of course. The only other person who knew, besides Dellar herself, of course, was the governor. He's long since passed away.

'We dressed her up in a WPC's uniform and that's how she went into the prison, just her and me. No one knew anything about it. I've never said a word before today. I hope that the press will respect the privacy of Lynette Bacon and her mother. Dellar's death means that it is a very sensitive time for them and all of the other families. We all have a duty to remember that.'

'But, but . . . Bill? I can use those quotes?'

'Yes. Any of them you want. I've cleared them with Mullins, and Lynette of course. You should have plenty there. Neither of them will talk to anyone else, not one single word. It's your story. I helped you with the background, but it's your exclusive.'

What else could Glasby do but take the hand which Davenport was holding out to her?

* * *

Later that day, Glasby was back at home and talking on the telephone:

'. . . so John, I just want to say sorry again for last night. It's been a complete nightmare at times, but the amazing thing is that I've got a story after all. It will be in next week's *Herald*, you'll see it. But if you'd still like to, I was really hoping that we could get together before then. To get to know each other better, like you said. And this time, I'd like to buy you dinner, so that I can say thank you properly, because it's worked out really well for me and it . . . it means a lot to me that you helped me and supported me like you did, really . . .'

'. . . you are so right! I had a bit of a sleep as soon as I got in, but Jesus, my head! We're not kids any more, are we? What do you mean, I never was? Bloody cheek! Anyway, we will keep in touch now, won't we, Lester? Only maybe not quite so much to drink next time . . .'

'. . . it has so been a weird weekend, yeah, I know. Isn't it amazing, about my story? I think it's going to be really big. And it's not just that. You know that guy I met at yours, Simon's friend John? Well, we're seeing each other next week. We kind of saw each other last week as well, you know. He's nice, I like him. You know, there're some things more important than work sometimes, don't you think? Yeah, of course I'm not feeling ill, Kate. Why do you keep asking?'

The child was frightened, lying in the dark, listening – but what was it? Quick, let's get under the sheet. Trembling, but it was a hot summer night, so sweating as well. What was that noise? Please God, take me in your care, keep me safe and hear my prayer. Not again not again not again not again. If I close my eyes it will go away. If I promise to be good nothing will happen. It can't. It can't. He's there! Outside the door. Why won't someone help me? It's not my fault, I didn't do anything wrong. Please! Please don't let him touch me. I've got to find somewhere to hide, somewhere he can't get me. If I'm really quiet I could get out of the window and he won't hear nothing. Sindy, you come with me and we'll tiptoe like Lynette learned us and then we'll push it open and—

He was across the room quickly for a heavy man and a drunk at that, but no one ever said that John Bacon couldn't hold his beer. Little bleeder! Out the bloody window, would she? One hand on her leg, fingers closing around her thin little ankle, but she kicked with the other, got him right in the gut, so he jerked her leg up, hard.

Crack! She hit the wall under the window, forehead against concrete.

Then, nothing. No more whimpering from the terrified little girl. No sounds of them struggling, half in and half out of the metal-framed window. Just the hoarse, rasping breath of her attacker, her father, getting deeper and faster, eyes screwed closed against the horror of what he had done.

Only the Sindy doll saw it all, lying on her back outside the window, a drop of blood slowly turning brown on her little white dress.

Epilogue

After two hours of sitting staring at an almost blank computer screen Bill Davenport gave up and settled down to the newspapers instead.

As usual, he turned first to the *Herald*, a gloomy front page full of yet another impending war, quite incongruous in the bright sunshine which was pouring in past the scaffolding into the still not quite renovated cottage. It wasn't until halfway down page eleven that anything caught his eye, under the headline 'Murder Could Be Professional Hit' with the byline 'Alison Glasby, Crime Reporter'. It wasn't a long story:

> Police are now understood to be investigating whether a brutal murder may have been the work of a professional hitman. Michael Fisher, 47, was found beaten to death in his own apartment two days ago. The crime, which was at first thought to be the work of a burglar, bore all the hallmarks of a gangland execution.
>
> Witnesses are said to have seen two men of military appearance shadowing Mr Fisher's North London home in the days leading up to the killing. Murder squad detectives have so far refused to make any comment.

'Hmmm,' was Davenport's only audible response, and the cats bunched up together on his lap didn't seem overly impressed either. A moment later the phone rang, scattering two of them in alarm and the third across the room to answer it.

'Lynette, how are you? I was so sorry to hear the news. I hope you got my flowers? And how did it go, as well as these things ever can, I hope?'

He said nothing for some time after that, but a look of surprise and alarm crossed his face. 'Please, don't do anything,

Lynette. I can be up tomorrow, if that's OK with you, and we'll sort everything out then. I promise.'

'. . . so the doctor, he told me that she was going so I rushed in and Mum looked terrible, like she was panting for breath, and I don't think she knew it was me at first. But then it was like she looked over to me and her eyes were suddenly all clear, and I had to get really close to hear her, she was talking so quiet. She told me, she said Dad had told her all along what he'd done with Donna, where he'd buried her, I mean. It was near Hoveton, by a big old willow tree next to the Broad. And then Mum made me promise to look after her – Donna, I mean – and then she closed her eyes and she was gone, ever so quiet, just like she was asleep.'

The damp little house had never felt so lonely or so cold.

'I want Donna buried properly, Bill. I've never been one for the church, not like some round here, but –' tears were rolling down her cheeks, but Lynette kept on talking – 'she's all alone out there, poor little Donna, and now I'm alone in here, and I want to be with her.'

The last few words were barely audible through her sobs. Davenport sat down next to her and comforted her like a small child, her tears soaking through his shirt front. She quietened and he held her again, this time as if they might once have been lovers. Then he spoke, leaning back now on the sofa.

'If you have her buried now it will have to be done officially. And that will mean the authorities, the police, and even if they're sympathetic we'll never keep it out of the press.'

'I don't care,' Lynette cried. 'I let her down when she was alive, I never looked after her like I should've done so I'll do it now at least. Mum's gone now and I don't care what happens to me no more, all I want is what's right for Donna. A proper grave with flowers for her. I want flowers on her grave.'

He paused, and spoke again, his voice quiet but intense. 'Listen to me, Lynette, listen please. You don't need a vicar for a service. You don't need a churchyard for a grave. You don't need to sacrifice your own life to care for Donna – as if you haven't given enough already, all these years. Now you know where she was buried you can honour her, and care for her, and love her, I promise you that. Have you been there yet, to where she is?'

'No.' Her voice was no more than a whisper. 'I couldn't, not on my own. I was too scared.'

'Could you go there with me, do you think?' asked Davenport.

Two people stood hand in hand, a man and a woman, neither of them young, their eyes closed but tears running freely down both their faces, in the warm late afternoon of a July day in Norfolk. Towering above them was an ancient willow, and at their feet was a small patch of muddy earth on which was scattered red and yellow rose petals. Pinned to the tree trunk, protected by a clear plastic bag, was a photograph of two girls at the seaside, smiling in the summer sun.